Hidden Gypsy Magic

by

Tena Stetler

A Witch's Journey, Book 3

Hidden Gypsy Magic

Cover Art by *Kristian Norris*

The Wild Rose Press, Inc.
PO Box 708
Adams Basin, NY 14410-0708
Visit us at www.thewildrosepress.com

Publishing History
First Black Rose Edition, 2020
Trade Paperback ISBN 978-1-5092-3255-0
Digital ISBN 978-1-5092-3256-7

A Witch's Journey, Book 3
Published in the United States of America

"This house may not have a history of magic, but I'd bet it's magical. Pepper is going to go nuts when she sees this. You're going to put an offer in. Right?"

"As I said before, it may be completely out of my price range."

"I have a feeling the house has been waiting for you." She flung her hand to her mouth, her face flushed, and her gaze swiveled to him. "I don't know what made me say that."

Looking thoughtful, he grinned. "Since the day I stumbled upon Pepper's secret—then discovered that you and I share the gift or curse of Gypsy blood, things have been different—" Pausing, he shoved his hand in his jean's pocket and jingled the change inside. "I've been different. It's as if knowing magic exists awakened something in me."

"Join the club. Years ago Pepper made a believer out of me. In fact, there were times I wished—never mind. Whether it was my outlook or as you said magic awakened. But to be fair, I've always had what I called a sixth sense with animals, attuned to their feelings, almost their thoughts, fears, that kind of thing. Pepper called it my talent. But as we became close, I noticed other abilities…you'll think I'm crazy."

"Try me." He moved closer to her and the front door banged open. Quickly he rushed to the top of the stairs.

Praise for Tena Stetler

Dedication

To my READERS for whom I write the stories!
To all the wonderful people in my life,
personal and professional,
who help me realize my dreams every day.
My Editor, Lill Farrell, Rocks!
She makes my books shine.
The staff at The Wild Rose Press are the best support
an author can have!

Chapter One
Baby Desert Turtles Dumped Along the Roadside—What's Wrong with People?

March came in like a lamb, but a few days later a frigid wind gripped the northeast region of the United States with a vengeance. Gwen covered the box with her tiny treasures inside and shoved open the vehicle door. When the SUV's door slammed against her legs, she yelped but continued to tightly hold the cover in place over the box. *I'll have bruises tomorrow.*

Once inside Brock's vet office, she glanced at the empty receptionist area. "Anybody here?" No one answered, so she eased into a seat and waited anxiously with the cardboard box on her lap. Weak scratching came from the box. Carefully lifting the cover, she peeked inside to make sure the little creatures were safe.

When the front door banged open, she jumped. A cold breeze swept through the waiting room ahead of Delta, the receptionist, who rushed in throwing her arms up in an exasperated gesture. "Sorry, I'm late. Traffic." She frowned while rounding the reception desk and glanced down at the appointment book, then back up to Gwen. "I don't have you on my schedule today." Leaning over the counter, the receptionist pointed to the box. "What's in there?"

Gwen's face flushed in anger. "Someone dumped

these poor innocent turtles or more accurately Desert Tortoises by the side of the road. They can't be much more than a few weeks old. Even the spring temps are close to freezing at night. Poor little things were cold, dehydrated, defenseless, and malnourished." She glanced at the receptionist.

"Wow. Desert Tortoises. Ya sure?" Delta momentarily peered at the door to the back room and returned her attention to the calendar. "How do you suppose they found their way here?"

Gwen gritted her teeth. "Human interference," she said savagely "Lucky for them, some kids found them by the side of the road. The youngsters' parents called the center last night and brought the tortoises in late."

Delta cocked an eyebrow and stared at her. "Wow. Some find."

"What's wrong with people?" Gwen huffed.

The receptionist shrugged. "You're preaching to the choir." She stared at her desk then switched on her computer. "Who are you seeing?"

"I called Brock early this morning. He said to bring them on in. They're in pretty bad shape." She stood up careful not to shift the box too much and lowered it so the receptionist could see in. "We warmed up sand for them."

"Awww… Aren't they cute."

"That's probably what nearly got them killed. Can't survive at this age and in this climate. At least I don't think so. Have to do research on desert tortoises. Never had anything like them in my care before."

Somewhere in the back of the office, a door creaked open and footsteps sounded on the tile floor. Brock strolled into the waiting room. "Let's see what you've got here." He took the box from her, reached in and touched one of the tortoises. "Poor little thing is warm now and starting to move around. That's a great sign. Come on in the back and we'll see what can be done."

Still seething, she followed him into the examination room chewing on her bottom lip as he gently examined each of the four.

"It may be best to start an IV for hydration, then we'll try tempting their appetite with grasses and leafy greens." He paused for a beat rubbing his jaw. "Maybe a bit of fruit. I'll send you back with a multivitamin high in D3 and calcium." He paused for a couple of beats. "I'd like you to leave them with me for the rest of the day. I'll drop them by your place on my way home."

He gave her a reassuring smile. "These little guys will be just fine thanks to you." He handed her several pieces of paper. "I did a little research after you called and found this information on housing and dietary needs for tortoises. If you need help getting their habitat ready, let me know."

She took the documents from him and gave them a cursory review. "Not necessary, I'll get what is required and have an enclosure ready by the time you drop them off." She smiled. "Running the rescue is so much easier with Pepper's regular donations."

He nodded. "Speaking of Pepper, how are they doing? What about Lobster Cove Rescue?"

"They're doing great. Lathen expanded the bird area and added more heated cubes. He's going to bring a few cubicles for Salem's sanctuary the next time they are up this way. The rescue keeps them pretty busy. But they're talking about coming up for a visit in a few weeks."

"Maybe we can get together with them. You've been pretty scarce around here too." He caressed her arm. "I've missed you."

"Rotating door of volunteers." She blew out a breath. "I'll have the new paid staff members trained in another month, so I'll have more free time." Giving him a sideways glance she batted her eyes up at him and grinned. "You could always stop by the sanctuary."

"Things were crazy around here too. Jacob, my business partner, will be off paternity leave next week. That'll help."

"Oh, I forgot you've been short-handed for a while. How are his new twins?" She snorted a laugh. "Bet his life has changed dramatically."

"You know it. Keeping him and Grace busy. Last I heard one of the twins had her days and nights mixed up, which blew the schedule they'd worked so hard on right out of the water." He snickered. "Bet, he'll be glad to get back to work."

She gave him the stink eye. "Nope, he'll just have less sleep and more stress. Aren't they going to hire help for a few months since Jacob is coming back to work?"

"Yeah, that's the plan at least it was the last time I talked to him. They're probably sifting through the applicants as we speak." He snapped his fingers. "Hey, how about I stop and pick up dinner on the way over to drop off the tortoises?"

"Sounds great. I was up most of the night worried about the little buggers and trying to figure out how best to accommodate their needs."

"You did a good job. Warming the sand to bring up their body temp was smart. Now relax, they'll be fine."

"I hope so." She lightly caressed the little creatures before padding to the exam room door.

"I'll walk you out."

"Thanks." She smiled and glanced back at the box on the exam table. "See you tonight."

"They'll be fine," he reassured her as he held the office door open. "Pizza and soda okay for dinner?"

"Sure." She climbed in her vehicle and started the engine. Backing out, she stopped to give him a wave while he still stood in the doorway to the office.

Inside her pocket, her phone buzzed as she turned onto the main street. "Never fails." Touching the screen on her vehicle audio hands-free system, she answered. "Hey Pepper. What's up?"

"Just got your message this morning. Never had Desert Tortoises here either. This is a first for you too. I bet." Pepper clicked her tongue. "Sometimes humans haven't a clue. Anyway, been in touch with a rescue in Nevada. They emailed a few blueprints for tortoise habitats. I've forwarded them to you. Wanted to make sure you got 'em."

"I'm just leaving Brock's office, so I haven't looked at my email since early this morning. When I get back to the sanctuary I'll check."

"So how's that going?"

"He's going to keep the tortoises today and bring them by the sanc…"

Pepper interrupted her. "I'm talking about you and Brock, not the turtles."

"Oh, both of us have been really busy, so haven't seen much of him. His partner is out of the office. I've been training the new staff on how I want things done. Maybe after the training is done, I'll have more free time."

"Gwen Taylor you're making excuses." Pepper chided. "Remember me—your best friend. Don't you dare shut him out of your life because you're scared."

"I'm doing no such thing. If you must know, he is bringing dinner over tonight with the tortoises."

"Okay. That's better." Pepper's voice lost the authoritarian tone.

"Brock thought it would be a great idea if we get together when you two come up to visit next month."

"Sounds great. But… it might be a bit longer. Not comfortable leaving an endangered owl we recently took in. Dylan, our vet, is out of town next week for a conference and the week after tending to her out of town patients."

She tried hard to keep the disappointment out of her voice. "Understood. Look forward to seeing you whenever. We'll hold off planning anything until we hear from you."

"Don't worry. We'll be there soon. We're hoping to be able to spend a week or so. I can't wait to see the tortoises." A door slammed open somewhere in the distance and someone called Pepper's name.

"Sounds like you need to go. Talk to you soon. Let me know your plans." She glanced at her watch.

"Yeah, the new hire is calling. It's the third veteran we've hired recently. They're working out really well."

"You don't by any chance have a lead on anyone looking for a position up here do you?"

"I'll ask Lathen and get back to you. Bye now." Pepper ended the call.

Making a wide turn into the sanctuary parking lot, she sucked in a breath. "What the heck are they doing here?" She pulled into a space next to a truck with the Mass wildlife logo emblazoned on it. The door to the vehicle was flung wide open. But no one was in sight. "I don't need this." She took a deep breath and blew it out.

Previously a visit from DOW meant trouble. But now she didn't have to run the sanctuary on a shoestring budget, their facilities met all requirements and then some. She gave her shoulders a little shake and straightened.

Clambering out of her truck, she sprinted into the office where the scarred wooden door stood open. She closed the door and headed toward a group of employees gathered around the reception desk. "George, is there a problem?" She pushed closer. There on the desk was a wood turtle drawn into its shell, except for one back foot that appeared flattened and missing a couple of nails.

Startled, the DOW officer whirled around to stare at her. "Yes. We have a problem. Vet on the other side of Salem treated this turtle as best he could a few days ago." He shook his head. "But it's going to need long term care. May never be able to fend for itself in the wild. Think it may have gotten run over on its left side." George picked up the turtle and turned it on its side. "See."

She grabbed his hand and eased it back toward the desk with the turtle upright. "Put that poor creature down. You're scaring it to death. How'd you like to be injured, someone jostle, and flip you all around?" Her voice was sharper than she intended it to be. Releasing his hand, she motioned to the desk.

He set the creature down carefully on the desktop and eyed her. "Sorry. Didn't mean to—"

She shook her head. "It's me that's sorry. It's been a long day already this morning, one that started last night." *It's been years since I've seen a turtle or tortoise in the facility and we've got 5 in the span of twenty-four hours.* She rolled her eyes heavenward. "What the heck?" *Geesh, did I say that out loud? By the look on George's face, I did.*

The wildlife officer took his hat off and ran his fingers through his hair, rubbed at the back of his neck. "Understand this is highly unusual, but the wood turtle is on the endangered list. Dr. Reed said you're the only licensed endangered species or reptile sanctuary in the area. Besides you're associated with Dr. Brock Scutter who specializes in wildlife medicine. We tried to get the turtle into Brock's clinic, but he was full. Figured this was the best place for the little fellow." He shrugged. "Not sure Dr. Reed sees turtles often. You know what I mean?"

"Yeah," she said absently. Kneeling down to eye level with the turtle, she cooed to the reptile, "So what happened to you?" She leaned to one side and held still. The creature slowly poked it's head out, and relaxed it's front legs to reveal orange skin, then yanked itself back inside the shell. The tortoise's back leg didn't move. "Jed, ready one of the reptile tanks and make sure there is a half log for hiding." She glanced at George. "I'll take it from here." She snatched the phone out of her pocket and called the Scutter Veterinary Hospital. "Hi, Delta. Can I speak to Brock? This is Gwen."

"He's with patients. Can I take a message?"

She tapped her fingers on the phone for a couple of beats. "No. I'll call back." She ended the call and tapped the speed dial for Brock's private number. It went to voice mail. "You are not going to believe this, but a Mass Wildlife officer just brought in a wood turtle. It appears to have been run over on one side. Dr. Reed saw it first but doesn't know exotics well so he sent it here. Needs to be seen. I want to make sure there aren't any internal injuries. Call me back."

Gently she picked up the turtle and carried him to the reptile enclosures. When she placed him in the cubicle, she covered the patient with the corner log. She eased down on a stool next to the turtle and filled out the intake sheet. Wood turtle, age unknown, sex unknown, size eight inches across. Right back leg immobile.

At the top of the sheet, she glanced at the name line. She grinned. "Guess we'll call you RoadTrip," she said quietly. Slowly leaning closer to get a better look, she noted its eye was swollen and crusty around the edges. She made another note on the file. "Possible eye infection." Setting down the chart, she crossed the room to the sink.

Inside the cabinet, she reached for a sterile pad and ran warm water over it. Returning to the turtle, she gently cleaned around the eye removing the crust. "There little guy, that's looks better and should feel more comfortable."

Chapter Two
House Hunting in Salem—an Adventure in Itself

Brock leaned over and held the iguana in front of its hind legs and behind the head. There was a soft growth on its front foreleg. He manipulated the growth and barely avoided the lashing tail. "How long have you had him?" he asked the teen owner and her mother.

"A couple of months. A guy at school had it. Said it wasn't doing well and was going to turn it loose." The girl turned her huge blue eyes up to him. "I couldn't let him do that. Iguanas are tropical creatures. After extensive research, I changed its diet, enclosure, increased humidity, but then it got that bump. We didn't know what to do."

The mother shook her head. "Rita is always bringing home hurt, abandoned or lost animals. I just don't think she was prepared for this."

"What kind of lighting do you have in its habitat?"

"A heat lamp about four feet away, so it stays warm but not hot," Rita said. "There's a thermometer on top of the enclosure."

He smiled at her. "You're on the right track. The bump could be caused by lack of a UVB light, uh…sunlight. You need a full spectrum light source to provide the necessary UVB rays. While natural sunlight is the best, full-spectrum will work in this colder climate. It's been a while since this guy had the necessary light which I suspect has caused this." He pointed to the bump. "Not your fault. What are you feeding him?"

"The info I found said greens, veggies, and occasional fruits. I feed him every morning before school." She stroked the lizard and it calmed down, trying to crawl up her arm.

He let it go. Pleased the iguana recognized its owner as he observed the interaction. It was apparent she cared for the creature. "Tell you what. I have an old lamp here at the clinic, I can sell you a new bulb at cost, then start him on vitamins. Bring him back in two weeks. We should see a shrinking of the bump and brightening of his colors."

"Fluffy will be all right then?" A hopeful expression replaced the down in the mouth look she'd come in with.

He raised an eyebrow. "Fluffy?"

"Yeah, different but less intimidating when introducing him to my friends. He's really sweet— now."

"With you. Might not want to hand him off to someone else unless he knows them. Trust is a big issue especially if there was a problem at his last home. Size… Are you aware…"

"He could grow to be six feet or more. I understand. Also interaction, socialization is a must or aggression could become a problem. No one handles Fluffy but me and Mom." Rita paused. "He can give you a nasty whip with that tail or bite. But he doesn't do either to us anymore. Originally he was so scared. But now, he's a sweetheart."

"Good. Sounds like you've done your homework.

See you in a couple of weeks. If other concerns arise, give me a call."

"Sure thing." Smiling she headed to the door.

"I'll meet you up front with an information sheet and the lamp, bulb, and vitamins." *That's one Iguana that won't end up in a rescue or die at the hands of an uninformed human. The morning is looking up. Maybe she'd be interested in helping out at the Salem Sanctuary.* He made a note in the file, printed out information sheets and went in search of the lamp and bulb.

The rest of the morning flew by. Finally, in the early afternoon, he had a few minutes to wolf down a sandwich, a banana, and gulp a bottle of water. He scooped his phone off the desk and plopped into the chair. There were several messages. Recognizing Gwen's cell, he listened to the message and returned her call. She answered on the first ring. "Hey, what's up?"

She proceeded to fill him in on her morning adding that she thought the turtle had an eye infection. "Do you have time today to see RoadTrip? I cleaned up the eye, but it's still weeping."

His snicker grew to full-blown laughter.

"What's so funny?"

After containing his mirth, he snorted. "I saw an iguana named Fluffy and now RoadTrip the turtle? But I understand your situation. Unfortunately, I'm double-booked all day. Shoot me a picture of the eye, leg and the overall turtle. Tonight when I bring dinner, I'll have the necessary supplies to set RT on the road to recovery. Depending on the extent of the leg damage, you may be looking at a life-time resident."

"Yep. Figured. See you tonight. You might want to bring something a bit stronger along with the soda." She sighed.

"I was thinking the same thing. See ya soon." His phone buzzed before he had a chance to put it down. Relieved it was his real estate agent and not another emergency. He regretted giving his personal number to a few of the clients in emergencies, some had passed it on. "Hi Bill. What you got for me."

"Good news. That property you had me keep an eye on. It's going to hit the market in the next week or so. A friend of mine has the listing and is giving me, us, first crack at it. Needs some work, but for a turn of the century house with acreage, and history, it'll be well within your budget."

"What kind of history? It's not haunted is it?"

"Brock, all the houses worth having in Salem are haunted." Bill laughed. "No ghost sightings. It's one of the rare gems here in Salem that has no history of haunting or witches. At least that we know of." He paused. "Only kidding. It's been remodeled and changed hands numerous times without a whisper of ghosts or rattling chains."

He blew out a breath. Remodeling or repair he could handle. Ghostly visits, noisy haunted apparitions, and witches or curses not so much. *I need my rest*. He shook his head, today was a prime example of that. When Bill cleared his throat, Brock's attention snapped back to the conversation. "I can handle that. When can I see it?"

"End of the week. You'll love the carved wood, craftsmanship in the tile work, and etched glass in the windows."

13

"Sounds great." He flipped through the paper calendar on his desk he used as a backup to his electronic calendar app. "Currently, I have a short day on Thursday. How about I pencil in an afternoon showing at say four-thirty."

"You got it."

"If an emergency comes up, I'll call you."

"The seller isn't going to wait very long. So do your best to make the appointment," his real estate agent warned.

"Will do." He ended the call and opened his calendar app marking unavailable from two o'clock on next Thursday and strode out of his office. Entering into the reception area, he leaned on the counter. "Delta, check my appointment calendar, make sure I'm blocked out of the office from two o'clock next Thursday. No exceptions."

The receptionist raised an eyebrow, but tapped a few keys and pulled up the calendar. "Yep, you're marked out. Got a hot date?" she whispered.

"Nope." He turned on his heel and sauntered to the exam room two. Pushing through the door he glanced at the unfamiliar vet tech who had toweled his next patient, a blue and gold Macaw. The bird screeched its displeasure at being held then managed to flip around and with an open beak tried for his assistant's fingers.

Quickly, he snatched another towel, calmly covered the bird's head and took the angry Macaw from her. He smiled reassuringly to the stressed owner who hovered in front of him as the bird calmed down under his soothing magic. "You're fine. This will only take a minute." Turning his attention to the vet tech he said. "Get Roberta in here."

"She's on break," the tech stammered. No sooner than the words were out of her mouth, a tall middle-aged woman rushed in. "I've got this." She shooed the other girl out of the room and expertly took the bird from him cooing at the Macaw.

After calming the owner and apologizing then explaining the vet tech was new and in training, he finished the exam, trimmed the bird's nails, then discounted the fee and sent the bird and its owner on her way. *Good thing she's a long-time client.* Before he could address Roberta, she raised her hands in a gesture of defense.

"I went to the back to get a bottle of water. Didn't realize Ms. Drew and Roady were here already. And… it would appear your new hire isn't an experienced bird tech."

"Roady didn't know her. The bird likes you. But… I'll have a talk with the new tech, Amy. Thanks for rushing in Birdie. All's well that ends well."

Roberta's defensive posture disappeared replaced by a slight grin. "I'll make sure Delta knows the new girl and I will be double-teaming birds for a while. And under no circumstances is Amy to be in an exam room alone. We could have lost a client or she could have injured Roady."

"Or been injured herself," he added. "Thanks. Good plan." In the hallway, he spotted Amy leaning against the wall, head down staring at her shoes. "Hey Amy, a word." He pointed to his office.

"I'm so sorry." She began. "I really have handled large parrots before. Not often, but…"

"Around here, we pair the new techs with the more experienced ones until everyone is comfortable with all aspects of my practice. Roady, the Blue and Gold Macaw, doesn't like people he doesn't know. That's a mighty big beak and could have caused you severe damage had he connected."

"I know sir. It won't happen again." Amy sucked in a breath. "Am I fired?"

"No, not this time. You'll shadow Birdie until your probationary period is up. Follow her instructions and you'll be fine. She's been with me since I took over this practice. She knows all the patients, the owners, and how to handle each one."

"Got it. Thank you."

Nodding he sent her a reassuring smile as she turned and fled his office.

The clinic was quiet as the last rays of sun reflected off the office window. He settled into his well-worn high back leather chair tucked behind his scarred oak desk. After reviewing test results and returning phone calls, he rubbed his eyes with thumb and forefinger then glanced at the clock that read seven-fifteen. *Dinner is going to be late.* He picked up his phone and touched in Gwen's number.

Her cell barely rang once. "You know I have a no-cancellation policy."

"In that case, I'm just leaving the clinic. Been a helluva day. I'll stop by the pizza place and be over shortly."

"Sounds good. Did you remember to bring supplies for RoadTrip?"

"Of course," he lied. Picking up his medical satchel, he gathered items and medication, he may need while shouldering the phone to his ear. "See you soon." Ending the call, he leaned over and tugged open the bottom desk drawer. A bottle of good whiskey, a patient had given him last Christmas, lay unopened nestled below a couple of folders. He smiled, adding the bottle to the supplies in his medical bag, closed the clasp, and turned off the light.

After putting the items in his vehicle, he started the truck and turned the heater on full blast, then returned to the clinic and checked the container of tortoises. They were all warm and moving around. After giving them fluids this morning, he'd offered a few wet leafy greens in a bowl. Three of the four had nibbled on the offerings. The smallest one hadn't been tempted by the food at first, but eventually, by late afternoon, it had finally eaten a little bit too, according to one of his interns assigned to watch over patients.

On a paper taped to the side of the container, he noted his vet tech had written all the weights, sizes, meds and foods liked by each tortoise. He made a copy of the document for Gwen, then tucked the original inside the turtles' file. *Gwen would appreciate that information.* He loaded the tortoises in his truck and headed toward Salem Sanctuary on the outskirts of town.

Twenty minutes later, he strolled up the path with the container of reptiles to Gwen's tiny cottage to the right of the rescue's main building. She was waiting at the door for him and took the container. He returned to the vehicle and grabbed the still-hot pizza box in one hand, tucked the bottle of soda under his arm, and grasped his medical bag in the other. Gwen opened the door, pointing to the coffee table between the fireplace and the sofa. He set the pizza box and soda on the table, then dropped his medical bag on the floor next to the sofa.

A large, worn upholstered chair sat in the corner of the living area with a heating pad covering the seat and plugged in. She deposited the box carefully on the chair and peeked inside gently touching each of the tortoises. "They look much better than this morning." Padding over to the sink, she washed her hands. Turning her attention back to him, she dried her hands on a towel. "Busy day, huh?"

He washed up and followed her back to the living area as she flipped open the pizza box lid and inhaled deeply. "Yum. I'm starved. It was nonstop around here also." She glanced at the little acrylic tub resting on another heating pad in a worn chair at the end of the coffee table. "Do you want to eat in the kitchen or crash on the sofa and relax?"

"Sofa is fine." As he passed by the chair, he gave the creature in the tub a cursory glance. "We'll get you taken care of after dinner."

Returning to the kitchen, she grabbed paper plates and two tumblers out of the cupboard filled them with ice then returned to the living area. "What went on in your world today?"

"Had a fiasco with a Blue and Gold Macaw." He waved his hand in dismissal." New vet tech, communication, and training problem."

"That's a big beak, heck that's a big bird to have a misunderstanding with." Her eyes widened.

"Yeah, but it ended up all right. Don't think Amy, the new gal, will make a move without Birdie our experienced vet tech." He sighed. *It shouldn't have happened. I'm stretched too thin. Be glad when Jacob gets back.* "Treated an iguana named Fluffy for a vitamin deficiency. The original owner hadn't taken proper care of the lizard so he developed a deformity in his front leg."

Gwen frowned. "Poor guy."

"Yeah, but Rita, the girl who has him now, took the time to research his requirements, change his diet, and enclosure. He's on the road to recovery, I think. She'll bring him back in a couple of weeks and we'll see how he's doing. Speaking of Rita, I thought she might be a good fit here at the rescue. Volunteer part-time after school, that kind of thing."

"I could sure use a few dependable volunteers. Got a name and number?"

"Yep. I didn't mention the rescue to her or her mom. Thought I'd bring it up with you first. See if you needed anyone."

She snorted a laugh. "I always need volunteers. I'll give her mom a call and go from there. You okay with that?"

He nodded sliding a large piece of pizza onto a paper plate. Handed it to her. "How about your day?"

Tilting the tumbler, she slowly poured the soda over the ice, but the liquid bubbled over the side and ran down the side of the glass. "Darn it." She grabbed a roll of paper towels and mopped up the mess. "Sorry about that. Warm pop and ice don't play well together."

Laughing he took the glass from her and took a long drink. "Ahh…it hits the spot." He poured the next one, filling it only half full and letting it settle down before adding more.

"Show off," she sputtered taking a bite of pizza. Chewing slowly, she paused and grinned at him. "Had to meet with the accountant. Gave him a stack of receipts for the remodel, new habitat and supplies. After it was totaled up, there are still enough funds, God bless Pepper and her donations, to purchase a few of those nice avian and reptile enclosures. I'd about decided to pass on the reptile enclosures but given this afternoon, I'm rethinking the matter." She took another slice of pizza out of the box, bit into it, and placed the slice on a plate.

"It couldn't hurt to have a few on hand. Especially if you can afford them."

"Yeah, things go in cycles. Looks like it's going to be a reptile cycle for your place." She took a sip from her glass of soda.

He took another bite of pizza and washed it down with the gulp of soda. "By the way, I heard from my real estate agent today. You know that house I was telling you about?"

She took the last bite of her slice of pizza and nodded. "That two-story house that takes up nearly half a block and the shutters are falling off?"

"Yep. It goes on the market next week. Want to come along and take a look at it with me? Bill's giving me the first option on it. He knows the real estate agent that has the listing."

"Are you in the market for a fixer-upper? Does it come with its own ghost? You may have to pay extra for it." She dissolved into a fit of giggles. "I'm tired. Can you tell?"

Grinning he pulled out the bottle of fine whiskey. "I don't imagine you want any of this." He wiggled the bottle in his hand.

"Like hell, I don't. I'll get glasses from the kitchen." She gathered up the empty pizza box and picked up one of the tumblers.

He put his hand over hers. "We can use the same glasses. Whiskey and coke should hit the spot and keep you from falling asleep on me."

She clenched her hands on her hips. "Are you saying I can't hold my drink?"

Putting his hand up in a gesture of surrender, he shook his head. "Absolutely not." He moved over to the chair and gently picked up the turtle. The creature flailed a bit with its good legs then gave up. "He's pretty weak. But he's got quite a bit of body fat stored up. Don't you fella." He took a light out of his pocket and shone it in RT's eyes. "I don't think the eye's infected, only scratched at the corner making it water. We'll put him on a few days of antibiotics just in case. Has he eaten anything since he's been here?"

"Wasn't interested in the mealworms we had on hand, but sure liked the strawberries and raspberries I had on my salad at lunch. I think the injured eye is causing him to miscalculate where things are. I set the berries in front of him and he pushed at them with his beak, but when I hand fed them to him, he ate several right down." She wiggled her fingers in front of him when he raised an eyebrow. "I still have all my digits too."

"So I see." He touched the injured back leg. RoadTrip hissed at him and flailed again. "Sorry fella, we gotta take a look." After a few minutes of examination, he took out a roll of vet wrap. "It's definitely broken below the knee joint, but the bone isn't smashed. We'll splint the leg and wrap it and see how he tolerates it. If you get a chance, supervised sunshine would be a good thing."

"Will do." She covered a jaw popping yawn with her hand. "Been another long day." Leaning into him, she peeked up at him through thick lashes. "How are you doing?"

"Better'n you, I'd wager." He slipped his arm around her shoulder, running his fingers through her sleek black hair streaked with green and pink highlights and gently tugged her close. "We gotta make time for us."

"I know." She sighed. "We've only seen each other a handful of times since we got back from Lobster Cove the first of the year." Her full bottom lip stuck out in a pout. "But we knew that could be a possibility given our occupations."

"I understand, doesn't mean I like it." A yawn he'd attempted to stifle a couple of times, burst through and he rubbed his eyes. "I gotta get home and get a few hours of shut-eye. I'll stop by tomorrow after work and check on our patients—and you."

"Good idea. I'm going to keep the patients here for the night. Hopefully, the weather will be warmer tomorrow and I can return to them to the heated cubicles in the reptile habitat." She checked the humidifier situated between the two containers. "They should be fine for the night. Don't want to disturb them anymore this evening."

"They'll be fine." Brushing his lips over hers, he murmured, "Until tomorrow." Squeezed her tight against him, then reluctantly let her go and crossed the room to the door. "Good night."

Chapter Three
A Fixer Upper with a Questionable History

She glanced at the clock and squeaked. Only one hour before she needed to meet Brock at the house he was interested in buying. And the desk was stacked with paperwork requiring her attention. But…she blew out a breath and sprinted to her cottage, changed clothes, brushed and braided her hair, then returned to the sanctuary to let Trinity, her part-time assistant, know she'd be out of the office for a while. "Hey Trin, if you get a chance, could you organize the stuff on my desk in order of priority. I'll get to it this evening when it's quiet."

"Sure thing. Oh, Charlotte said the turtles are doing well. The little ones are eating on their own, trashing their water regularly. Roadtrip hasn't gotten his bandage off—yet but is more active today. The eye looks much better."

"Great! Thanks for letting me know. I checked in on them earlier. RT was snoozing but the four others were at their bowls."

Once inside the SUV, she texted Brock to let him know she was running late, started the engine and took off in the direction of town. Slowing down, she checked the house numbers then spied Brock's truck. She slowed and parked behind his vehicle, pushed open the door, and stepped out of her vehicle as he exited the truck.

Stopping to stretch his legs, he grinned at her pointing to his watch. "You made it with two minutes to spare. Bill's the one that's late."

"Lucky for me." The hair on the back of her neck prickled and she gave a little shudder.

He raised an eyebrow and glanced at the sky. "You can't be cold with the sun still shining and no wind. 'Bout time Spring gave us a gorgeous day."

She glanced at the bright blue sky with only a few fluffy white clouds floating on the horizon. "Nooo… not cold. A strange feeling came over me when I got out of the SUV."

The rambling two-story home needed paint. The front garden had green sprouts poking through the dirt and a few blades of green grass showed promise of mature landscaping well cared for. "Have you been inside?"

He shook his head. "Only to peek in the windows after the owners moved out. I hoped they were going to sell it."

It was her turn to raise an eyebrow and stare incredulously at him.

A slight crimson crept up his neck as he cleared his throat. "I don't usually go peeping in other's windows. But I've had my eye on this place since I returned from vet school and joined the practice. Even before I bought it."

She shrugged and couldn't keep the grin from her lips. "I didn't say a word."

"You didn't have to."

"I was yanking your chain. So what's so special about this property?"

He paused as a grimace crossed his face and gave a slight shake of his head. "I don't know. Except it's within walking distance of the clinic. I like that. Every time I drive or walk by I get a feeling of home and contentment. I know it's crazy."

She shrugged, her arms up in the air palms up.

"As I told you, I asked Bill if there was any spooky history. He claims it is one of the rare homes in Salem that doesn't have a history of witches or hauntings. Otherwise, it'd been snatched up by some historical society and opened to the public."

"Magic doesn't only happen with witches. If they didn't want anyone to know, that could be arranged. If it was up to me, I'd enlist Pepper's expertise. If it matters to you."

"I'm not sure it does." Scrubbing his hand over his face, he shrugged one shoulder. "I like the house. Depending on the price, I'll probably buy it. Real estate is a sound investment. Not to mention the tax deduction for owning a home. I can't keep throwing my money away renting. Especially now that the clinic is turning a profit. Adding wildlife care to the practice seems to have brought in several new customers."

"Glad to hear it. It probably doesn't hurt you now have regular hours and vets on call. The newspaper article on the clinic when you got certified for wildlife care didn't hurt either. Even though Doc Hamilton retired a couple of years ago, he'd lost interest in his practice when his health started to decline several years before. He'd even stopped helping out at the sanctuary."

"Yeah, that's when I approached him to purchase the practice." He smiled. "It took me a while to convince him this "young whippersnapper" his words not mine, could handle the job and had the funds to keep it afloat. I think he was planning on closing it."

"When I offered to buy the practice and suggested it would give him a nice nest egg, that's when he decided to sell. Still, he wouldn't accept what was considered full value. What he wanted in writing was a guarantee that I'd take care of the clientele even if their owners couldn't pay much. Once I said no problem, he was on board and actually excited to retire."

"It was a good solution for him and a great one for you. Not to change the subject, but I see your point. Pepper is always harping at me to purchase a property away from the sanctuary. But funds have always been too tight. Now with her generous yearly donations for staff and equipment, I can even afford a salary for me. I'm still getting used to the changes. She suggested that I turn my cottage into a vet quarters. In the event, we need a vet in residence for a week or longer."

"Could be handy. Especially if you have animals in need of round the clock care for a period of time. My sister actually had to sleep on the floor next to a large animal in her care. Not fun. Thank goodness it doesn't happen very often. But it happens when you have a mobile vet as well as a clinic practice."

Her eyes widened and a smile spread across her face. "Are you planning to add mobile services?"

"Yeah, I kinda have to in order to comply with the requirements of the certification. Jacob and I are going to set things in motion as soon as he's back full time. We'll probably need to hire another a vet intern part-time then offer a full-time position if he/she works out. I'll be the mobile vet which will take me out of the office on occasion."

She tilted her head up to peer at him. "You'll like going out on location?"

"Yeah. That's why I wanted to qualify and obtain permits for the treatment of wildlife. I enjoy bringing the baby Desert turtles back to you after they stabilized. Then being able to to treat RoadTrip on location rather than having you bring him into the office which would add more stress to his injured body." He chuckled. "To switch gears just a bit, how did you take over ownership of the sanctuary?"

She rolled her eyes. scrunched her face up and waved her hand in dismissal. "Oh, that's a long convoluted story."

"I'd love to hear it." He glanced at his watch. "Bill seems to be running late." Right on queue, his phone rang. Brock touched the screen. "Hey Bill, where are you?" There was a pause as he listened intently. "No, I don't want to reschedule. It was hard enough to juggle this afternoon off, so I'll just wait. See you in a bit."

Switching his gaze to her, he snorted and threw a hand up in the air in frustration. "He got caught up in a closing that is running late. He'll be another thirty minutes or more. So if you have to leave, I'll understand."

"No, I took the afternoon off too. I wanted to look at the house with you but it also gives us a chance to spend time together. As you mentioned, we haven't had a lot of time together since the holidays."

"Don't I know it. Now back to your take over of the sanctuary." He wiggled his eyebrows as if about to learn the juicy details in a scandal.

"Not really much to tell. Roger owned the

sanctuary when I started there. Worked my way up to assistant manager. One week he was away on vacation and investors wanted to look at the books. When I reviewed them before allowing the investors access, something wasn't right. Then I discovered another set of books.

"Roger was cooking the books and showing the investors a fake set of books. He squandered the money and made it look like it went to the sanctuary. When he returned I confronted him. Well, actually Pepper and I confronted him. I'd confided in Pepper and showed her what I found to verify I was right. Unfortunately, I was."

He let out a low whistle. "That's serious business."

"The IRS got involved and it got ugly. The losers were the animals in our care. Pepper and I pooled our resources to keep the sanctuary afloat. Between the two of us, we figured out what permits were needed and certifications then filed them in my name. Roger and the non-profit he supposedly created owned the building which the IRS seized.

"Because we couldn't find a place for the animals, and I threatened to go public if the IRS tried to euthanize them, finally, the IRS let me buy the property at a tax sale. I got a bank loan and paid only pennies on the dollar, thanks to a lawyer my banker knew. It was a community effort and I couldn't have done it without Pepper's help."

"Wow, was this before or after she left to start her own rescue?"

"Before. When we eventually got the sanctuary on an even keel a magic storm hit during the anniversary of Salem's witch trials. Pepper had to use her magic to protect and save the animals."

"Good thing she was here." He continued to listen intently.

"Several other buildings were destroyed in the area, but yet the sanctuary remained unharmed. The bank executives didn't like the rumors swirling that Pepper wielded magical powers to save the sanctuary and the animals inside. Of course, we all know there is no such thing as magic." She winked. "Thousands of tourist dollars flood into Salem every October trading on magic and witch trials, still the bank threatened to call the note due if Pepper remained an employee."

He scratched the top of his head. "Were they afraid of her?"

"Don't know. I wanted to call their bluff. There was no way in hell, they'd have won. We'd made every payment on time. But Pepper wouldn't hear of fighting it. She said we'd have to use funds for a defense that should go to the care of the animals. I had no doubt we'd win, but she was right about the money and left. I hated the whole situation. But…seems fate stepped in and we're both better off."

"So you and the bank actually own the sanctuary?"

"No. It's mine and I've restored its non-profit standing. Pepper paid the loan off at the bank with some of her inheritance. You should have seen it." She snickered. "Pepper actually marched into the bank, walked right up to the banker that issued the ultimatum, and handed him a cashiers check. The expression on his face." She fanned herself attempting to hold back a laugh.

"Don't you love it when the good guys win?" He leaned back against the truck.

"It was priceless. But I digress. She demanded he mark the note paid right then and give her the original. When he balked, she threatened to tell the bank's Board of Trustees what he'd done." Unable to hold back her mirth any longer, she burst out laughing at the memory and continued. "Pepper handed him her lawyers' card and said in a low voice what you did was illegal, it's called discrimination. You know that right? He turned bright red then all the blood drained out of his face as his mouth opened and shut without a word coming out. Finally, he marked the note paid, gave her the deed, and she recorded it. Then…." Gwen paused for effect. "She wrote a letter to the bank's Board of Trustees detailing the whole sordid affair. Accusing an innocent of being a witch, in Salem, forcing her to leave town, and threatened to go public if he wasn't fired. The board terminated him the next day."

"Wow, what an interesting tale. No wonder you and Pepper are so tight."

"Yeah, when she left, I missed her something awful. Ten years we'd had each other's back, spent night after night up taking care of the animals. But when she called, told me about her aunt, the inheritance, and building a rescue on McKay land, I knew it was meant to be."

Suddenly, a car drove up and skidded spraying gravel in its wake before coming to a stop beside Brock's truck. A young woman got out and sprinted to over to them, leveling her gaze at him. "Are you Brock?"

"Who wants to know?" His eyebrows knitted together as he watched her.

"I'm Joan. I work for Bill. He's still tied up in the

closing from Hell but wanted me to give you the key to the house. Go ahead and look around. He'll join you later." She popped her gum and handed him the key. "If he doesn't get here by the time you are ready to leave, lock up, and he'll get the key from you later." Sprinting back to her car, she gunned the engine and took off again.

They watched the trail of dust her car left, then Brock held up the key. "Shall we?"

"We shall." She grinned and followed him up the cobblestone path to the house and waited on the wrap-around porch for him to unlock the door. While the porch needed painting, the craftsmanship on the carved newel posts and railing around the porch was fantastic. It had to have been well cared for over the years, until lately. The oval glass in the top half of the heavy wooden door was etched with a picture of a fairy riding a dragon. He turned the crystal knob, pushed the door open and she gasped.

Chapter Four

If You Aren't Aware of the Magic, Is It Still There?

It was like stepping back in time. A carved mahogany newel post formed a dragon's body complete with an intricately detailed dragon head, the banister curving upstairs was a tail of the dragon complete with etched smoothed scales. Brock closed the door behind them.

Gwen stood in the entryway turning in a complete circle. "Wow...just wow. This house is beautiful." Walking to the staircase, she touched the individual balusters. Each one was intricately etched to look like a tree or had vines and leaves carved around it. She turned her gaze to the ceiling, then tugged on his shirt sleeve and pointed.

The crown moldings were carved to depict a fairy garden in the main room off the entrance. "You know I didn't notice any of this when I peered in the windows, only the spacious rooms and the feeling it gives off if that makes any sense."

"It does. Let's tour the rest of the house." She reached for the light switch. "Is the electricity on?" Her question was answered as she flipped the switch. A warm glow lit up the room from a sparkling chandelier hanging from the center ceiling. Upon closer inspection, the chandelier was a bit dusty, but she stood in awe. "This place will cost a fortune."

"May be out of my price range." He took her hand and towed her up the stairs to the second story landing. In the top half of each wooden door was an oval carved to depict either a dragon, fairy, moon and star scene, or flowers. "If I didn't know better, I'd say an old hippy decorated this house. But it dates back to the 1700s or so the title records claim. A few hundred years before the hippies." He chuckled. "The craftsmanship in the woodworking seems authentic to the time period."

Running her fingers lightly over the wall, she murmured. "The cream-colored walls need a little paint maybe a bit of plaster or drywall, in contrast with all the woodwork." She shook her head in amazement. "I don't see a nick or sign of wear. Do you?"

"No." He walked along the hallway pushed the first door open and his jaw dropped. The crown molding was carved in a moon and star pattern matching the oval in the door. "Look at this." He pointed to the ceiling molding.

The air whooshed out of her. She paused for a moment then sprinted to the next door with a dragon carved in the oval and pushed open the door. "Brock, you're gonna want to see this."

Tearing his gaze from the first room, he bolted to the next where she stood in the doorway, one hand held to her mouth the other pointing to the ceiling. Inside the light streamed in the dirty windows to reveal walls in need of paint, but again the crown molding was delicately carved in dragons and castles.

"Quite a contrast from the walls to the perfectly maintained moldings." He glanced at the baseboards. "They're carved in the same wood, but in rounded edges fit flush to the wall. "Bet I know what is on the next door and molding." Catching her hand, he strode to the next door, a fairy was carved into the oval. She peered up at him as he twisted the knob and pushed open the door. Releasing her hand, he pointed toward the ceiling. "Yep, as I expected. Carved images of fairies dance amongst the flower garden."

"This house may not have a history of magic, but I'd bet it's magical. Pepper is going to go nuts when she sees this. You're going to put an offer in. Right?"

"As I said before, it may be completely out of my price range."

"I have a feeling the house has been waiting for you." She flung her hand to her mouth, her face flushed, and her gaze swiveled to him. "I don't know what made me say that."

Looking thoughtful, he grinned. "Since the day I stumbled upon Pepper's secret—then discovered that you and I share the gift or curse of Gypsy blood, things have been different—" Pausing, he shoved his hand in his jean's pocket and jingled the change inside. "I've been different. It's as if knowing magic exists awakened something in me."

"Join the club. Years ago Pepper made a believer out of me. In fact, there were times I wished—never mind. Whether it was my outlook or as you said magic awakened. But to be fair, I've always had what I called a sixth sense with animals, attuned to their feelings, almost their thoughts, fears, that kind of thing. Pepper called it my talent. But as we became close, I noticed other abilities…you'll think I'm crazy."

"Try me." He moved closer to her and the front door banged open. Quickly he rushed to the top of the stairs.

"Sorry I'm late," Bill stood at the bottom of the stairs grinning up at him. "Wow, this is quite a house. Never been in here before. Have you?" Ascending the stairs, his hand lightly on the banister he stopped occasionally to examine the balusters until he reached the top. "Kinda creepy in a way. Don't you think?" A nervous laugh bubbled out of his throat.

Raising an eyebrow, he shook his head. "Not really. Any idea what the owner wants for the house?"

Bill pulled his phone out of his pocket and touched the screen putting the phone to his ear. "Not sure. Haven't had time to do much research or talk to my friend who has the listing." He paused for a moment holding up one finger. "Hey Rod, what's the asking price for the house we talked about. I'm here with my client and he could be interested." Another pause. "That seems a little steep. I'll run it by my client and get back to you. The listing doesn't go live for another week, right?"

Brock mouthed to Gwen. "Told you, out of my range."

Bill waved an arm in dismissal. "Oh, got ya. I'll get back to you before—Hey email me that info. We'll keep the key for a couple more days. Thanks. I'll be in touch." Bill ended the call shaking his head. "I can't believe it."

He glanced around, backed down the stairs and poked his head into the downstairs rooms, then returned to the bottom of the staircase, touched the newel post, and jerked his hand back. "Creepy. Anyway, the asking price is well within the range that you set. Even on the lower end." He tucked his phone in his coat pocket.

Brock met him at the bottom of the stairs. "Didn't you say the price was steep?"

"Of course. You want the best deal, don't you?" he laughed. "Bet I can get the price down with the promise of an immediate contract and quick closing." Bill rubbed his hands together gleefully.

He cleared his throat and narrowed his eyes. "I don't want to take advantage of anyone either."

"Hey, it's eat or be eaten in the real estate world son." A tri-tone sounded from Bill's phone. The real estate agent yanked out his phone, touched the screen, smiled, and turned the screen toward Brock.

"Wow, that's the asking price?"

"Yep, we'll counter offer less ten grand and see what happens. You got cash for escrow and a down?"

"Yes, but…"

"You come up with the funds and let me worry about the negotiations." Bill paused staring at him. "You do want this house?"

He glanced at Gwen descending the stairs slowly while chewing on her bottom lip. "Yes. I do."

"Then let me do my job. I'll be in touch tomorrow morning." Bill texted something on his phone then strode toward the door. "I'll be in my car. Technically, I'm not supposed to leave you in the house alone." He paused.

"I believe you already did when your assistant dropped of the key and took off." He grinned. "But I understand."

Bill narrowed his eyes then snickered. "It not like I don't know where to find you. Go ahead, finish looking around. I'll wait. We're going to keep the key anyway. Since you're going to purchase the property." Bill grasped the knob. The door creaked when he tugged it open.

"I don't think he likes it in here," Gwen whispered as her gaze followed Bill out the door.

"I was going to say the same thing." He shrugged. "Bill is acting strange. But... he is a real estate agent."

She snorted a laugh. "How well do you know him?"

"Pretty well. He's a friend of the family. Helped me negotiate the purchase of my vet office building. Though there wasn't much to it. Come on, might as well check out the rest of the house while we have the chance." He took her hand and led her toward a swinging door. Holding the louvered panel open, he paused in the door frame to peer into a state of the art kitchen. The appliances were polished to a gleam. Letting out a low whistle, he turned to see Gwen standing on tiptoe behind him.

Her hand resting on his shoulder, she peeked around him. "Looks like the appliances are new or were never used much." Lowering herself, she shoved at his arm still holding the door open and walked inside. Staring at the floor, she frowned. "Not a good place for a klutz like me. Drop a dish or glass on the tiled floor, it'll shatter in a million pieces."

"Good to know, won't use the fine china when you're around." He snickered and walked to the double wall ovens on their left. Tall oak cabinets lined the other three walls. A huge side-by-side fridge stood across from the large center island where a cooktop with grilling capability took up one-third of the possible granite counter space, a divided stainless sink occupied another third leaving a large portion for counter space.

"Whoever designed this knew their way around a kitchen."

"Stange it wasn't used much—or maybe household help spent a lot of time cleaning." She opened one of the double ovens, ran her finger inside. "Spotless."

He pointed to a copper carousel with hooks over the island and around the recessed lighting. I have a copper set of cookware that would look fantastic hanging there."

"Sounds like you enjoy cooking." Gwen closed the oven and turned around to face him.

"I do. When I have time."

"How did I not know that," she mused. "Seems there are a lot of things I don't know about you." She rubbed her hands on her jeans and tugged the strap of her backpack up on her shoulder.

"I guess there were a few things that didn't come up while we were in Lobster Cove. After we returned to Salem, we've both been busy."

"Yeah, payback for taking time off," she groused.

"I'm about changing that starting tonight. How about dinner?" He snapped his fingers. "I know just the place. Howling Wolf Taqueria. Made from scratch Mexican food, sometimes they have live music, and a bartender who knows how to make a fantastic margarita."

"I'm not much of a drinker, but love Mexican food. So you're on."

When he pushed the door open it squeaked loudly. He glared at the hinges. "This has got to go. I want a tall and wide archway here that connects the kitchen to this dining room. This door is such a noisy nuisance. You can't talk to the people in the dining room from the kitchen."

He pushed through the door. "You don't know if someone is on the other side. A recipe for disaster."

"Gee tell me how you really feel." She giggled. "The house isn't even yours yet."

"Oh, but it will be. How about we take a peek in the other rooms on the first floor. Then go home and change, I'll pick you up in an hour. And don't let anyone waylay you."

"As if I'd allow such a thing." She sniffed, turned the knob to a room off the main living area, and flipped the light switch. The study was lined with built-in bookshelves, a mahogany desk and a leather high back chair arranged in the far corner. A sheet of glass covered the desktop and dust covered everything. "Guess the former owner forgot something."

"Or didn't want it." She ran her fingers over the intricate carvings on the edges and corners of the desk leaving a trail in the dust. She bent down and tilted her head. "Would you look at this. I've never seen anything like it." The four short stout legs ended in lion or dragon feet. "This desk must be an antique and could be worth a fortune. Why would you leave it behind?"

Hesitating only a moment, suddenly he knew the answer, but had no idea how. "Because it matches the staircase, upstairs doors, and moldings."

"So it does." She glanced at the ceiling moldings dragons and castles had been etched here too. "We need a history of who owned this place since it was built." Her stomach growled loudly and her face turned scarlet. She flung her hand over her midsection. "After dinner or tomorrow."

"Sounds good." He touched his hand to the small

of her back and guided her toward the door. But when he turned the knob and tugged nothing happened. *How could the door be stuck?* Tugging again the door made a scraping sound like nails on a chalkboard, but moved only a half-inch.

She glanced quizzically at him. "What's wrong?"

"The door doesn't seem to want to open." Puzzled, he stared at the door. "Didn't have a bit of trouble opening it."

When she placed her hand gently on the wooden surface and murmured, "We'll be back." The door released and swung open a crack. A sliver of sunlight streamed through the crack and spread across the polished hardwood floor.

"What the hell?" Pulling the door open wide, he held it while she exited and he followed. "Why did you do that?"

"It's something I've seen Pepper do. I figured it was worth a try." In a whisper, she confided, "I don't think the house wanted you to leave."

He raised an eyebrow. "Now you're using personification to describe an inanimate object. The door or the house."

She shrugged. "It worked didn't it?"

Tapping on the window to Bill's car, Brock dangled the house key in front of the glass.

Bill rolled his window down. "Have you made a decision?"

"Yeah, make an offer and let's get the ball rolling." He slung an arm around Gwen's shoulders.

Glancing from Brock to Gwen, Bill's lips curved into a self-satisfied grin. "Well, all right then. That's what I like to hear." He tapped send on his tablet. "That was the offer we discussed. I'll let you know when I hear something." Bill started his engine. "We should be able to get the deal wrapped up in a couple of days."

His eyebrows winged up and his eyes widened. "That fast?"

"Yeah, the seller is motivated. He's moving his family out of the area and has already put an offer on another house across the country. You have financing already in place. Correct?"

"Yes, depending on the purchase price." He pursed his lips. "You're going to stay within my budget?"

"Of course. Well below, if I have my way." A smug grin spread across Bill's face as the real estate agent waved his hand. "Got another client appointment in five, so better get going. I'll be in touch."

He coughed and fanned at the dust kicked up by Bill's car disappearing down the road. "Never allows grass to grow under his feet."

"I guess not." As the dust settled, she switched her gaze from the road just in time to see the porch light flicker on and off. *Yeah, there is something about this house.* She tilted her face up to meet his gaze. "Did you see that?"

Chapter Five
What on Earth Is Going On?

"See what?" His eyebrows furrowed adding to his already puzzled expression.

"Oh, nothing." She looked at the dark porch light, then waved her hand in a gesture of dismissal chalking it up to a combination of not enough sleep and an overactive imagination.

His hand slipped to her waist as he guided her back to her vehicle. "What's the weekend look like for you?"

She hesitated, going over her schedule in her mind. The full-time staff had completed training and certification. Trinity, her assistant, had been with her for nearly a year, it was time to let her handle things on her own. Not being tied to the sanctuary twenty-four/seven would be a new but welcome experience. The last time she left for an extended time over Christmas, she'd come back to a paperwork nightmare.

Trinity had handled the day to day operations like a pro, but because she hadn't planned on being gone so long, she hadn't trained her assistant on all the necessary paperwork and the end of the year, well her mind had been elsewhere. Which is why she was trying to keep Brock at arm's length. But every time she was with him, her common sense and self-control went right out the window. Like now, she wanted nothing more than to spend time with him, but her obligations to the sanctuary had to come first. Didn't they?

Leaning over, he waved a large hand in front of her face. "Gwen… are you in there?"

Giggling she caught his hand, twined their fingers and rubbed his knuckles over her cheek. *What the hell am I doing?* Sucking in a breath, she gave him a coquettish look. "Yep, she's here. What do you have in mind?"

"Awww, wishful thinking. Tomorrow will be hellish because I took this afternoon off. I'm on call Friday, but Jason is due back and taking the weekend calls. So… how about we take off for a couple of days, somewhere no one can find us and…

"I'll pencil you in for the weekend and we'll see how things shake out.Hopefully, Trinity handled the things this afternoon. I just finished the year-end paperwork I came back to from the holidays." She scrunched up her face and blew a strand of hair out of her face.

"I see." He escorted her over to her SUV, opened the door, and held it for her.

"I don't think you do. Every time we make plans something comes up on your end or mine. Maybe if we leave it vague, fate will allow us time together." She slipped into the seat, just as she tossed her bag on the passenger seat a familiar tune about the devil in Georgia began. She frowned, glared at the offending object, dumped her bag out and grabbed her phone. "Gwen here."

A man's strained voice echoed over the phone. "There is a man snooping around the sanctuary. Guess he's from the MSPCA. He's chasing the mutt you've been feeding and coaxing to trust you. Stopped his truck on the road, the dog bolted onto sanctuary property and headed for the barn. The guy is still after it. What do you want me to do?"

"Sam?"

"Yeah. It's me."

"Can you go out, close the barn door effectively capturing the poor thing? It's got to be scared out of its mind." She shook her head. "This will undo all the progress we've made, but better than going to the pound. Do you know the guy?"

"Nope. Never seen him before. Must be new."

"I'm on my way. If you get the dog in the barn, don't open it for anyone. Including the dog catcher. If you have a conversation with the guy, inform him he is on private property. Ask him nicely to leave. My ETA fifteen minutes, give or take." She tossed the phone on the seat, grabbed her keys and started the engine.

Brock reached through the window and closed his hand over hers on the steering wheel. "Want me to come with you?"

She started to shake her head no, then reconsidered. "Yeah." Gunning the SUV, she took off, spewing gravel in her wake. A quick glance in the rearview mirror, she saw Brock sprint to his truck then pull into the street behind her. "This is the last thing I need."

Stopping beside the unfamiliar truck, she shoved her vehicle in park, turned the engine off, and ran toward the barn where Sam appeared to be having a heated argument with a man she didn't recognize. He didn't have on the MSPCA uniform either. Slowing her pace, she reached for her phone. "Shit." Her phone was still in the SUV. A quick glance over her shoulder, she saw Brock sprinting toward her. "Call the humane society, something doesn't feel right." She picked up her pace.

Brock grabbed her sleeve and put his phone in her hand. "You call them, I'll handle this." With a burst of speed, he left her behind and reached the barn quickly skidding to a stop. "What's going on here? You're aware this is private property?"

"We received a complaint about a dangerous feral dog acting aggressively. I'm here to take it in."

Joining the group breathing hard, she narrowed her eyes at the man clenching her hand at her hip while holding the phone to her ear. "What gives you the authority to be on my property chasing one of my animals?"

"I'm with the Northeast Animal Shelter. A dangerous dog is nothing to mess with." The man shifted from foot to foot and tugged on his worn black ball cap.

Brock put his hand on her arm then switched his attention to the man. "We need to see some ID." He sidled closer to Sam a tall muscular man who was standing feet a shoulder-length apart with his back leaning on the barn door. Sam was the sanctuary's security when necessary and maintenance ordinarily.

"It's in the truck." He pointed toward the parking lot.

"I suggest you go get it. Otherwise, the dog isn't going anywhere." A low growl then a series of barks erupted from behind the barn door.

Phone to her ear, she waited only a moment. "Hello… This is Gwen from the Salem Sanctuary. Did you send an employee out here?"

The man took off at a dead run toward his truck, jumped inside, and took off. Brock started to give chase, but Sam held out the sanctuary's cell phone.

Gwen leaned over to see what Sam had. On the screen was a picture of the man and the truck, license plate prominently displayed.

Brock skidded to a halt. "Good job. Let me see the phone."

"You didn't? That's weird, there was a man here impersonating a person from your office."

"Sorry we have no record of a complaint or dispatching someone to your location," the Northeast Animal Shelter representative explained.

"Thanks." She disconnected the call. "Why would someone be snooping around here, then chase a strange dog, pretending to be someone he wasn't? I don't have anything to hide." Her brow furrowed as she shifted her gaze from Sam to Brock. "Nothing worth stealing…"

"Unless you count all the state of the art equipment and medical supplies you've invested in recently. What about medications? What do you keep on hand?"

"Nothing a drug addict would want. If that's where you're going."

"Figured. Look here, Sam took pictures of your visitor, vehicle, and got a license plate. Probably should alert the police to the intruder." Brock returned the sanctuary phone.

"For what, chasing a dog that isn't even mine?" As if on cue, the dog growled and barked again. She handed the phone back to Sam, glanced at the double barn door, and opened the top half a crack. "We gotta do something about you," she crooned. "It's not safe for you on your own right now." The dog quieted and cocked its head peering up at her.

Brock touched her shoulder to get her attention. "No, he was trespassing on your property. You don't know what his intent was. What if he comes back?"

Sam straightened. "I'll make sure he regrets it."

"Now hold on." She placed a gentle hand on Sam's shoulder. "We don't want any trouble. I'll call the police and report the trespass. We'll all be more vigilant. Pay more attention to the security and monitoring system we recently had installed." *At Pepper's insistence*, she added silently. Which was one of the conditions for the ongoing donations. Her friend's voice wound its way through her mind. *Never can be too careful, the animal's lives depend on you.* Mentally she ticked off the types of creatures and their conditions that called the sanctuary home. *Nothing housed here would attract trouble.*

Sam slapped his hand to his forehead. "I should have reviewed the surveillance footage. I was headed out the door for rounds when I saw him. The door banged shut and alerted him to my presence. How stupid. At least I remembered to take photos."

She shook her head and flashed him an understanding smile. "Not used to having to worry about security. It's not your fault. Perhaps we should assign a volunteer to monitor the system." She took the phone from Sam, touched the sanctuary phone's screen, and scrolled to the police station's number and tapped an entry. "Hey Jess, it's Gwen. We had a trespasser here a little while ago. Sam caught him skulking around outside of the sanctuary. He took off after one of our skittish dogs. Sam intercepted him, secured the dog in the barn. But here's the weird part, the man claimed he was from Northeast Animal Shelter. I checked he wasn't. We have a photo of him, his truck, and it's license plate. Can I forward them to you?"

"Sure. I'll take a look, run the plate. But since he's gone and nothing happened or missing… Right?"

"Right. I know, but felt it should be reported since we don't normally have this type of problem out here."

"Understood. I'll contact Northeast Animal Shelter too. Oh, by the way, DOW is trying to get a hold of you. George said your phone just goes to voice mail. He left several messages. Didn't say it was urgent though."

"Oh, crap my cell is still in the SUV. I'll go get it now and find out what he wants. Thanks for letting me know." She disconnected the call and relayed the information to Brock and Sam.

"Wow, this day is never going to end." Sam took off his wide-brimmed hat, slapped it against his leg, then combed his fingers through his sandy blond hair and shoved his hat back on. "What do you supposed George wants?"

"One way to find out." She started for her vehicle then stopped. "Why don't we go take a look at the video surveillance first? I've got a funny feeling about all of this." Pausing again, she was torn. The surveillance, the DOW, the dog, and Brock…her head swam. She took a deep breath and blew it out slowly.

"Why don't you two go view the surveillance. I need to see the dog." Hand on the door handle, she turned. "Hey, could one of you bring me kibble and a bowl of fresh water?"

She opened the bottom half of the door, scooched inside closing it slowly behind her. The dog backed several feet away, ears flat to its head, and tail hanging down. Its fur was so badly matted it was hard to tell if its hackles were raised. Canine body language didn't lie.

This dog was scared, but not aggressive as she'd suspected in their prior encounters. Slowly she knelt, keeping her gaze down watching the dog with a sideways glance. "Sorry about this. Things got a little carried away today. I know you're scared, but it's going to be all right. I promise." She eased onto the floor and sat cross-legged.

The dog relaxed its stance, ears twitched and tongue licked at its muzzle as the dog held its ground. She watched the animal's chest rise and fall as its panicked breathing slowed to a somewhat normal rhythm. *A good sign.*

"No one is going to hurt you," she crooned. The canine's ribs were less visible than a couple of weeks before. So it was eating the food she'd left out. "Bet you could use some water." Inside the barn she located an old blanket slung over a stall gate. Slowly she got to her feet, reached for the blanket and slid it onto the floor. The dog's gaze was wary as it watched her every move.

Housed in the stalls at the other end of the barn, Blaze and Star nickered softly, tossing their heads and pawing the ground nervously. Not the ideal situation, but she had to make it work. Footsteps shuffled outside the door.

"I've got water and food. Where do you want me to put them?" Brock's deep calm voice soothed her nerves.

Easing backward till her foot touched the bottom half of the wooden door, she twisted then reached out to the open top. "Hand them to me." The stainless steel bowl of water sloshed over the side as she took the bowl and bent to set it on the floor. She arranged the bowl of kibble beside it. The dog's tail flicked and curled half-way over its back. The animal's gaze switched from her to the bowls and back again.

We're making progress. In a smooth movement, she sidled along the stall gates to the ones occupied by Star and Blaze. The gate latches were secure. *Good.* In a non-threatening manner, she returned to the barn door. The dog turned to keep her in its sights but still moved closer to the bowls.

"I'm going to leave you for a little while. No harm will come to you."

The dog cocked its head as if understanding.

Pepper had always told her she had a way of communicating with the animals, easing their fears. Over the years they worked together, she'd watched Pepper work her magic on the sick and fearful animals they'd rescued, but until today, she… Well, she hadn't believed she possessed that kind of talent. Gypsy magic Pepper had called it. She smiled thinking back to all the creatures she'd cared for as a girl growing up. Pepper was right.

The door *creaked* when she pulled it open slightly and slipped out, leaving the top-half open slightly, but not enough for the dog to escape. One last look back and she was satisfied the dog would settle for the night. Brock slouched, one shoulder leaned against the barn waiting for her when she exited.

His phone buzzed in his pocket. Glancing at the screen, his eyebrows knitted together as he motioned to her. "It's the DOW." He put the phone to his ear. "Dr.

Scutter." There was a long pause. "Really. I'll meet you in my office in a few." Another pause. "Gwen is here with me. I'll bring her along so you can bring us up to speed.

She blew out a breath. "Now what?"

Chapter Six
More Drama Amongst the Leagues of Wildlife Rescue

"Not sure. George indicates they have a situation that needs our attention. He's going to meet us at my office."

"In that case, I need to check on the turtles before I leave and see if Trinity can hang around a while longer." She glanced at her watch. "I don't want to leave the animals and property without proper oversight. The incident today has made me a bit nervous. Looks like I'm going to need to hire more help."

"Not a bad idea. We've had to hire a twenty-four-hour security firm at the clinic for the safety of the animals and employees there overnight. I keep a few controlled substances on-premises. They're locked in a cabinet. I have the only key. But insurance now demands stringent security measures or our premiums could go through the roof." He paused for a beat. "Tell you what, I'll check on the turtles while you bring the staff up to speed. Meet you out front."

"Sound's good. Yeah, guess I've had my head in the sand regarding security. Pepper insisted on all the security upgrades. Though at the time, I thought she was crazy. Guess not."

Sam met them at the sanctuary office door. "Need

me to stick around?"

"I'd appreciate it. Oh, have someone put a Do Not Disturb sign on the main barn door indicating the dog is inside. If you need to get at the horses, do it from the outside stall doors. I'll handle the dog when I get back. DOW wants to meet with us at Brock's office. Not sure how long that will take."

"No problem."

Gwen was still with Trinity and the staff when he headed outside after checking on the turtles. Scanning the area for anything unusual, he found nothing, it was a calm beautiful evening. The sun disappeared behind the horizon in a spectacular array of orange and yellow fading to red and purple across a blue sky as dusk fell. He slid his cell out of his pocket and called the security guard on duty at the clinic to bring him up to speed.

A feeling of foreboding washed over him when Gwen exited the office, the screen door banging behind her. He pushed the feeling away. *Too much drama lately.* "Turtles look great. RoadTrip was busy trying to get his bandage that splints his leg off, but so far no luck. The longer RT keeps it on the better the leg will heal. The eye is healing, but not sure if he has sight in that eye or not. We'll give it a little more time."

"Yeah, I was kinda afraid of that. When I approach him from his blindside, he swings his head around to watch me with his good eye." She sighed.

"I noticed that too." He paused for a beat. "On the bright side, according to their charts, the baby Desert Tortoises are eating, drinking, and moving around in their heated enclosure."

A slow smile turned up the corners of her mouth. "Once it warms up, we'll move them into the outside enclosures during the day where they'll have a lot more room and defused sunlight."

"Good idea. Figured the babies would be fine. We'll evaluate RT again after his course of antibiotics is through." He wrapped an arm around her and pulled her in close for a kiss before opening the passenger door and helping her into the truck. "Not the way I had the evening planned."

"Me either. Maybe this thing with George won't take long. Then we can have a nice dinner and relax."

"Sounds like a plan." He slid behind the steering wheel, started the engine and guided the truck down the street toward the clinic. It was back. That feeling of foreboding and it was getting stronger. His grandmother always had a second sense about danger. Heck, she had the reputation of being a seer in the old country. His mother claimed it was the ramblings of an old woman. Yet she always smiled at his grandmother, as if they shared a secret.

His mother had the same reaction to the Gypsy magic his grandmother claimed ran in her blood. When he was a boy, his grandmother would wink at him as his mother denied there was such a thing as magic. Any kind of magic. His grandmother would point with her bony, crooked arthritic fingers at him and say "Boy, you've got the magic, don't be afraid of it or to believe…" then she'd nod in his mother's direction and cackle. He was never sure if Grams did that to infuriate his mother, which it did, or because she believed.

When he slowed in front of the clinic, a DOW truck was already there along with a police cruiser. Both men were out of their vehicles standing in front of the clinic conversing. "Wow, what the heck?" Circling behind the clinic, he parked by the back door. "Ever feel like you are walking into a hornets' nest without protection?"

She snickered, a wicked sparkle lit up her eyes. "Yes, and it's never good."

"Mind out of the gutter please, Gwen. I meant a beekeeper suit or something." He couldn't help but chuckle at her lower lip stuck out in a pout like a scolded child. The security lights above the door cast pools of white light on the surroundings as he unlocked the door, stepped inside and was met by the security guard. "Trey, I'll handle this, continue on with your rounds. Meet you at the control center. Anything odd on the monitors tonight?"

"Nope. Quiet, just the way I like it." The guard moved off toward the back of the clinic with one final glance at the people standing outside the front door.

Automatically his hand felt for the main light switch on the wall and flipped it. The room was bathed in a warm golden glow which he found made the animals more relaxed than the harsh light of the fluorescents previously used.

Gwen made her way to the front door ahead of him. Unlocking the door, he ushered the men into the clinic's waiting room. That's when he noticed George was carrying a box with what appeared to be burlap sticking out of the top. "What do we have here?"

"We talked to the individual who found the wood turtle I brought to Gwen and retraced his steps. After scouring the area away from the road, we found three burlap bags stuffed behind a large oak tree." He pointed to the box. "Three more Wood Turtles not in the best of shape."

"Wood Turtles are globally-endangered," Gwen bit out clenching her hands on her hips. "As a long-lived species with low reproductive rate, Wood Turtles are especially susceptible to mortality and disturbance. The new subdivision going in along the creek is eliminating their natural habitat. Then you have low-lifes come by and scoop 'em up. Disgusting."

"Someone has done her homework." George shot her a quick grin.

"Yes, and I had a long discussion with Pepper. You remember her."

"Sure do. Great talent in the rehab specialist realm. Too bad those stupid witchcraft rumors chased her off. I believe the city fathers do that ever so often to keep the Salem Witchcraft Trials' memory alive and well. Tourist dollars line the city's pockets."

"Yeah, but it cost me a wonderful employee." Gwen shrugged one shoulder. "But it all worked out for the best, she's happily married to a man who is as passionate about wildlife rescue as she is. Our loss was Lobster Cove's gain. Her rescue is doing wonderfully well."

"Of course it is. Back to the turtles, they are often targeted by the pet trade, brings a hefty price, even though collecting Wood Turtles from the wild is illegal." George shifted the box and glanced at Brock.

"I didn't know that about the pet trade. Pepper didn't mention it. Heck a few days ago was my first encounter with the species." Gwen peeked into one of the burlap bags. "Yep, looks like RoadTrip."

George raised an eyebrow and shifted his attention to Brock. "Not even going to ask."

"Wise man." An exam room door squeaked when

Brock pushed it open and turned on the light. "Let's have a look. You can set the box down on the exam table." Out of the lower cabinet, he pulled out three towels and spread them over the cool stainless steel surface.

Unfolding the top of the first burlap bag, he reached in and brought out a turtle approximately nine inches in circumference, with vibrant orange on its front legs, yellow striping on it's under shell and a tan top shell. He gently placed the turtle on the towel and bent down eye level with the reptile. "Don't like the looks of what I can see of that right eye. Gwen watch this one."

"You got it." She slid her hands under the edge of the towel forming a barrier around the front of the turtle.

George held the remaining bags open. One bag had a large red stain on it. Brock removed the second turtle from that bag and eased it onto the exam table. By this time the first one had its head, legs and tail out. "The vibrant orange on legs, neck, and chin confirm this is a male, unlike RT." He murmured. "It's all right fellow, let me have a look at the foot." After several attempts at getting the foot out where he could see it, Gwen took the turtle from him.

She gently stroked the shell and cooed, "No one is going to hurt you. You're safe with us." To his surprise, the turtle angled its head out and pressed its foot against her hand. Giving him a sideways glance she smiled. "It's one of my superpowers." Turning her attention back to the turtle, she clicked her tongue. "Oh, that's a nasty gaping wound, might need stitches to close."

Brock nodded and moved on to the third turtle, a

juvenile with two missing toes on the left front foot. "These turtles were treated rough by someone who didn't know what they were doing. Appears they were being kept in a wire cage. That would explain the abrasions to the eyes. Looks like this one got her foot caught in the wires." He grimaced. "Possibly cut them right off in the struggle to get free. All the trauma to the foot made it swell. These wounds are badly infected." He pointed to the turtle with the eye injury. "He may lose sight in that eye."

"Apparently these three were injured and left behind." Gwen said with disgust.

"A sick or injured animal or reptile isn't going to be of any value in the pet trade. Which brings us to the reason Officer Tucker accompanied me this evening."

The officer rocked back on his heels and glanced at each of them. "We may be dealing with a poaching ring. By the condition of the reptiles, these people are inexperienced and looking to make a fast buck on the back of these turtles. Either way, they're dangerous individuals. And the people they may be working for more so which brings us back to your reported trespasser today."

"But I don't have...Oh, you mean they were after RoadTrip?" She frowned. "He won't be any good to anyone, with a broken leg and possible loss of vision."

The officer shrugged. "No, but perhaps they thought the rest of these were at your facility also."

"How would they know RT was even there unless you have someone in your organization feeding them information?" Gwen stared accusingly at George.

"Now wait on the finger-pointing until we're sure what we're dealing with." George bristled.

"It's late and it's been one hell of a day. How about we call it a night. I'll treat the turtles and keep them overnight. After that, we'll see how they're doing in the morning. We can make any necessary decisions then when we are fresh and rested."

Grumbles ensued from the two officers, but finally, George nodded his head in agreement. "Probably best."

"Be right back." Exiting the room, Brock returned in a couple of minutes with three tubs. He placed a turtle in each tub and glanced at Gwen. "You up for a long night?"

"Do I have a choice?" Stifling a yawn with her hand, her stomach growled loudly. "Need to get something to eat soon though."

"We can manage that." He washed his hands, waited for Gwen to wash hers, then escorted the men to the door, closed and locked it behind them. After watching the men walk to their cars, he led Gwen to the command center where the security guard was waiting.

She snapped her fingers and pulled out her phone. "I need to call Trinity and have her re-work the schedule. Security will be tricky with the staff I have, but we'll manage." Gwen walked outside the control center and put the phone to her ear.

Trey motioned toward the computers. "Nothing unusual on the monitors. I went back to this morning." He eyed Brock with interest. "Gonna tell me what's going on?"

"Not sure yet. The DOW and police think there may be a poaching ring operating in the area." He jerked his thumb toward the exam room with the turtles. "You'll need to be extra vigilant until this situation sorts itself out. No unauthorized personnel allowed inside the clinic outside of business hours without my knowledge."

"Understood, sir."

"Gwen and I will be here for the next couple of hours. I'll let you know when we leave." His mind wandered to the frozen pizzas he usually kept in the freezer for emergencies and long nights. This one definitely qualified. Gwen returned to the room. He took her hand and strode to the small kitchen area in the back of the clinic near the break room.

When he yanked open the freezer, he breathed a sigh of relief. One large pizza rested inside. *I'd better restock soon.* Next, he opened the door to the fridge and took out two bottles of cola and handed one to Gwen. "This should keep us going for the time being." He turned the small oven on and popped the pizza inside. "Let's take a better look at those turtles while the pizza bakes."

She took a long drink from the soda. "Ahhh, just what I needed—caffeine." Twisting the cap back on the bottle, she left it on the counter and followed him to the exam room.

Chapter Seven
Ask and Ye Shall Receive

It was well after midnight when Brock flicked off the lights and notified the guard they were leaving. Gwen was looking forward to her cozy bed and a few hours of sleep.

After Brock dropped her off at the cottage she checked on the dog. It was asleep. Once in bed, she spent the rest of the night tossing and turning and considering her options. Before dawn, she'd given up on sleep and made herself a quick breakfast.

Security had never been an issue at the sanctuary, but now, even if it wasn't a confirmed crime, they'd had an uninvited guest. With no security protocols in place, she'd had to scramble to staff the sanctuary for the overnight hours. Sam had done a great job under the circumstances, but he was going to need help.

She pushed aside her empty cereal bowl, took a sip of her orange spice tea and set the cup back in the saucer tapping her fingers on the table. Picking up the last bite of toast, she popped it in her mouth then stared at her phone. Willing it to ring. Nothing. So much for that idea. Reaching for the pad and pencil she always kept on the table, she roughed out a security plan to review with Sam and Brock before putting it into action.

Disgruntled at her lack of ability, she rinsed her

cup and bowl then set them in the dish drainer. When she turned around her phone played a merry tune. She all but leaped at the device. "Hey Pepper, I was just thinking about you."

"I know. I was in the middle of working with our new staff member. Your vibe was so strong, I had to excuse myself and call. What's that important?"

"Wow, that's great. I mean, that I could get to you."

"You had the magic all along just had to believe in yourself." Pepper chuckled. "Now, tell me what's going on?"

She brought Pepper up to speed, on the turtles or tortoises, the intruder, and their meeting last night at Brock's clinic. "Have you had a chance to talk with Lathen?"

"As a matter of fact, I was going to call you later this evening. One of the guys he was mentoring is in dire need of a job and he lives in your area. Needs work on his people skills, but Quintin is a hard worker. He'd be a good fit at your place, likes animals better than people. He has a wife and a baby on the way. He needs to be able to support them. The other guy…"

"Wait you have more than one? Wonderful. I'll take 'em."

"Why don't you let me finish?" Pepper laughed. "The other guy, Paul Thorp was also special forces, he has a security background and computer experience. He walks with a limp, so chasing down someone isn't going to happen. Also, he suffers from PTSD and social skills are not his strong suit. He's on meds and doing well. He'd be a good fit for you too. He lives within walking distance of the sanctuary and needs a job that will build his self-worth. It's been a stumbling block in his recovery. "

A male voice came on the phone. "Gwen, if you'll take a chance on this guy, I know he'll work out. He needs a break. Few employers are willing or flexible enough to work with him. They see PTSD and shy away. I know you won't, and the other guy, Quintin Rico, we're sending over was in rehab with Paul, so… Both know I'll be checking in on them regularly."

"Do you have phone numbers for them? As you probably heard from Pepper, I am really short-staffed. I'll let her fill you in on the specifics."

"Well, here's the thing, I told them about you and possible employment. Paul was so excited he wants to stop by this afternoon. Quintin can be at your office after therapy tomorrow. If those times work for you—if not we can do something else."

"I'll make it work. Their skill sets are what I need. We can work on the people skills as long as they show up, work hard, and don't offend anyone."

"As I said, Paul's people skills need work. Be patient with him and it will pay off. I'm positive."

"Good enough."

Pepper huffed into the phone. "If you're through butting into my conversation, I'd like to talk to Gwen about our trip to Salem in a couple of weeks. Like can we bring her anything."

He chuckled. "Of course. I've finished anyway."

"I'd love more of those larger heated cubes you guys created. With the turtles here now, we can use them. Other than that, I can't wait to see you two. Oh…I almost forgot. Brock has been house hunting."

"Ohhh, sounds like you and Brock are getting

serious. Glad to hear it."

"I said Brock is house hunting. Not us. Anyway, the house he's had his eye on for a long while came on the market. He invited me to come look at it with him. You aren't going to believe it. The staircase is out of this world. Newel post is carved in the image of a dragon with his tail forming the entire banister including the balcony thing in front of the bedrooms upstairs. The door panels of each room are different and carved to match the crown molding around the ceiling." She took a deep breath before continuing. "And… you are going to have to see and feel the rest to believe it."

"Are you claiming this house is enchanted?"

"Not at liberty to say. But the real estate agent claims it's one of the few houses in Salem that doesn't have some type of witch connection or magic. Can't say as I believe him. The reason Brock had his eye on the property is—" she clapped her hand over her mouth. "Not allowed to discuss that either."

"Why in heaven's not?"

"He wants an unbiased opinion when you see the house. Brock is going to do his own history search on the house. Thought I'd give you a heads up and see if you happened to be aware of anything." She rattled off the approximate address. "It's near Essex Street, I think. Crap, I've probably said too much already."

"Don't worry, I'll play along. But right off the bat, I can tell you Essex Street is known for haunted houses, whether they are real or a creation of Salem's Chamber of Commerce is another thing. Supposedly 310 Essex Street was the home of Judge Jonathan Corwin in Salem, Massachusetts, known as The Witch House. The only structure still standing in Salem with direct ties to the Salem witch trials of 1692."

Gwen let out a low whistle. "So the house could be….haunted?"

"Didn't say that. Corwin investigated the claims of diabolical activity when witchcraft accusations arose. He took the place of Judge Nathaniel Saltonstall, who resigned after Bridget Bishop's execution. Corwin supposedly sent nineteen people to the gallows for witchcraft. Most of which were innocent."

"Gee, familiar with Salem's history?"

"As all witches are. It was a dark time for witches and innocents. It came to the point that a lot of children died because people with knowledge of the healing arts feared for their lives, lest they were accused of witchcraft. Now don't get me wrong a number of witches lost their lives too. Ugh, let's get off this morbid subject."

"Agreed. I, uh, we just wanted your opinion on the house. If Brock buys it, you'll get a first-hand look. But hopefully before."

"He could keep it locked up in escrow until we get there. If the house is evil, his best bet is to walk away. Before you ask, yes there is such a thing." Pepper's voice took on a serious tone.

"Wasn't going to ask. I have enough problems as it is, not looking for the supernatural kind." She paused for a moment. "Unless they can help with my staffing shortage and our interloper." Laughing, she added, "Only kidding."

"The poaching matter is not a laughing matter. We know first-hand how many creatures are maimed or lose their lives to poachers." A door banged in the background of Pepper's side of the conversation. "I've got to finish up with our new staff member."

As she was about to disconnect the call, a tall man with well-defined muscle mass under his tight black t-shirt, jeans molded to his trunk-like thighs leaned his wide shoulders against the door jam and nodded toward her. His long surfer blond hair was tousled by the breeze. In a deep, confident tone, he inquired, "Would you be Gwen?"

She held up a finger and turned to the side. "Pepper before you go," she lowered her voice to a whisper, "give me a quick description of Paul?" *How had he found his way to my cottage?* When Pepper's description matched the man standing in her doorway, she ended the call with, "He's here now. I'll call you tonight."

Sam appeared in the doorway, out of breath, and gripped man's shoulder. The man narrowed his eyes at Sam, gave his shoulder a shake and returned his attention to Gwen.

"It's all right Sam. Mr. Thorpe has an appointment. Friends from Lobster Cove sent him. He has security and computer experience."

Narrowing his eyes, Sam looked Paul up and down. "Okay. But if you need anything, I'll be right outside." Sam hesitated with a backward glance then turned and sauntered a few yards from the cottage.

She stood drawing herself to her full six feet. He still towered above her a good six inches."Mr. Thorpe. Nice to meet you." Extending her hand, she walked toward him. He took her hand. His handshake was firm, business-like, but not overly aggressive. She hated men that tried to assert their dominance with a hand crushing grip. "I just got off the phone with Lathen, I understand you're interested in a job here." After motioning him inside, she glanced out at Sam and closed the door.

"That's correct." His eye contact never wavered as he handed her his resume.

Taking the paper, she quickly perused the document. *Lathen was right. The sanctuary could use his skills.* "Have a seat." She pointed to the chair at the kitchen table.

He shifted from foot to foot then moved to the chair and eased into it. "Thank you."

She joined him at the table and sat across from him. "What makes you think you'd be a good fit?" She met his intense gaze. "Working here is not easy, but the rewards are great. The pay would be less than you'd make in the private sector given your security and computer qualifications."

"I don't play well with others. But I'm working on that. I still need time off to meet with my therapist. I'll make up the time if need be. In the corporate world, people like me don't fit." He paused for a couple of beats. "I can't chase down anyone, so that's another point against me in the security world." Shifting in the chair, he stared at his right leg.

"Okay. I like your honesty. Recently, we've had a wakeup call. Our needs, match your qualifications to a tee." She shoved the pad she'd been jotting ideas on toward him. "Here's what I've been thinking regarding revamping our security protocol and surveillance system."

"You only have one security person?"

"Yes, and he doubles as maintenance. Around here we wear many hats."

"Understood. Security and surveillance isn't

something you can do part-time and be effective. There are a few changes I'd make, but you have a good solid start." He slid the pad back to her.

Through the open kitchen window, she heard a snort and looked at her watch. *I really need to get to work.* "How about this? Ninety days probationary period at an hourly rate of— " She wrote down a figure on the pad. "If you pass the ninety days, you'll get a raise and your pay will be salary like all my paid employees. Benefits are two weeks of vacation, medical insurance, and sick leave. I'm working on a retirement plan, but… We have a great crew here, I'll introduce you around. If you have a problem with any of the employees, you come to me. We don't tolerate disrespect of anyone. Fair enough?"

"Sounds good. When can I start?"

"Now." She raised an eyebrow questioningly.

A wide grin spread across his face. "Sure."

"Hey, Sam. Come in here," she hollered through the open window.

"Yes, ma'am." Sam strode through the door glancing from her to the new guy.

"I'd like you to meet Paul, you'll be working together. Computers and security are his things. Show him what we have. Review my draft for an updated security protocol." She tore off the sheet of paper and handed it to him. "Let's work together to come up with a plan we can all live with and keep the sanctuary safe. Paul, this is Sam, he'll be your immediate supervisor."

Paul nodded and clasped Sam's offered hand. "Good to meet you."

"Likewise." Sam glanced at her uneasily. "Supervisor?"

"Yep. No one beside me knows this place better than you. We'll be adding staff over the next few weeks so bring him up to speed quickly." She winked at Paul. "After Sam gives you a tour of the place, including where we have the cameras set up, he'll take you to Trinity. She's in our little office inside the bird habitat. You'll need to fill out your new hire paperwork before your first assignment." She glanced at Sam. "I want you to familiarize him with the computer system, software, and monitor system. You two put your heads together and see what we could be doing better."

"Will do." Sam gave her a salute.

"I need to go check on the dog. Figure out how to make it more comfortable and willing to stay within the confines of the sanctuary without caging." She chewed on her bottom lip. "It wouldn't react kindly to that. Eventually, we'll have to cut out the mats and give it a bath. I saw a couple festering sores yesterday when I left food and water." *This is not how I wanted this to go. I wanted to win the dog's trust, not force…*

After the men left, she picked up her cell phone, stuffed it in her pocket, and sprinted out the door closing it behind her. Inside the reptile building, she checked on the turtles, reviewed their charts for progress. Pleased with what she read, she hurried to the supply room and picked up a retractable hands-free leash and belt, snatched a harness, and dashed for the barn. *I hope this works.*

Chapter Eight
An Emergency Ends the Day

Despite a busy day, Gwen danced around his thoughts, interrupting his concentration more than once. Most of his clients were dogs, cats, a couple of bunnies and a guinea pig. The highlight of his day came as he was closing up. He'd just flipped the sign to closed and was locking the door when a semi-truck bobtail, swerved into the clinic's parking lot. The driver jumped out of his cab, paused at the front of his cab for a split second, then sprinted through the mist toward the building.

Brock opened the door and before he could get a word out, the trucker barreled in.

Out of breath, the man gasped, "I was on my way home. It flew right in front of me. I couldn't help it. The owl smashed into my grill and radiator. I stopped right away. When I went to extricate the bird from my grill it hooted and flopped one wing. Poor thing was still alive. I looked around and that's when I saw your sign. Can you help it? It's not moving now."

Brock grabbed several clean towels from a pile kept at the reception desk and followed the man to his truck. Snowy white feathers were covered in crimson. He moved a few head feathers, then the wing closest to him, but couldn't see where or how badly it was hurt. "We gotta get this bird out of the grill so I can assess its injuries." He watched for the rise and fall of its chest. "Still alive, but the owl has gone into shock."

The driver rushed around the side of the truck and yanked out a toolbox. The man flipped open the box and took out a large pair of cutters. "I can cut the metal around the bird so we can get it into the clinic. Rather than spending time trying to extricate her from the grill."

"Excellent. The sooner we get it inside, the better its chances of survival." He carefully supported the owl's body, covered the head as a precaution, while the trucker carefully cut through the metal bars around the unconscious creature.

An hour and a half later they'd cut the owl out of the semi's grill. He took it directly to surgery. The most damage was to one wing, the chest and shoulder area. The right foot was swollen but an x-ray verified it was only a bad sprain. Head trauma was unknown until or if the bird regained consciousness. Stress is a common killer of birds. This one was lucky to be alive at all.

The Snowy Owl may never fly again, but after surgery its vitals were stronger than he thought possible, considering... The owl was a survivor and he intended to give the bird every chance to do just that. After settling the bird into a special enclosure, he made sure the door sealed shut, then hooked up oxygen, removed his gloves, and leaned against the counter his shoulders sagging. With a deep breath, he trudged into the reception area and picked up his cell from the counter. Next to his phone was a scrap piece of paper with a phone number, name and a message scribbled on it. "I'd like to know if the bird survives." He shoved the paper in his pocket, tapped the phone's screen, and slid into a chair resting his head against the back eyes closed.

"Hello. Brock? I expected you three hours ago. Are you all right?"

He opened his eyes and glanced at the clock on the wall. It was nearly ten. "Wow, I'm sorry didn't know it was so late." He related the events of the evening. "I'm going to stay here with the owl. If it makes it through the night, the bird's chances of recovery increase dramatically. I want to be here when it wakes up."

"Oh, wow. You must be exhausted. I'll come by with something to eat and drink."

"That'd be great. But you don't have to," he said wearily.

"Be there in twenty."

A loud banging awoke him. Disoriented for a moment, he blinked and saw Gwen waving in the window glass of the door. She pounded again. He waved and pushed up from the chair. *Must've fallen asleep?* Hurriedly he strode to the door and flung it open. As she entered, he spun around and rushed to where he'd left the owl. Its eyes were still closed. The rhythmic rise and fall of its chest told him the owl was still alive. Turning, he crashed into Gwen. "Sorry."

"How's it doing?" She peered over his shoulder.

"About the same." He sighed. "Though the breathing has evened out, not as ragged as it was.

"Brought you roast beef, potatoes, and gravy." She held out a brown bag. "Probably need to warm it up a bit. Hey, where's the security guard? I brought enough for him too."

"I called and told him not to come in until midnight. Figured I'd be here at least that long. Thank you." Inhaling deeply, he touched his rumbling stomach that echoed his sentiments.

She reached into the bag, brought out paper plates, plastic ware and a couple of travel mugs. A thermos swung from her other hand. "Looks like you could use fresh coffee." Grinning, she poured him a cup of the steaming liquid.

He sipped the coffee. *Mmm, that hit the spot.*

With the roast beef dish in hand, she disappeared around the wall to the tiny kitchen. "Be back in a flash."

Suddenly, the delicious aroma of roast filled the room and his mouth watered. Until now, he hadn't realized how hungry he was. She returned with a steaming plate piled high with potatoes, roast beef all smothered in brown gravy. He picked up a fork and dug in. After a few fork fulls, he smiled at her. "This is delicious. Another of your talents?"

"Yep, Mom insisted all us kids learn to cook. An important life skill, she claimed." She stole a little piece of meat from the side of his plate. Popped it in her mouth. "It was a flavorful roast. Real tender."

"You know how my day went." He rolled his eyes and glanced toward the back. "Tell me about yours."

"Talked to Gwen. Lathen has two vets that might work out for security positions."

"Uh-huh. Look promising?" He forked up mash potatoes, topped it with a piece of roast and bit of gravy.

"I hired the first one." She told him about Paul's qualifications and the possibility of another interview tomorrow. "I sure hope they work out as well as the guys Pepper has working for her. Then there is the dog." She blew out a breath and threw up her hands in frustration. "We were doing so well, until that trespasser. Locking the dog in the barn undid all the progress we'd made. Though it did clean the food bowl. When I opened the door to attempt putting a harness on it, the dog bolted through my legs and out the barn door."

"You didn't close the— "

"Of course I closed the door." Her eyes narrowed. "It apparently didn't latch. I didn't see the dog at first when I walked in. The pup appeared from my left side and hit the door with its front paws so hard it jarred open. I didn't chase it. Figured we'll have to start all over."

"At least it left with a full belly." He chuckled.

She crossed her arms across her chest and glared at him. "I don't find anything funny about the events that led to its escape."

He held up his arms in a gesture of surrender. "It's a little funny. Face it, you were outsmarted by the creature. He/she heard you coming, hid and waited for the opportunity to escape."

"Never would have happened if I'd been on my game."

"Hard to be on your game with only a few hours sleep over the last—what—week? Know the feeling. How about we take in a movie and enjoy a nice quiet dinner Friday night? Jacob is on call over the weekend. They finally hired a nanny."

"Sounds—" She paused, held her finger to her lips. A weak hoot sounded from the back.

He pushed up from the desk and strode through the hallway, turned into the in-patient area where the owl was unsteadily trying to get to its feet inside the cubicle. Haunting yellow eyes wide open peered at him then blinked once. Allowing a few feet between him and the bird, he slowly lowered himself to its eye level.

In the soft light he'd left on, he could just make out both pupils were the same size. He breathed a sigh of relief. *I can rule out head injury, so far anyway.* The bird toppled over hitting its injured side against the enclosure and screeched.

"Its okay girl," he cooed. "No one is going to hurt you."

Gwen sucked in a breath behind him. "What a beautiful bird. And huge."

Only Gwen could see the beauty in the blood matted feathers of an injured owl. He shook his head. It was the reason he was drawn to her. There was no way he was going to let her get away.

"Never saw one up close before." Her gaze was full of compassion and understanding as she turned to him. "You're going to need a bigger enclosure. That one's not even big enough for her to spread one good wing. She does have one good wing. Right?"

"I think so." Concern creased his forehead as he watched the bird try to balance on only one foot gingerly touching the swollen foot to the floor of the enclosure in an attempt to steady itself. Finally, the bird gave into to exhaustion and leaned against the corner of the enclosure, its beak open breathing hard, and its eyes slowly sliding closed.

She wrapped her arms around his neck, pressing against his back, she whispered. "It's going to be fine. That bird is a fighter."

He leaned his head on her arm. "I hope so. It's

been through so much and it probably will never fly again. If it survives, do you have room to rehab it?"

"Of course. We're expanding the aviary in the next few months. As soon as I get a contractor worth a damn. I've had two bail on me."

Turning in her arms, he nibbled on her neck, along her jawline and kissed the corner of her mouth. "So glad you're here."

"Me too. Not enough time for us since Christmas. I miss—." Standing on tiptoes, she brushed her lips across his and deepened the kiss.

He groaned and pulled her tight against him. "To hell with dinner and a movie, let's disappear for the weekend." Her firm breasts against his chest were almost his undoing. Remembering where they were, he reluctantly pulled away keeping his arm around her waist, he lowered the lights and closed the door so as not to disturb the sleeping owl.

In the dark hallway, he pressed her up against the wall and slid his hand under her shirt feathering his fingers along the side of her breast through her lacy bra. She gripped his shoulders and wrapped her legs around his hips. Her warmth penetrated the crotch of his jeans driving him crazy.

They hadn't been intimate since Christmas when for the first time things got carried away and…he'd learned what a wild creature she really was. Making love to her had never been far from his mind since that night. She stirred his blood like no other. He had to get this relationship back on track.

Tilting her head to the side, she peered coyly at him from under her long, thick eyelashes. He trailed kisses down her neck, to the cleavage bared by her scooped neck shirt. Flicking his tongue between her breasts, he slid his hand behind her back, released the clasp of her bra, and licked his way further down until he could almost suck on her hard nipples.

She moaned, grabbed the bottom of her shirt and yanked it over her head baring both breasts to him. He smiled and took the first one nipple in his mouth, teased it with the tip of his tongue then moved to the other. *Oh God, where was the night security guard? Was it past midnight?*

Fumbling with the buttons on his shirt, she managed to unbutton several, tug his shirt out of his pants before she paused, fingers on the last button and cocked her head.

Shoes scuffed on the polished tile floor of the reception area telling him exactly where the guard was. A least he hoped it was the guard. Quick as lightning, he wrapped an arm around Gwen securing her against him, snatched her shirt off the floor, and slipped from the hallway into another exam room. Silently he let her down until her feet touched the floor.

She let out a soft giggle and slapped her hand over her mouth.

He straightened his shirt, tucked it inside his pants and opened the door. "Trey?"

"Yes, sir." The footsteps increased in speed toward him. "Figured I'd do an outside perimeter check before coming inside."

He stepped out into the hallway, bathed in a soft glow from the security lights, and closed the exam room door. "I'm going to be spending the night with the Snowy Owl in the clinic. So you won't have to patrol in here. Just the perimeter and stick close to the control center monitors."

"Got ya. There's another vehicle parked in the lot. Do you want me to check it out?"

"No. It's Gwen's SUV. She brought me supper tonight. She'll be leaving shortly after we check on the owl once more."

The corners of Trey's mouth curved in a smile. "Of course. Let me know when she's ready to leave, I can see her to the vehicle."

"Not necessary. But thanks. I could use a few minutes of fresh air." Hand on the door handle, he waved the security guard away and pushed the exam room door open.

"Whew, that was close." Gwen straightened her shirt and snickered. "I forgot you have a security guard."

"You'd think I'd know better," he grumbled. *What am I a horny teenager?* The expression on her face was that of an unrepentant teenager caught in the act. He couldn't help but laugh. "Been a while since I've been nearly discovered in a compromising position."

"The keyword there is nearly." She succumbed to a fit of giggles. Putting her hand over her mouth, she shook her head and finally mouthed "sorry".

Chuckling, he pulled her to him. "Confirms what I've suspected for a while now."

She drew in a breath. "What's that?"

"We need time alone— together." He snapped his fingers. "And I know just the place. My family has a cabin in the wilds of Maine." He grinned. "My parents are in Ireland on vacation, my brother and two sisters are busy with kids in school or summer camp or something. And you know Dylan is up to her earballs with her veterinary practice in Lobster Cove. So the cabin should be ours for a few days…. How about we take a long weekend end of next week. I'll check with everyone tomorrow so being gone the extra days won't throw a wrench into things at the clinic."

"Sounds like a plan, provided I can arrange the schedule so I can get more than a couple of days off."

He held up four fingers. "Four days maybe five. We need a break."

"What about the deal with your house?" She tilted her head up and blinked at him.

"We put in a bid and are waiting to hear if they accept it. If they do while I'm gone, Bill has the authority to counter-offer or accept the deal. I'll call him and let him know I'll be gone for a few days."

"I'll do my best, but I don't know. Two new hires this week."

He lowered his head and took her mouth with his, hot and demanding. Crushing her to him, he teased kisses along her jawline and lower, then slowly eased away. "Think what you'll be missing."

Breathing heavily again, she huffed, "Okay, okay, I get the picture. I'll arrange the time off somehow." She paused for a couple beats her brow creased in concentration. "If Sam runs into trouble with the new hires he's got my number. Since Lathen vetted them, I'm not worried. " She glanced at her watch. "I have to go if I am going to be worth anything later this morning."

"I'll walk you out. First, I'd like to check in on the owl. You okay with that?"

"Sure." Pausing she glanced up at him. "Why does this creature have you so…protective? We deal with life cut short all the time."

He blew out a breath. "Don't know. It's such a brave soul struggling to survive. I have to do everything I can to save it. Most creatures would have been dead upon impact. Not her."

"It's female?"

"Not sure. But guessing by the large size, I'd say female." Twining his fingers with hers, he led the way to the owl's enclosure. In the low light, he could see the bird's beak was closed and the rise and fall of its chest was regular. "Resting comfortably."

Gwen nodded and silently slipped through the open door. Neither spoke until he unlocked the outside door and held it open for her. Once outside he breathed in the cool night, scratch that, morning air. As she climbed inside her vehicle, he bent toward her and brushed his lips over hers.

"I'll call you in the morning. Let you know how the bird is doing and what I find out about next weekend. Regardless of whether or not the cabin is available, we are disappearing for a few days."

"Remember our friends will be here in a couple of weeks give or take."

"Can't wait to see them." With a wave, he watched the red tail lights to her SUV bob down the road until they were out of sight. Trudging into the clinic, he flipped the sign to Closed, locked the door, and notified Trey where he'd be.

At the supply closet, he took out a blanket, pillow and folding cot then quietly set it up outside the owl's room. It seemed like his head had just hit the pillow when a series of weak hoots greeted him. He scrubbed his hand across his face and blinked at the first rays of sunlight streaming through the front windows and down the hall.

Chapter Nine
A Cozy Cabin in the Maine Woods Provides the Perfect Getaway

On her rickety porch swing, Gwen sipped a cup of orange spice tea and waited, her overnight bag at her feet. Except for the dang recurring dream she'd had over the past few nights, she'd slept like a log and awoke rested and ready to go. She mulled over the dream, the strange feeling she awoke with and wondered what prompted it to keep returning. *Is my subconscious trying to tell me something?* She waved her hand as if to push thoughts of the dream to the corner of her mind where she'd deal with it later. Determined to enjoy the impromptu vacation, she took another sip of tea and enjoyed the view.

The screeches of the birds in the aviary as they greeted the day, along with barks and howls of the canines that were recovering or permanent residents filled the air. Sounds she'd become accustomed to and even enjoyed. *If the morning was quiet, something was wrong.*

Two large stainless steel bowls were arranged at the edge of the porch. One bowl filled with kibble the other she'd filled with freshwater this morning. No sign of the dog she'd dubbed Misfit. The one she'd been trying to befriend when things went south in a big way. Damn that poacher. She'd like to wring his neck if she ever saw him again.

Yet his appearance had set into motion necessary changes in security and led to hiring two competent workers that needed the jobs as badly as she needed their expertise. *Funny how things work out*. Thank God for Lathen and Pepper. The men were a perfect fit. In fact, the staff had started referring to Sam, Paul, and Quintin as the three musketeers. It was a good thing. A final sip of tea and she'd check on the turtles once more.

Quintin had installed a lock on the reptile building and bars on the windows as a precaution against anyone trying to get in. Something she'd never considered until recently. The larger reptile enclosures her friends from Lobster Cove would bring with them could be put to use right away. RoadTrip would be a permanent resident. The other Wood Turtles' futures were still up in the air.

Movement at the edge of the cottage had her getting to her feet until she saw Misfit creeping along the ground. She eased back in the swing. It was hard to tell with all of the dog's fur but it appeared to have lost weight since bolting out of the barn. At the bottom of the stairs, it froze, eying her then switching its gaze to the bowls. When she didn't move, the dog put one front paw on the bottom stair then another until finally, it reached the bowls. Close enough now, she could tell it was female.

It gobbled up the food in a matter of seconds while keeping an eye on her. When it had finished the pup backed away pausing to give her a sideways glance. A couple of slurps of water and it barreled down the stairs, stopping several yards from the porch to stare at her. Then the canine was gone. But in those few moments, something had changed, something in Misfit's demeanor and a gut feeling told her they were back on track. Thrilled, she jumped up and refilled the bowl with kibble, nearly spilling it into the water in her excitement. She picked up her phone and tapped the #1. Trinity answered on the first ring.

"I thought you were gone by now." She chuckled. "Your sexy hunk stand you up?"

"No, not at all. He'll check on things at the clinic before he picks me up. Misfit was just here. She looks thinner than before, but she ate, drank and stared at me before disappearing into the woods."

"That's the first time the dog's been seen since the uninvited guest incident. Right?"

Gwen bit the side of her cheek to keep from laughing. Trinity didn't want to believe there had been a poacher on the premises stalking some of their residents, even though the police had all but confirmed it. The trespasser remained at large. "Yes. What I need you to do, is make sure there is freshwater and the bowl of kibble is full every morning until I get back."

"Sure no problem. Do we need a volunteer to stake out your cottage?"

This time Gwen did giggle. "Won't be necessary; just have Sam tell the guys to watch for the dog on surveillance cameras and keep track of the time and date of sightings."

"Will do. Have a great time. We got things handled here."

"I'm sure you do." She reconsidered sprinting across the compound to check the turtles and verify that Sam received the message. Her staff was quite capable of handling the sanctuary for the few days she'd be gone. She eased back down on the swing.

A dust cloud rose from the bottom of the hill announcing the arrival of a visitor. She smiled when Brock's truck came into view and parked in the gravel lot. The last consecutive days off she'd had was the previous Christmas when she'd gone to Lobster Cove to visit Pepper. The sanctuary had been nearly empty except for the few permanent residents. That was different from the current situation of nearly a full house. However, now she had a trained staff of paid employees, a core security staff, and volunteers she could trust. They had this.

Spring was quickly warming into summer. Inhaling deeply of the fresh rain-washed air, she sighed. *I'm ready to leave it all behind for a few days*. Quickly, she rinsed her cup out in the cottage, closed and locked the door. Then she leaned over to pick up her bag and met Brock at the bottom of the stairs.

A mischievous twinkle in his eyes, he swept her off her feet and twirled her around. "Four glorious days, no clinic, no sanctuary, no emergencies—just you, me and the cabin in Puffin Cove, Maine."

"Wow, you are excited." She grinned. "Me too. But, I gotta ask. How's the owl?"

He set her down on the ground and kissed her lips affectionately. "She's doing great. Doubt she'll ever fly again, but we'll be transferring her to you when we get back. She needs rehab on that busted wing and to strengthen the other. Cuts and scrapes are healing well."

"Great to hear. We look forward to having her. Everything is all set up for the birds arrival. I'll see to her rehab myself. Though Pepper is going to consult.

She did such a fantastic job with Kaylee years ago. In addition, she's had a couple of endangered owls in her care recently."

"Figured. Between the two of you, that's one lucky owl." He took her bag and wrapped an arm around her waist. "Ready?"

"You betcha."

****

After tossing her bag in the back seat, he opened the passenger door and offered her a hand. She took it and climbed into his truck. When they passed the office she waved at Trinity and Sam standing outside the building. "You know they're checking to see if I really leave with you."

"Yeah, Jason was at the clinic bright and early this morning. Gave me a hard time about sleeping there until I filled him in on the owl. Then we went over the pending cases before I left him to fend for himself." He turned the truck onto the street leading to north MA114 out of town. "We'll catch I-95 at Salisbury, NH. From there take the coastal route to Owls Head. It's been a while since I've traveled to the cabin but should make it there without a problem."

"Won't need a map, huh? So exactly where is this cabin?" Gwen watched out the window.

"It's west of Owl's Head and south of Rockland in a little cove. It's a small fishing village made up of mostly summer homes, a few families remain there all year around. Most are caretakers for the cottages or are employed by the state or work in Rockland. The cabin and land have been in my family for generations. My great-great-great-grandfather was a lobsterman."

"Really. He owned his own boat?"

"Yep. Did right well too. He bought up parcels of land around our cabin when he had the opportunity. Our property is one of the largest in Puffin Cove with acres of ocean access on the northern border of Owls Head State Park. We have one beach area that is kinda sandy, but most are rocky. If you want a sandy beach, Crescent Beach south of Owls Head is great."

"Oh, I've seen pictures of Owls Head Lighthouse. Always wanted to visit there, tour the lighthouse, but the sanctuary kept me busy."

"Can't believe you've never been there."

"I've never been to a lot of places. I spent all my time and energy at the sanctuary. Until Pepper inherited the McKay land and set up an endowment fund for the sanctuary, we were on a shoestring budget and most the time the string was knotted in several places." She laughed.

"Owl's Head Lighthouse it is. We'll go there tomorrow morning or Sunday, can't remember what days the public has access. I remember the wide path surrounded by pine trees and spectacular views of the water off the sheer cliffs to the right. There are a series of stairs to get up to the lighthouse, but you can walk right up to it."

"Sounds like fun."

"The lighthouse which was built in 1825, is owned by the U.S. Coast Guard and licensed to the American Lighthouse Foundation. It stands twenty-six feet tall. The docents take visitors up the winding stairs to the top of the lighthouse to take in the breathtaking views of Penobscot Bay."

She clapped her hands together. "How exciting. I can't wait." Pausing to enjoy the scenery out the window, she turned toward him. "You sure know a lot about the lighthouse."

"When I was a kid, we spent most of the summer and vacations at the cabin. Lighthouses intrigued me. I made a nuisance of myself at the lighthouse when it was open." He chucked, "I imagine people who manned the lighthouse were glad when I went off to college."

"Not been back since then?"

"Well, not to the lighthouse. Visits with family once in a while. When I took over the veterinary practice, there was a lot of work to be done to make it a profitable clinic again and vacations went by the wayside. Jason had twins and life took over."

"I know that feeling well." She shifted in her seat and resumed enjoying the view. Her shoulders relaxed for the first time in she didn't know how long. She was one of those people who held her stress in her shoulders. On a bad day, she felt like her shoulders were up around her ears.

A feeling of calm washed over her, as it always did when she was with him. *Maybe Pepper was right, there was someone for everyone.* When Pepper first spouted that sentiment, she was sure it was the rose-colored glasses of a woman in love. But now, she wasn't so sure. Pepper and Lathen were so happy together, even after the bossy ghosts, her mother's stalker, and the other events they'd conquered. *Could I find that with—Brock? Whoa. One step at a time.* Avoiding his attention, she drew in a deep breath and let it out slowly. *I'm going to have fun this weekend and not worry about anything.*

Time flew by as she settled in and watched the breath-taking cliffs, evergreen forests, hard-scrabble towns zoom by out her window. The truck slowed and turned onto a two-lane paved road. Brock drove slowly through the little village. People stopped and waved, the store windows were decorated with flags and red, white and blue streamers. The middle of June and these people were ready for the Fourth of July. *Interesting, my kind of people.*

"We're here. Gonna stop for gas and a few supplies before heading to the cabin." Brock jumped out of the truck.

She stepped out of the truck, stretched and glanced around. *Only one gas station in the village? Huh?* Talk about a one-stoplight town. The old fashion lamp posts along Main Street were decorated with hanging baskets filled with colorful flowers and a nice sized flag tucked in each one. Planters filled with a wide variety of blooming plants with more streamers adorned the street corners. People stopped to chat on the sidewalk and several people did a double-take as Brock drove through town.

A gray-haired withered old man shuffled out of the gas station office, his sparkling green eyes wide. "Hey, aren't you Brock Scutter?"

Brock grinned wide. "In the flesh. Mr. Prescott. I figured you'd be retired by now." He reached out and shook the old man's hand. "How's the family?"

"Ornery as ever. The wife wants me to sell the place. But what am I gonna do? Sit on the front porch and watch the world go by? No sir. Not me. Besides, how am I going to find out what's going on? Guess they can bury me out back." Mr. Prescott's eyes twinkled with mischief as he turned his attention to her. "Who's this beautiful gal? Finally settled down, did you?"

"Not quite. This is my friend, Gwen, she operates a wildlife sanctuary in Salem. We're here for the weekend for some R&R." He finished pumping the gas and returned the nozzle to the holder.

The old man pushed his ball cap back on his head and glanced at Brock. "Good to get away from the big city rat race once in a while. Haven't seen your mom and dad for a while."

"Their spending a couple of months in Ireland. I think Molly and her family went with them, to help settle Grandda's estate."

"That's too bad. I mean about Shamus's dad. He was here several years ago with your mom and dad. Nice fellow. Talked kinda funny. I think you were in vet school at the time. Heard you bought a practice in Salem."

Brock's eyebrows winged up, nearly to his hairline. "You heard right. News travels fast, even when you aren't here."

"Yep. Just because you don't come around anymore, don't keep people from flapping their gums about you. Family is mighty proud of you young man."

"I hope so." Brock smiled.

"Parents and sisters keep us up-to-date on your accomplishments. Riva's three kids are getting big. Reckon oldest boy will be a teenager this year. Husband works too hard. She's always here by herself with the kids. Sometimes he joins her for a couple days."

"Well, I gotta get going Mr. Prescott. Need a few supplies from your general store. It's been good talking to you. Probably see you before we leave."

"You can count on it. The Mrs is going to want to

see you before you high tail it out of here." The old man took off his ball cap, slapped it again against the side of his leg, and repositioned it on his head.

"We'll be out and about most days, want to take Gwen to Owl's Head and Crescent beach. Do a little hiking. Show her around where I grew up. But should be home in the evenings. Look forward to visiting with you and your wife."

Mr. Prescott took a rag out of the back pocket of his overalls and polished the driver's side mirror. "Nice truck." Stuffing the rag back in his pocket, the man moseyed back toward the building that housed the office and general store. "'Spose you can call me Jack, now that you are all grown up."

"Thank you. Jack." Brock took her hand and they picked up some marshmallows, chocolate bars, and graham crackers, along with cold soda and a six-pack of beer, eggs, bread, and a few other essentials. Taking his wallet out of his pocket, he paid for the items and turned to her. "Ready?" He picked up the bags with one hand, wrapped his arm around her waist and whispered, "Give 'em something to talk about."

She picked up the other two bags, giggled, and brushed a kiss on his cheek. "Yep."

After loading the groceries, Brock swung into the truck and started the engine when his phone rang. He frowned and yanked the cell out of his pocket, glared at the screen, then his expression relaxed. "It's Bill." Touching the screen before he put the phone to his ear, he said. "Hey, Bill. What's up?"

A voice boomed through the phone so loud she could hear him. "Where are you?"

"Taking a little vacation."

"The owners agree to our price. Want to close next week? You going to be back?"

"Maybe Thursday. But schedule-wise the following week would be better. Provided all our stipulations are met."

The volume of the voice quieted. Brock nodded. "Set it up." With a tap on the screen, he ended the call. A wide grin spread across his face and he pumped his fist in the air.

She eyed him questioningly. "What?"

Chapter Ten
Expect the Unexpected Where Magic and Mystery
Meet

"They accepted Bill's lower offer. So we're all
set."

"On the house?"

"Yep. It's not a done deal yet. Gotta put the money
down and tie up a few loose ends, like new carpet,
house inspection, and roof replacement. But Bill
doesn't see a problem. We'll get the contract in writing
and nail everything down. Closing could be in the next
week or two."

"You might want Pepper and Lathen to walk the
house first. I get a twitchy feeling inside it. But then
again, it's not my house." She sighed. "It is a beautiful,
unique old home."

Oh, don't say that it could be our house, if...
*P*ausing for a beat, he scrubbed his hand across his face.
I gotta make this work. A turn off loomed ahead, he
turned up the gravel road, glad to see it had been
recently graded, then followed the familiar twists and
turns until the two-story cabin came into view.

The years seemed to melt away as he followed the
circular driveway up to the cabin and brought the truck
to a stop in front. The gas lanterns still lead the way up
the path to the cabin. *Wonder if they still work?*

Flashbacks of growing up here, the gatherings of a

large Irish Gypsy family, a sense of loss welled up in him for his grandparents on both sides who'd passed away in recent years. They were so much a part of his fond memories in this place. As were the squabbles between his four siblings regarding the chores, who got to take the boat out, who had to paddle, and who went to town with Grand Da.

They'd all raced for his old beat-up truck and jump into the passenger seat, pushing and shoving until a couple of them were forced out. They'd have to wait until next time. His sister, Dylan, nearly always got to sit next to Grandda. Even today, he wasn't quite sure how she did it.

He grinned and opened the truck door. The sea breeze heavy with brine buffeted his face. He inhaled deeply brushing the hair out of his eyes. "We're here." Gwen sat slack-jawed staring at the cabin. "Not what you expected for a Gypsy clan?" he teased. His brows furrowed. *I never asked or she never mentioned much about her family other than—actually had it been Pepper who mentioned first that Gwen had Gypsy blood in her veins? Yes.*

On that fateful day, he'd brought a little owl, wrapped in a blanket to Pepper's new wildlife rescue on Dylan's instructions. He'd followed the path to the lake on Pepper's property. It was there that he was gobsmacked by the discovery that ghosts existed, roses blooming around the lake in the dead of winter, the beautifully hand-carved wooden arbor that just appeared out of thin air. Magic was real and part of Pepper and Lathen's wedding ceremony. He shook his head. *What an eye-opening experience.*

Gwen had escorted him back to Pepper's house

where the McKay's, and Pepper had explained everything to him. *Witches. Enchanted land.* He'd never quite forgiven his sister, Dylan, who had a clinic in Lobster Cove, for not warning him. He shrugged one shoulder. *Probably wouldn't have believed her without seeing it with my own eyes. See it I did.*

Pausing he rubbed his chin with thumb and forefinger. *When was the last time Dylan was here? Heck, when was the last time I was up here. Five maybe eight years ago?* The Christmas holidays in Lobster Cove seemed so far away now. *Though it's only been six months.* The sound of Gwen's voice brought him back to the here and now.

"Not exactly. It's absolutely gorgeous. And so much land. Does it all belong to your family?" She sucked in a breath and stepped out of the truck to stand on the running board getting a better look at her surroundings. "Wow."

He waved a hand toward the beach behind the cabin. "Our land stretches from where we turned onto the gravel road, all the way to the beach and several acres in both directions." Spreading his arms wide, he motioned from side to side. "We can take a hike after we get settled."

"I'd like that." She jumped off the running board and opened the back door to the pickup tugging out her bag.

"Let me get that." He rushed around the front of the truck.

Stubbornly she held onto the bag. "I've got it. You get yours and the door. We'll have to come back out for the rest of the stuff." She grinned up at him. "Since you do have the key."

Suitcase in hand, he stopped to finger one of the gas lanterns, then sprinted to the door and opened it. Inside a little fire burned merrily in the fireplace, not a speck of dust in sight. The kitchen table was set for two and the aroma of lobster stew wafted through the air. "What the heck?"

Peering over his shoulder, Gwen gasped. "Someone expecting you?"

"Not that I know of. It's been a couple of months since anyone has been here." A warm feeling of family he remembered from childhood enveloped him as he closed the door behind Gwen. The polished golden oak floors shone as if Molly's kids hadn't been the last to tramp through here. Not that Molly wouldn't have cleaned up after her three boys, but…

Gwen put her bag on the floor and glanced around. "Who takes care of the cabin when no one is here?"

"Nobody as far as I know." He made a mental note to call Molly and ask her. The door stood wide open as a gentle breeze wafted through the cabin.

Gwen put her hand on her hips. "Someone does. It doesn't magically stay this spotless. And who went to all this trouble to fix a delicious meal" Her stomach growled loudly. "Let's get the groceries in and put away so we can eat." She jerked her chin toward the kitchen in the open air concept cabin.

Inside the cabin was as he remembered. No walls downstairs, furniture his ancestors had built and carved by hand separating the rooms decorated in bright yellows, oranges, and turquoise. Hanging from the floor to ceiling window frames, shimmering crystals spun and threw rainbows around the room in the late afternoon sun. White-crested waves crashed to the shore as the sea birds screamed defending their territory or maybe searching for dinner. How he loved this place. "Sure."

She stood at the big picture window as he sprinted out the open door and slid to a halt beside the truck glancing back at her.

Jogging back to the cabin, arms full of bags, the breeze tousled his hair, flinging strands over his forehead as he grinned wide. Dropping the bags on the floor of the kitchen he backtracked and yanked up the duffel bags. "I'll take our bags upstairs and join you in a moment to put away the groceries. Then we can eat."

Sprinting up the stairs, he skidded to a halt at the first door at the top. Pushing it open he saw the old queen-sized bed had been replaced. In it's place stood a new king bed with an intricately carved forest scene into the head and footboard and matching dressers. *Wow. Mom and Dad have upgraded the place.* Without a thought to sleeping arrangements, he dropped the bags beside the bed and bounded back down the steps two at a time. On the landing, it hit him. Would she want to sleep in her own room, separate from him? Would she share his bed this weekend?

After the fiasco at the clinic, he was pretty sure they were both on the same page. He was giving this whole situation way to much thought. The stew's aroma had his mouth watering as he entered the warm friendly kitchen. He'd simply let things play out. By the time he got back to the kitchen, Gwen had all the groceries put away.

She stood in the kitchen ladling stew from the crock-pot that now sat in the middle of the table into bowls. A bottle of wine, rested in an ice bucket, crystal wine and water glasses were arranged next to each china plate. The folded light blue napkins were embroidered with the family crest, a raven over a colorful shield and the initial S. He remembered those napkins from when he was a kid. Yet the cloth was like new starched and folded. The silverware placed appropriately. "Hey, Gwen, where'd you find all the…"

"It was all here. I moved the crock-pot to the table so as not to spill anything. The pantry is full, there is also a pot of fresh-brewed coffee. If you want some. You have great neighbors or one heck of a maintenance staff."

"As far as I know, there is no maintenance staff, and neighbors are like us in and out of vacation homes— Someone must be playing a joke."

"Well, I like their joke. Let's eat. Homemade rolls are warm from the oven. Weird huh?" Gwen plopped in the chair and spooned up the stew. "Mmmm. This is delicious."

He picked up a roll, tossing it from hand to hand until it was cool enough to take a bite, he chewed, brows knitted in concentration. "I'll call Molly or Riva after dinner and see who I need to thank for all this wonderful hospitality. I know Dylan had nothing to do with it. She's been away from here longer than me."

"Yeah, her vet practice and Pepper's rescue keep her hopping." Spooning up another bite of stew, she blew on the hot liquid and glanced at him. "So you have three sisters and one brother. Where are you in the lineup?" She popped the spoon in her mouth. "Mmmmm. This is delicious."

He popped the cork and poured the wine in the glasses. The burgundy liquid winked in the firelight as it sloshed against the glass. "I'm the youngest. My three sisters are older. There's barely two years between each of them, then there are only eighteen months between Jeremiah and I. Dad thought he was going to have a brood of girls." A chuckle bubbled up from his throat. "Dad wanted to even the numbers, but Mom said she was through after me. Tough pregnancy and delivery, I'm told." He put his wine glass down, picked up a spoon, and sampled the stew.

A melodic giggled bubbled up from her throat. "You're the baby."

"Yep. Not nearly as fun as people are led to believe. I had three bossy sisters and a brother who didn't want me tagging along with him. But given all that, we are a close-knit family. How about yours?"

She took a sip of her wine and hesitated a moment as if considering what to tell him. "I was the middle wild child. Danced to the beat of my own drum, so as to speak. Dad was a law professor, he's retired now. Mom was the polar opposite of Dad, an artist, free spirit until she had kids. She deferred to my father's strict idea of raising children. I didn't fit the mold. Dad and I were like oil and water. I left the day of my eighteenth birthday. Haven't seen any of them since."

"You appear to have found your niche."

"Yeah, I worked my way through college, then went to work for Salem Sanctuary. The rest you know. Pepper was a Godsend—until…the magic storm. The barely-scraping-by years make me appreciate all that Pepper has done for our little sanctuary."

"Is that when you discovered you could understand the feelings of animals?"

She glanced at her wine while swirling it in her

glass. "I've always had a connection to creatures. But yes, Pepper, recognized it as being able to understand how they were feeling and what they were thinking. Kinda scary at first. But after she had to leave, I had no choice, if I was going to continue to help the animals in my care." She shrugged. "How about you? Why become a vet?"

Remembering back to a prior conversation that was interrupted, he decided to push a little more. "Do you have other talents I don't know about?"

She narrowed her eyes. "Not really."

His phone played a tune and he glared at it. *Every time I get close to getting an answer. It's almost like…* He jerked the phone out of his pocket and checked the screen. "Hi, Molly. Strange, I was planning to call you later."

"Hey, lil' brother. Figured it was you I felt. Find the cabin to your liking after all these years?"

"Sure. But you didn't need to go to all this trouble."

"What trouble?"

"The lobster stew, the rolls, the fireplace."

"You been working too hard bro. I've no idea what you are talking about. Besides I just got back from Ireland."

"You didn't arrange all this?"

"Nope. Was just hoping that one of the boys didn't leave a frog or worse in the cabin last time we were there. So I called to check."

"Then who would have set a fire in the fireplace, lobster stew in the crockpot, and homemade rolls in the oven. Oh, and a bottle of wine chilling."

"Not me. Wish I could take credit for…" She

paused mid-sentence and sucked in a breath. "You might want to call Mom or Dad. There are a few idiosyncrasies about the cabin that haven't been experienced in decades."

"What do you mean?"

"Call Mom or Dad. They can explain the phenomenon." She huffed. "Figures it would happen to you." A crash and squeal sounded. "Gotta go, the boys are at it again." She disconnected the call.

Staring at the phone, he finally swiped the screen and pocketed it.

"What was all that about?" Gwen raised her brows as she swept her impossibly long lashes over her enormous dark chocolate brown eyes.

Her expressions never failed to get a rise out of him. He shifted in the chair. "I'm not sure. We can finish dinner and take a walk along the beach. I could use some fresh air." *Neither Mom or Dad would appreciate a call at midnight their time in Ireland. Why couldn't or wouldn't Molly answer my questions?* He shrugged. *She always loved being mysterious.* A half-smile curved the corners of his mouth.

They picked up the dishes and put them in the dishwasher. He grabbed a huge beach blanket from the couch, a couple of large beach towels from the closet, and opened the door, waiting for her to exit then locking it behind him.

They stepped out into the cool evening air, sauntering down the lighted path to the beach, their fingers twined together, and arms swinging to and fro.

"Those path lights look like they are held in the claws of a dragon." She stopped, bent over and examined one. "Yep, that's exactly what they are."

He chuckled. "Yes, my parents and grandparents had a fetish with dragons. If you look closely at the brass door knocker when we return, you'll see two green eyes light up as you use the knocker. Used to freak out the new neighbors when they stopped by. I'll show you the back yard tomorrow, there's a blue scaled dragon fountain in the middle of it. Stepping stones from the porch to the fountain are shaped like blue and green dragon scales."

"Sounds interesting, I can't wait to see." The waves splashed along the shoreline, she leaned against him to remove her shoes then sprinted into the surf.

"The water's cold…" The words were no sooner out of his mouth than she squealed as a large wave engulfed her to the waist, the ocean spray covering the rest of her. She looked adorable standing there after the wave receded, clothes soaking wet clinging to her curves, rivulets of seawater streaming down her face and dripping from strands of her dark hair.

"Right you are." She laughed and rushed back to him, wrapped her arms around his neck and arched against him soaking the front of his clothes.

He slung the blanket and one towel over his shoulder then wrapped the other towel around her. Good thing she was cold or her actions would have caused a reaction. As she warmed against him his arousal stirred.

"Ohhh, you're sooo warm." She drew the words out as her teeth started to chatter.

"Better get you out of these wet clothes." Smiling seductively, his hands slid down to her waist then slowly tugged her wet tank top out of her jeans and feathered his warm fingers under her top, along her ribs lightly caressing the sides of her breasts. Tilting his head, he kissed her cold lips, then took her mouth with his. She seemed to revel in his possessive kiss. He wanted her here, now. *Glad I brought the blanket.*

Shivering, she unbuttoned his shirt and cuddled against his bare chest. He cupped her cute ass in his hands and lifted her. The towel slid to the ground. To his delight, she wrapped those long, sexy legs around his waist and squeezed.

****

The sun hung low in the sky and it would be dark soon. Glancing around the beach, he carried her toward an alcove that was protected from the rising tide and any prying eyes. He groaned as she ground her center against his crotch. Tossing the blanket on top of the smooth flat-topped boulder warmed by the earlier sun, he eased her down on the surface, unzipped her pants, and slid them off her legs. His fingers caressed and teased her soft folds as she reached down, unbuttoned his pants, and slid her hand inside to grip his velvety hardness. *He was definitely built to please a woman.*

She wiggled her foot between his legs and shoved his pants to his ankles. He kicked them to the side and leaned her back positioning himself between her legs spreading them wider. *What would it be like to take him in her mouth?* Before she could contemplate the action further, he was running a hand gently down her naked body caressing her breasts. He leaned over and kissed first one then the other, teasing the nipple with his tongue until it was a hard little berry.

All the while his fingers feathered between her legs teasing, exploring and dipping into her center. She loved the feel of his hot hands on her cool body heightening the erotic sensations.

Kissing a scorching trail down her body, he ignited a firestorm between her legs. She could barely breathe as the tip of his tongue teased her belly button. No one had ever taken this kind of time to ensure her pleasure. He nibbled lower, teased her hip bones lightly with his tongue then paused to smile up at her before he lowered his head and brushed his lips over her most intimate parts, his tongue swirled around her sensitive nub.

She writhed under him as he continued his teasing torture until she could stand no more and crashed over the cliff of ecstasy, gripping his hair with her fingers holding him in place until the last waves of pleasure washed over her. She'd lost track of time or place as he slid up and kissed her. He teased her center and slipped inside with a groan. "You feel so damn good."

"Mmmm," was all she could muster as together they found the rhythm that bound their bodies together until he increased the tempo and she succumbed to the rising passion like molten lava flowing out of a volcano and cried out. He followed her over the brink of ecstasy. Breathing hard, he lowered his forehead to hers, then kissed her tenderly pulling her upright against his chest. She wrapped her quivering legs around his waist again.

She raised a brow a mischievous grin curved her lips. "So that's it?"

"What do you think?" He grinned undulating his groin against her playfully.

She felt him stir inside her, he was still… she returned the favor. "I think it's my turn to be on top." Releasing one leg from his waist, she shoved against the rock pivoting him around so his backside was on the rock, folding her knees against the outside of his strong thighs, she braced her hands on his muscular chest. Twisting to the side, she grabbed the other towel from the rock and wrapped it around her letting the sides fall around them. "Ready for the ride of your life?" She giggled rubbing her center against the tip of his arousal.

"You bet," he growled grasping her hips and pulling her down on him.

Chapter Eleven
Surprise, Surprise—Unexpected Visitors

Wearing only his t-shirt which fell halfway down her thigh, she padded silently down the stairs and into the kitchen. The aroma of fresh-brewed coffee wafted through the room as a dark stream of the steaming liquid filled the glass pot. He must have it on a timer, she mused, opening one cupboard door after another in search of a mug and dishes.

Finding everything she needed, she set the table and placed the cast iron skillet on the stove then arranged slices of bacon in the pan. At the scent of frying bacon, her stomach growled loudly. She glanced out the window, the sun high overhead reflected on the white-capped waves crashing to shore. Her phone was still upstairs in her backpack. She glanced around the room for a clock. I*t must be close to noon.*

A pile of damp clothes in the middle of the living room made her smile. Last night had been fantastic. Never had she felt so cared for, so satisfied, though a bit sore this morning. Touching her finger to her still slightly swollen lips, she closed her eyes reliving the velvet warmth of his kisses and her whole body tingled at the memory. She sighed, turned toward the counter and plowed right into his bare chest. Squealing, she grabbed his shoulders to steady herself and stared into his smoldering gaze.

Laughing he wrapped his arm around her waist and kissed her soundly murmuring against her lips. "You should always open your eyes before you take a step."

She giggled and cuddled into him, noting he wore nothing but a pair of black silk briefs that did nothing to disguise his arousal. His usually sleek raven hair was tousled from sleep and made him the sexiest man alive in her book.

He reached for the bottom of the t-shirt she wore. "Got anything under there?"

"Wouldn't you like to know." She slapped at his hand, backed away and yanked at the hem of the shirt.

"Indeed I would."

"You'll just have to guess. The bacon is burning and I have the scrambled eggs ready to go into the pan. Orange juice is on the table, coffee on the counter. This place is well stocked."

He paused for a moment. "But I'm hungry for something else." Quick as a wink, he looped an arm around her waist, letting his hand slide lower to cup her behind, and pulled her to him. "As I suspected, nothing under here." Reaching behind her, he flipped the burner to off.

Her stomach rumbled again. He raised an eyebrow and snickered. "Guess we'll have to wait until after brunch."

She chewed on her bottom lip as she considered her options. Her traitorous body ready to jump him again.

They both turned toward the sound of gravel crunching under tires as a vehicle drove up the driveway and stopped out front. Two car doors slammed.

"Are you expecting someone?" She whirled on him.

"Nope." He walked to the front window and peered out. "The SUV is pulling a trailer and both are from Lobster Cove Wildlife Rescue and Rehab. It's got to be Pepper and Lathen. What the hell are they doing here and how'd they find us?" He picked through the pile of clothes on the floor, yanked on jeans from last night and stuffed the rest behind the couch.

She shrugged and giggled. "Remember we are talking Pepper here." Sprinting toward the front door, she flung it open to a surprised Pepper before remembering she was only wearing a t-shirt. When Lathen cleared his throat and Brock chuckled behind her, she felt the heat rise in her cheeks.

"I was about to ask if we were interrupting anything, but clearly we are." Pepper roared with laughter turning to cover her husband's eyes.

"How'd you find us?" Brock wanted to know, putting an arm around Gwen's shoulder.

"I called the Sanctuary. Trinity told us you left with Brock for a long weekend. Then I called the clinic, Jacob told us you went to the family cabin and proceeded to give us directions. It was on the way to Salem. Soo…" She laughed. "We decided to surprise you. If you're hiding out, you gave way to much information to the powers that be."

"I'm going to get dressed and we can all have breakfast." Gwen pulled at the hem of the t-shirt.

Pepper snickered softly. "Sorry to interrupt."

"That's all right." Gwen started.

"We didn't dress for breakfast. That's all." Brock finished.

"We'll be right back. Make yourselves at home." She fled upstairs, her cheeks still heated with Brock right behind her.

Laughter ensued from downstairs as she dumped out her bag and stared at the contents. A pair of jeans and a t-shirt seemed the best. "Are we still going to Owl's Head?" she asked popping her head out of the t-shirt, then wriggling into comfy blue jeans.

"Sure. Bet they would enjoy a scenic drive to the park. We could tour the lighthouse then stop for a nice dinner." Standing on one foot, he pulled off his still damp jeans and tossed them in the corner. Quickly, he dressed in clean jeans and a polo shirt, then pulled on socks and shoes.

By this time she was dressed and opened the door to the bedroom. "Good thing you assumed we'd be sharing a bedroom, and put both bags here."

He grinned. "I wasn't sure at the time I brought them up, but things worked out." Reaching out he caught her wrist and spun her to him, kissing her on the lips. "Ready."

"Yep."

At the bottom of the stairs, they turned and padded into the kitchen to find Pepper scrambling the eggs and Lathen patting grease from the bacon with a paper towel. Several pieces of toast were buttered and placed on a paper towel. "If you tell me where to find two more plates and a couple of mugs, breakfast—scratch that—lunch is ready."

Gwen opened the cupboard door and pulled out two plates and mugs. "Have a seat, let's eat. I'm starved."

The conversation around the table was pleasant

with Gwen telling them she'd hired Paul and Quintin. Brock filled them in on the Snowy Owl and the turtles.

Pepper shook her head. "You don't do anything by half, do you? We never had turtles when I was there, then bam in the course of a couple of days you have—what—three, four?

"Yep, at least two will be permanent residents." She grimaced. "RoadTrip is kinda growing on me though."

"Great. We brought larger habitats more geared to a permanent reptile resident." Pepper smiled at her husband.

"Yeah, Pep wanted to bring most of the extra stuff for reptiles we have at the rescue." He pointed his thumb over his shoulder. "Hence the Rescue's SUV and trailer."

"Oh, quit exaggerating." Pepper switched her attention to Brock. "Now tell me about your Snowy Owl."

"Well, she's another one that will be a permanent resident at Gwen's place. Doubt she'll ever fly again." He reiterated the story about the trucker, cutting the owl out of the grill and the rest of the incident. "Figured we'd move her to the sanctuary when we return."

"The timing is great. I could really use your help in setting her up at the facility." Gwen popped the last piece of toast in her mouth.

"Happy to help. How about this house you are buying?" Lathen asked, scooping up the last bite of egg and popping it into his mouth.

"Won't need as much work as I thought, but Gwen seems to think there is more to the house than—well you'll see."

Pepper and Lathen exchanged glances. "So are you going to tell us? Or let us guess?"

"I want you to discover for yourself. Prefer you to go into the house without any preconceived notions." Brock stood, picked up the dishes, rinsed them, and put them in the dishwasher. "Hiking or a leisurely ride around the stomping ground of my youth?"

"Oh, I want to see the lighthouse. Driving by, we noticed they were open today. Looks like a nice hike to the lighthouse and interesting jaunt inside."

Gwen nodded her head in agreement. "Let me pack snacks and we'll be off. Soda, iced tea and water okay? I have a few sandwiches we picked up in town before we knew supper was already prepared." She opened the pantry door and grabbed the bag of potato chips she'd stuffed in there the night before.

"Sounds fine." Pepper got to her feet. "Let me help. Hey, wait a minute. Who prepared your supper out here?" She gathered up the items Gwen put on the counter and put them in a box she handed to her.

"That's a story for another time. Now, we're all set." She handed the box to Brock and they all trooped out of the cabin to his truck. "Wait a second." She rushed back to the cabin. "We may need jackets. The wind can be chilly off the ocean, as you know."

Lathen ambled over to the SUV and took out their jackets.

When she returned, Pepper grabbed her arm. "You will tell me before we leave."

She shrugged.

Brock touched the fob to unlock the truck doors. "Everybody in."

Lathen glanced at the rescue's SUV, took the fob

out his pocket and locked their vehicle, then clambered into the back seat of the truck beside Pepper.

"And we're off." As Brock pulled on the road, clouds boiled up on the horizon, the sky turned gray and the mist was rolling in. "Looks like we could encounter a storm. If the lighthouse is shrouded in fog, the long flight of stairs leading up to the lighthouse may be treacherous."

"Yes, but what a wonderful ambiance to tour the lighthouse in the fog." Pepper squealed. "What fun. Will the light come on?"

"I imagine. Since the lighthouse is owned, manned, and maintained by the U.S. Coast Guard. Believe it is a working lighthouse." Brock scrubbed his hand over his face. "In fact, the Fourth order Fresnel Lens from 1856 is still in use.

"Only you'd know that," she teased.

The farther they traveled over the normally scenic county back roads, the denser the fog became. He switched on his fog and headlights then proceeded at a snail's pace.

"Ohhh, this is positivity spooky." Gwen watched the fog float in waves across the road and crawl over the side until you couldn't see where the road stopped and the shoulder began.

"Dangerous is what I'd call it." The breeze kicked up and the fog lessened the closer they got to the lighthouse. A mist slowly replaced the fog by the time he pulled into the large deserted parking lot. "Aww—I thought we might get to hear the two blasts every 20 seconds for the fog signal."

"You sure know a lot about the lighthouse."

"As I told you I was a fixture here as a child.

Nothing more exciting than to watch the fog roll in and wait for the horn to sound."

"Maybe they're closed for the day because of the inclement weather," Pepper said glumly.

"Oh for heaven sakes, it's a lighthouse. Why would they close for a little fog—and mist." Gwen chirped. "Only one way to find out." Unfastening her seatbelt, she jumped out of the truck. Turning her face to the sky she giggled. "I've always loved the way mist feels when it kisses your face." She stared up at the white lighthouse trimmed in black perched atop the bluff on the southern side of the entrance to Rockland Harbor. Shrouded in mist, she could imagine it a prop in a horror story. She shivered. *I gotta quit letting my overactive imagination run amuck.*

Pepper chuckled. "I remember you cursing the freezing mist at the sanctuary years ago. When the bowls were frozen to the ground and we had to pry them off before we could continue getting the animals fed then finish the chores."

"That was different. This isn't frozen, it's just a soft mist." She wiped her face with her hand and scampered across the parking lot to the wide path surrounded by pine trees and water views of the sheer cliffs to the right.

Brock grabbed her hand and slowed her progress up the path. "There is a gift shop in the light keeper's house. Do you want to do shopping first or after we've seen the lighthouse. We may not get to do both."

"The lighthouse first." Their friends chorused.

"My thoughts exactly." At the bottom of the long stairway, she paused peering up through the light fog. Tendrils of mist crept along each step all the way to the lighthouse.

A gentleman in a raincoat stepped out of the lighthouse onto the landing at the top of the stairs. "Be careful…Watch your step," he called down to them.

"It's still open." Pepper grabbed the metal railing and started up the stairs. "Let's go before they do close it."

"Right behind you." Gwen wondered how her friend had gotten ahead of them then glanced back at Brock. "Come on slowpoke."

He grinned good-naturedly and reached for her hand. "We've plenty of time. Appears we are the only ones here." Their sneakers squeaked as they ascended the steps.

"Kinda like a private tour." She snickered pulling her jacket closer around her wishing she'd brought her rain slicker.

Once inside the docent gave a history of the lighthouse, then led the group single file up the red spiral staircase to the top of the lighthouse. The mist was starting to clear, she gasped at the spectacular view of Penobscot Bay and took out her camera. First, she photographed the bay then turned skyward to capture a section of the lighthouse and the dissipating puffy white clouds reflecting a few golden rays as the sun tried to peek through. There were even patches of blue sky.

"Hey, it looks like the weather is going to cooperate." Pointing at the alternate path down to the rocky beach below she squeaked, "We could follow that trail down to the beach and have a picnic with the snacks I packed since the wind has died down and the sun is making an appearance."

Pepper chewed on her bottom lip and glanced at

her husband then back to her friend. "Or we could visit the gift shop then have our little picnic if the weather holds."

"Good idea. Let's go." She led the way back down the spiral staircase and out on to the landing.

An hour or so later they were perched on rocks at the beach savoring their peanut cluster bars and iced tea. "Now tell us about the cabin when you arrived." Pepper took a swig of her soda, set it on the rock and rubbed her hands together, then glanced expectantly at Gwen.

She relayed the experience with Brock adding a few details and his conversation with his sister.

Pepper's jaw dropped open and her eyes rounded. "Really. I've heard of witch's homes that had a mind of their own, rearranging things, producing hidden items, even cooking up a meal or two. But— is there hidden Gypsy magic in your family, Brock?" She rubbed her forehead. "There would have to be…it had to be magic."

"Not that I know of." Pausing for a couple of beats, he rubbed his hand over his chin. "Well… now if you believe my grandmother's tales, it's possible. Mom and Dad never confirmed or denied her stories. With Molly being so secretive, I gotta wonder. But she always loved a good mystery, even if she had to create it herself." He chuckled.

Chapter Twelve
Secrets Are Neither Confirmed nor Denied Unless Magic Awakens

Long past dinner time, Brock pulled the truck into a little diner at the edge of Puffin Cove. "How about we grab a bite before heading to the cabin? I'd hate to tax the cabin's magic to prepare another meal." He shook his head and laughed. "A year ago if someone had told me magic, witches, and werewolves were real, I'd have questioned their sanity. But now…"

Pepper giggled. "Gwen, you're a bad influence on our veterinarian. Even, Dylan, his sister says so."

"Me?" Her eyebrows rose nearly to her hairline as she feigned an expression of shock and jumped out of the truck. "I'm not the one who produced roses in the dead of winter, had an ancient arbor appear out of thin air, surrounded by family ghosts in front of a mere mortal."

"Hey girls, I'm standing right here." He opened his arms wide and glanced around carefully closing the vehicle door.

She turned her attention to Brock. "By the way have you told her about the house you're considering purchasing?"

"Mere mortal isn't exactly the words I'd use after hearing the story of your arrival at the cabin." Lathen chuckled climbing out of the back seat.

"Hey, whose side are you on?" He whirled around to face his friend then switched his attention to her. "Not yet. Don't you spill the beans either."

She made a zipping motion across her lips with a Cheshire Cat smile.

"Depends on who is winning." His friend motioned toward the girls. "In my experience, it's usually the ladies who win."

The good-natured bantering continued into the fifty's style diner. The booths were red leather with chrome accents, red and white checked curtains hung at the windows, and a colorful, old-fashion jukebox sat in the middle of the floor. They took a booth in the center of the diner.

A middle-aged waitress with her tawny hair pulled into a ponytail and pom-poms on her sneakers sauntered up to the table handing out plastic menus framed in yellow. "What can I get started for you?" She paused and stared at him. "As I live and breathe, it's Brock Scutter."

He laughed. "Jackie, how have you been? Still waiting tables I see." He stood and gave her a hug.

"Yeah, but now I own the joint." She blew on her nails and polished them against her pink uniform. "Heard you're a big-time vet with your own practice in the city."

"Yep, you heard right, if you consider Salem a large city." He slipped back into the booth.

Jackie snorted. "If it's bigger than Puffin Cove, it qualifies." She surveyed the others in the booth. "Your city friends?"

"Sort of." He motioned to his friends. "Pepper and Lathen run a wildlife rescue in Lobster Cove up the coast not far from Bar Harbor. He glanced at Gwen sitting beside him. "Gwen manages the Salem Wildlife Sanctuary in Salem."

Jackie grinned. "Molly mentioned you were seeing a gal in Salem. Said you were off the market. There were broken hearts all around that night." Jackie put her hand over her heart.

Heat rose up his neck and spread across his cheeks. "Molly has a big mouth. And you, tell a whale of a story."

"I'm going to take that as a yes." Jackie snickered. "Occupational hazard. What'll it be?"

"Cheeseburger, fries and chocolate shake," Gwen piped up.

"I'll have the same. Only make my shake a strawberry." Pepper picked up her menu and handed it back to the waitress.

"Make that three and a chocolate shake." Lathen slid his menu over top Brock's.

"Might as well make it unanimous. Chocolate here too, only make mine a malt. I'd like to add one of your cherry pies to go. Still make them from scratch?"

"Sure do. My claim to fame."

"Good, I'd like ice cream on the side to go also."

"You're in luck. I have one whole pie left. I'll box it up and put the ice cream in an insulated container when you're done with dinner."

"You're a doll." He flashed a grin at Jackie then turned to his friends and Gwen. "Believe me when I say her cherry pie is the best in the state. Heck probably on the eastern seaboard, maybe even the universe."

Pink patches bloomed on Jackie's cheeks. "Well, now I wouldn't say that. But thank you." She hustled toward the kitchen.

When Jackie was out of earshot, Pepper rubbed her hands together and lowered her voice to a conspiratorial whisper, "So about this house in Salem?"

Brock glanced around. "I don't want to spoil the surprise. When we return to Salem, I'll arrange a tour." He paused a beat indicating the subject was closed. "What goodies did you bring for Gwen's place?"

A few minutes later, Jackie appeared at the table with four milkshakes on a tray.

Gwen huffed out a breath and pulled out her phone, flipped through a few pictures and grinned. "Here is a picture of the dragon staircase."

He reached over to grab her phone but Pepper was quicker. Rolling his eyes, he leaned back against the booth and sighed. "The subject is still closed."

Lathen leaned over to get a look at the phone and whistled. "No wonder you want the house. That is quite a selling point. Pepper tells me it's touted as one of the homes that has no paranormal history."

"Well, not exactly." Gwen began, then clamped her mouth shut at Brock's glare. "I don't see what the problem is." She sucked on the straw to no avail, then spooned up the creamy chocolaty goodness and popped it in her mouth. Closing her eyes, she savored the treat. "Mmmm made the old fashion way."

Motioning to the shake, he gave her a smug look. "Of course." He paused for a moment. "Is it too much to want an unbiased opinion with no possibility of swayed judgment on the property?"

"Okay," Gwen said sulkily as Pepper flipped through a few more pictures before handing the phone back to her with a raised eyebrow and a wink.

"Goodies?" He glanced at his friend ignoring the silent communication between the best friends. *Choose my battles.*

Pepper interrupted with her arms crossed over her chest. "You'll have to wait till we get back to the cabin."

Jackie returned with food on a tray carried on her shoulder.

"Saved by the meal." He chuckled. "Smells fantastic."

The waitress placed the plates on the table. "Enjoy. By the way, the pie is on the house."

"You don't have to do that."

"I know it. I want to. An enticement to return more often." She flounced off to the other table with her order pad open.

They quickly ate their meals. He paid the bill and the couples departed with the promised pie and ice cream.

Climbing in the truck after everyone was settled, he turned to Pepper. "How is it that you've lived and worked not far from here, but never visited?"

"Too busy. First I spent summers with my aunt at her place in Lobster Cove, she taught me a lot about wildlife rehabilitation. From there it was on to college. Then, I spent ten years working with Gwen at the Salem Sanctuary until… the magic storm. Now as you well know, I have my own wildlife rescue. Doesn't leave much time to cavort around the countryside."

"I see your point. Glad you decided to join us for a long weekend. You two probably need it as much as we do." He gave a quick sideways glance at Gwen, reached down, and squeezed her knee.

"We didn't mean to invade your weekend." Pepper began.

"Oh, sure you did." He chuckled. "After all you went to great lengths to track us down. But we're glad you're here."

****

The next morning well before dawn, he was glad he'd set the coffee maker on a timer. The aroma of freshly brewed coffee made his mouth water as he pulled a mug out of the cupboard, poured a cup and pondered the activities for the next couple of days. The text alert on his phone sounded. He glanced at the screen. A green text cloud appeared.

"Can you come home early. We're ready to close on the house." Bill.

"Nope. Won't be back until Wednesday, then I have a full schedule of appointments Thursday and Friday. However, I would like another peek at the house before we close. I have friends in town that I want to see the house. How would Saturday morning be?" Brock.

"You still have the key." Bill

"Okay. Can we set the closing for next Tuesday? Mondays are a nightmare at the clinic." Brock.

"I guess that will have to do. Call me when you get back." Bill.

"Will do." Brock.

He ended the text conversation and stuffed the phone back in his pocket as footsteps sounded on the stairs.

Gwen padded around the breakfast bar into the kitchen. "Good morning. Up early aren't you? I didn't even feel you get out of bed." She smiled and brushed her lips over his.

"Wanted a little solitude before the day gets started. An old habit."

She nodded in understanding. "I heard Pepper and Lathen in their bathroom, so guess we'll catch the sunrise as you planned. How far to the point?"

"Ten minutes at the most. Then we can hike the trails and relax on the beach weather permitting. Looks like there could be more afternoon storms. Clouds are roiling over the horizon again this morning."

She squinted out the window into the darkness. "How can you tell?"

Reaching up, he flipped the light off. "Let your eyes adjust. Then look to the horizon."

"Hey, who turned off the lights?" Pepper chirped entering the kitchen with Lathen on her heels.

He smothered a laugh. "Wanted to show Gwen the clouds over the horizon. Might be an indoor afternoon or evening."

"Aww shucks. It'd be terrible to have to drink cocoa, eat popcorn, and enjoy a movie in front of a crackling fire," Pepper teased.

"Gee don't know how we'd deal with that." Lathen let out a hardy laugh.

"We better get going." Gwen glanced down at her new high top hiking sneakers.

He handed everyone a to-go mug of coffee and led the way.

By the time the group reached the rock point that provided the best view, the sun peeked over the horizon, filtered by the clouds painting the blue sky in a spectacular array of yellow, orange, red and magenta edged in purple.

"Wow. What a sunrise." Gwen sucked in a breath and snapped several pictures.

"You were so right. Is it always this fantastic?" Pepper wanted to know as her hubby took pictures of his own.

"Yep, most mornings. Once in a while, you'll get a clear dawn and the sunrise lacks the purple hues the clouds and dust particulates cast." He paused to enjoy the scene in front of him in silence. After a few minutes, he pointed toward the trail that led around the tops of the rocky outcroppings and eventually led to his beach. Frowning at the little shadows near the tiny boathouse his family used to store kayaks, beach loungers, and coolers. "Let's head down the path."

Gwen put the lens cover on her camera and peered in the direction he pointed. The guys took the lead while she and Pepper brought up the rear chatting amicably about the surroundings, the rescues, and life in general.

"Hey Brock, you have kayaks stored in the boathouse? I haven't kayaked in ages. It would be great fun. If we have time."

"Used to be kayaks and life jackets in the building. Not sure what shape they are in, but we can take a look."

"I've never kayaked. Is it hard?" Chewing on her bottom lip, Gwen glanced out at the rolling ocean waves as their group made their way down the rocky sloping path.

"Not at all." He assured her. "In our little cove, you'll see lots of wildlife early morning and just before dusk."

A while later they rounded the last curve leading

down to the beach. Brock skidded to a stop at the view a few yards in front of him. Four loungers were set out facing the ocean, and two umbrellas provided shade over the chairs. On the table in the middle of the semi-circle of chairs rested a cooler. He flipped open the top to discover bottles of orange juice, soft drinks, and bottled iced tea. Beside the drinks was a closed picnic basket.

"What the heck?" Brock took off his baseball cap and ran his fingers through his hair then looked behind him at the rest of the group.

"Don't look at us." Gwen piped up. "We were with you." She paused. "Is this like the night we arrived?"

"Maybe. I don't know. But I am sure going to find out." He took out his phone, calculated the time difference between Maine and Ireland and tapped the screen.

"I don't know about anyone else, but I'm starved." Pepper skipped to the table and opened the picnic basket. Gwen grabbed orange juice out of the cooler and handed one to each of them.

"Wow, there's watermelon, cantaloupe, peeled hard-boiled eggs, and English muffins." Pepper took out plates from the basket and set the food bowls on the table. Grinning she sniffed the air and said, "My magic is no match for your Gypsy magic. Unless you have a staff here that takes care of this stuff."

"We don't." He held the phone away from his face and held up an index finger. "Mom. How are you?"

"Brock, what a nice surprise. What are you up to? Something wrong?"

"Oh, no not at all. Got a few questions regarding some strange occurrences that Molly said I should run

124

by you."

"Strange. We missed a call from Molly last night while out with friends. We're going to call her back later today. Where are you?"

"At the cabin. I brought Gwen with me and a couple of friends joined us. You remember me telling you about Pepper and Lathen."

"Yes, dear. Those are your friends that run a sanctuary in Lobster Cove. She's a witch. Right?" His mother apparently covered the speaker of her phone. Her voice sounded muffled telling someone it was him and that he was at the cabin.

"Mom is Dad there with you?"

"Yes, he is. Let me adjust the phone so you see both of us." After a few clicks and scraping noise, his mom and dad appeared on screen. "There that's better. Now you were saying?"

"Good morning son." His father's voice boomed over the phone as he waved. "It is still morning over the pond."

"Yes, dad. About the cabin. When we arrived last night, there was a fire in the hearth, lobster stew in a crockpot, and homemade rolls in the warmer. No one but the family knew we were coming. When I called Molly, she hemmed and hawed around then finally told me to call you claiming she had to go."

Silence greeted him from his parents' side of the conversation. They exchanged glances. "If that wasn't strange enough. This morning we went to the point to watch the sunrise, then we hiked around the path along the ridge above the beach ending at the boathouse." He told them what awaited on the beach. "Now I know none of the locals have this kind of time. Want to tell me what is going on?"

Again silence for several beats. "It's kinda of a long story." His dad began.

"Your friends are waiting for you. So why don't we call you back this evening?" his mother interjected.

"My friends don't mind waiting. They're rather curious too. In fact, Pepper stated this morning that her magic is no match for the Gypsy magic she sensed around here. Is she right?"

"Well, sort of." His mother tapped her fingers on something near the phone. "Remember the bedtime tales your grandmother used to tell you?"

"Yes, but you claimed…"

"You were so young. We weren't sure how, if at all, any magic was passed down. It skipped your brother entirely. Apparently, you got his share." His mother and father both laughed nervously. "After the McKay's introduced you to their magic—we wondered if yours would awaken. Guess it did by what you are telling us."

"You're telling me, I'm causing this?"

"If the wand fits," his mother teased. "Not exactly. Your great-grandmother was a product of love between a Gypsy man and a Fae woman. A forbidden match at that time. They braved all the scorn in Ireland but escaped across the pond to raise their children and live their lives without—well—the way they wanted. Your great-grandfather built the cabin. Great-grandmother blessed it with welcoming magic for her family."

"Gee it would have been nice if…"

His mother shook her head and continued, "Generations since discovered it also awakens the magic in those that inherited not only Gypsy magic but

Fae magic. Which is what you witnessed upon your arrival and this morning and last evening. Those members of our family without magic are unable to cause the magic to perform. The Fae magic skips generations. You and Molly are the only ones that received the Fae talents. Though it appears you may have inherited the Gypsy magic as well. Riva and Dylan got the Gypsy magic but it skipped poor Jeremiah entirely. Or at least that's what we think. Maybe if he…"

"Son, you don't remember us cooking much at the cabin do you?"

"Not really, but I was too busy exploring or at the lighthouse."

His mother chuckled. "I bet the Owls Head lighthouse was the first place you went upon your arrival."

Thinking back to his first night at Puffin Cove, he smiled. "Not exactly but it was a close second. We were there yesterday."

His father cleared his throat. "Too much information son."

"What?" He feigned innocence. "I only meant we went down to the beach the first night after the interesting situation at the cabin. So what you're telling me is that everyone knew our family history but me."

"Afraid so. Except for your brother. A least he's never shown any aptitude for magic. Like you, he was intent on making his mark in the world. The girls, well, they were in the cabin more and demanded explanation when you two weren't around."

"To be fair, I don't think your brother has ever been back to the cabin as an adult and never alone," his dad mused.

"Your journey and belief began at Lobster Cove." His mother paused for a beat. "Now you've come full circle. Be honest son. If we'd told you and you'd never experienced it for yourself, would you have believed?"

He was silent for several minutes as he glanced at his friends. "Probably not. But still…"

"When we get back, we'll have a family get-together at the cabin, sort all of this out, and have a great time. Gwen, Pepper, Lathen are invited too," his mother said excitedly. "I love a good party. Maybe end of summer shindig would be perfect. Huh? Better yet, Halloween. Costumes required. Never know who may show up. The veil is thin at that time of year." His mother touched her fingers to her lips as if considering then waved a hand nonchalantly. "We'll have to see how it works out."

"Halloween? Yeah, wait, what do you mean? Who will show up? Given the weather, an end of summer shindig may work better. If you're back. Oh, I'll harass Jeremiah into coming. Then we can see what's what."

"I'm not sure that's a good idea. How'd you feel when unexplained things began happening without warning?" His mother's voice held an ominous tone.

"Then you'll have to explain it to him." He chuckled. "Well, I better let you go, my friends are waiting and have heard half of the conversation. I imagine they want to know the rest. Love you. Talk to you later." He considered telling them about buying a house, but that was a subject he'd rather wait on until Pepper visited it.

Especially now. He wasn't sure how he felt about all the revelations his parents bestowed on him. If he was honest with himself, he'd been a little envious of his friends' talents before. Now he was—what? Did Gwen have hidden Gypsy magic as well? Did this type of situation arise in other Irish Gypsy families? All good questions to mull over as he ended the call and turned to his friends. Gwen had prepared a plate for him and set it on the table in front of the empty chair.

"Well…" Gwen peered expectantly up at him.

He filled them in between mouthfuls of food.

Chapter Thirteen
Effects of the Revelations and Sharing the Magic

After Brock's explanations, the couples relaxed on the beach discussing the possibilities. Gwen wondered if she'd used her talents to the best of her abilities. *Do I have more I'm not using?* She shrugged and glanced at her friends. Her magic had come into its own when Pepper was forced to leave Salem.

Up until then, her friend had done most of the communication with the creatures at the sanctuary. Out of necessity, she'd honed her skills to the point she could tell if an animal was in pain, She could also tell what had happened to them and was able to sooth and communicate with them as well as Pepper.

Lathen pushed up from his chair and stretched. "Okay, enough lounging around. Let's check out those kayaks. The ocean is calling me."

"I could use a bit of physical exertion. But don't know if the kayaks are seaworthy anymore. Saltwater is hard on them." After getting out of the lounger, he led the way to the boathouse.

Pepper hung back then winked at Gwen. "You mean to tell me you've never been on a kayak?"

"Nope. Never had time as an adult. Didn't have the opportunity growing up."

"It's fun and it can be relaxing." Pepper grabbed her arm and propelled her forward. "No stalling."

Brock unlocked the boathouse, threw open the doors, and let out a low whistle. Glinting in the stream of sunlight were four bright orange kayaks and two blue ones slimmer and longer than the others. "I guess someone replaced the old ones. These look brand new. Guess we got a couple of sea kayaks and the rest are recreational. As I remember we only had four and had to take turns." He chortled.

"There were several knockdown, drag-out fights among us kids." He shifted one shoulder up and down then grabbed the sides of two of the wider kayaks with larger open cockpits. "Our little cove is perfect for these." Nodding toward the two blue ones, he glanced at his guests. "Best leave the sea kayaks for the professionals. Probably Molly's husband or Riva's. Going out on the choppy sea isn't my idea of fun." Pausing he grabbed two sets of paddles and put them in the kayaks. "Just look at these paddles, not a scratch on 'em."

"There will be after today." His friend chuckled and grabbed the sides of the other two boats. "Pepper you want to get the other paddles?"

"Sure thing."

"Don't you think we should ask someone to borrow the kayaks?" Gwen stood off to the side letting the guys carry the boats out the door to the shore.

"Naw, if they're in the boathouse, they are for family members use. Otherwise, they'd be chained down." Brock pointed to the U-shaped metal bars beside the racks.

"Okaaay." She drew out the word as Pepper gave her a nudge forward.

At the shore, the guys lowered the boats near the

water's edge, took the life vests out of each kayak, tossed two in her and Pepper's direction. Brock glanced up at her. "If you don't want to go— you don't have to." He clambered back up the beach to where she stood picking at the catch on her life vest. "You okay?"

"Oh, she's a little nervous about trying new things. She'll be fine." Pepper patted her back and grinned. "Won't you."

"Sure. I mean, I guess so." She popped open the clasps and slipped the vest on. "I'm not very coordinated on land, let alone on the water."

"You'll be fine. I'll stick right beside you." Brock slung an arm around her shoulder. "You guys go ahead. We'll be along shortly."

After donning their life vests, Pepper and Lathen hopped in two of the kayaks and paddled a short distance from shore making it look easy.

Hesitantly, she edged toward the boat while Brock plopped the watercraft into approximately two feet of water and offered her a hand.

"Brace your hands on each side of the cockpit and swing your legs in. Nothing to it." He demonstrated where to put her hands.

She did as instructed. The kayak bobbed and shifted from side to side but evened out quickly. *This isn't so bad.* Stretching her long legs out she found the little footrests inside the front.

He handed her the paddles and shoved her boat out toward deeper water. The boat bobbed up and down on the incoming waves. "Give me a minute to get my boat in the water and I'll show you how to paddle and steer." In a smooth motion, he put the boat in the water and slipped inside. Paddling out a few yards, then in circles around her, he showed her how to propel the kayak forward, steer right and left with the paddles, then back paddle to stop or slow.

The water shoved her boat into his. Swiftly he used the paddle to put space between them. "Now you try it."

Slowly at first, she paddled around, testing her ability to steer the boat. Finally, she nodded to Brock and they headed out toward their friends. Only twice did she lightly ram one of the other kayaks because she didn't back paddle fast or soon enough.

"There's an art and timing issue to this." The rolling waves rocked her boat, but she rode them out and rather enjoyed the motion. Her paddles slapped the water scaring the wildlife and fish while her friends' paddles cut smoothly through the water.

She laughed when Brock floated up beside her. "I think my paddles are defective."

He reached out and twisted the paddles at different angles in her hands. "Try this."

Using one paddle, she shoved away from his boat and paddled to where her friends were waiting. *Still more of a splash than the others, but much better than before.*

The breeze was a welcome relief from the sun. She splashed water on her arms and legs in an effort to stay cool. The sunscreen she used made the water droplets bead up on her skin. A few fluffy white clouds dotted the bright cerulean sky casting shadows over the water occasionally.

"I don't know about you all, but I'm ready to head to the beach. It's been years since I've guided a kayak in the water, let alone through the ocean's constant waves." Pepper stretched and rubbed her upper arms and shoulders, clenching and unclenching her fingers. "River or lake kayaking is different than the constant wave action of the ocean. Even in this cove."

"Me too." Lathen chimed in.

"Back to shore, it is." Brock floated beside her, giving her kayak a gentle shove to turn it toward the shore.

"Hey, I can do it myself. Move out of the way." It took her only a few minutes to direct her boat toward the shore. Her paddles cut smoothly through the water leaving little splash in their wake.

On the shore, she slipped out of her life jacket, dropped it in the boat and picked up the front end of her watercraft by the handle. It took two trips to get all the boats back in the boathouse.

"How about we start a fire and roast hot dogs and brats."

"That would be great if we had—"

"Check the cooler. Lathen and I will gather wood."

She peeked into the cooler and ran her fingers through the slushy ice pulling out a pack of hot dogs and a pack of smoked brats. "Well, doesn't that beat all."

Pepper peered over her shoulder. "Now all we need are skewers or pointed sticks." She snapped her fingers and pointed. "Several skewers were in a bin next to the door of the boathouse." She dug her bare toes into the warm sand and raced toward the building. Flinging sand with her every step.

Gwen started to follow her, then hesitated. Her gaze swept over the previously used fire pit, the rocks around the pit arranged willy nilly. Large pieces of blackened wood were partially buried in the sand.

Rearranging the rocks into a circle, she dug out the burnt wood placing it inside the circle leaving gaps between the wood for air to circulate.

Maybe we could use those for a firebase. Furrowing her forehead in concentration, she tried to remember the fire building skills her childhood friend, who was a scout, taught her. *Wood arranged in a teepee shape then papers stuffed inside, smaller sticks in-between the bigger ones. Right? Or was it the other way around?*

She straightened peering at the campfire circle. "The guys will know how to build a fire." Dusting off her hands, she turned to see Pepper marching toward her waving four skewers in triumph high above her head.

"Got 'em. Needed a little cleaning up. I scrubbed them in the sand. If we put 'em in the fire until they turn red, they should be safe to use."

"Good job. All we need are the guys and the wood."

"Hey were there buns or condiments in the cooler?"

"Not that I saw, but I didn't check the picnic basket. There were chips in there."

Pepper set the skewers on the table and rummaged through the basket pulling out whole wheat hot dog buns. "Geesh, healthy magic. We need to get this service at the rescue." She giggled and glanced at Gwen. The guys' laughter proceeded their appearance.

She turned in the direction of the sound just as the men rounded the bend and came into view. "So Brock is this magic in the land, cabin, boathouse, or…"

"My grandmother or great grandmother. Oh, Hell

who knows." He shrugged one shoulder careful not to drop the wood. "I've nothing to do with this." Brock sauntered up the path, arms full of wood, followed by his friend. "This should hold us for the night." They dropped the wood on the ground. Brock glanced at the horizon where the storm clouds had hung all day without advancing.

She held her breath for a moment, then released it thankful as Brock knelt down in the sand, crumpled newspaper, stacked wood in a triangle, interspersing small kindling between the larger logs. "Anyone see a charcoal starter?"

"Oh, for heaven sakes." Pepper snapped her fingers. The fire consumed the paper, crawled up the kindling, then blue-tipped orange and yellow flames whooshed into a full-fledged campfire.

Gwen and Brock stumbled several steps back from the rock circle she'd arranged. "Wow. Play with fire much?"

"On occasion." Pepper grinned.

"Ahhh…What happened about not using magic for personal gain?" She pointed out.

"If I didn't step in, we'd all die from starvation. So it doesn't count as personal use. Can't have you all starving to death." She snickered when her husband coughed to hide a laugh. "Now where are those weenies and the skewers?" Pepper pulled out a bag of marshmallows, a couple of chocolate bars, and graham crackers out of her backpack. "Never go to the beach without the proper campfire dessert."

Gwen tossed the packages of meat toward the men and picked up the skewers. "Let's get this party started." She passed around the soft drinks and cans of iced tea.

Pepper took out the plates and tore open the chip bag.

After the brats and dogs were roasted and consumed, she leaned back in her chair and yawned.

"Don't you dare fall asleep. We must make s'mores." Pepper tossed the fixings on the table, ripped open the bag of marshmallows and stuck two on her skewer and set about prepping the graham crackers and chocolate on a plate.

"You're going to be sick," Gwen warned.

"The way I figure it, I burned a huge amount of calories kayaking, now I have to replenish those." A pop, sizzle and her marshmallows were on fire. "Shoot." She blew the fire out and carefully placed each ooey-gooey confection between the crackers and chocolate square. Putting the skewer down, she took a bite of her s'more, stringing marshmallow from fingers to mouth, finally, a string settled down her chin. "Yummy." Attempting to wipe the sticky stuff from her chin with her hand, she effectively smeared it over her face and now her fingers stuck together. She licked her lips to remove the last trace of chocolate.

Lathen laughed, dipped a paper towel in a five-gallon bucket of water, for putting the fire out, and wiped at Pepper's face and hands. "I can't take you anywhere."

Unabashed, Pepper stacked two more marshmallows on her skewer and held it over the fire. "You can have the other s'mores. I'll make more."

"Hand me the plate with the graham crackers and chocolate on it." Brock examined his perfectly golden brown marshmallow, took the prepared stacked crackers and squished the marshmallow between the grahams and chocolate. "Perfect." He took a bite careful to avoid stringing the gooey substance and grinned triumphantly.

"Hey, you can make mine." Gwen stuck marshmallows on a skewer and handed it to Brock.

"Traitor." Pepper giggled.

By the time everyone had eaten their fill, the bright full moon shone over the water casting a silvery shadow over everything. "Hey, we probably should head back. Traversing the path in the dark could be treacherous."

Lathen doused the fire. Brock dumped the slush out of the now empty cooler onto the fire as an additional precaution. When he stepped onto the rocky trail, path lights flickered on lighting the way to the cabin.

"Oh, yeah. I forgot Dad installed these with motion detectors so the path was safe at night."

"Oh, too bad. Thought it was more magic." Gwen wrapped her arm around his waist and kissed the side of his cheek and whispered. "I'll keep you anyway."

****

The sun was high overhead before someone turned on the shower and the pipes rattled. Gwen opened her eyes and stared at the man softly snoring beside her. His tanned muscled arm wound around her. How quickly she'd become accustomed to having him by her side. Friday afternoon when they'd began this trip seemed a long time ago. So much had happened, just like Pepper insinuated it would if she'd just relax and not overthink it.

"When it's right, you'll know it." Her friend's words from last Christmas echoed in her mind. "But was it?" She shoved the thought to the back of her mind. She was here to relax and unwind and that was exactly what she intended to do. *Only one day left.* A feeling of sadness crept into her chest. *Don't be silly.* Pepper and Lathen would be accompanying them to Salem.

Excitement at the thought of her friends meeting the owl, RoadTrip and the rest of the new residents, in addition to showing them the house Brock intended to purchase replaced the melancholy of leaving. The feeling of being in the house surged, the dreams she'd had come into focus. *Could it be all the magic revelations this weekend? I can't wait to discuss all this with Pepper after she sees the house.*

The water pipes banged and screeched again. Brock stirred and blinked open his eyes. "Good morning Sunshine." He smiled sleepily and brushed his lips over hers. "I like waking up with you. We need to make adjustments in our lives to accommodate this."

"Hey, one step at a time. Remember?" She rolled against him and reveled in his warmth and strength.

A loud banging on the bedroom door broke the moment. "Are you guys going to sleep all day? What's on the agenda for our last day in this magical place?" Pepper called through the door. "Coffee is brewing. I'll start breakfast if you two are going to be downstairs anytime soon." She cackled and two sets of footsteps sounded in the hallway and down the steps.

"Well, I guess we better get up or we'll never hear the end of it." She sat up and swung her feet to the floor.

"We allowed them to crash our romantic weekend—Why?" Brock chuckled.

"Because they're our best friends and due to our schedules we rarely get to see them."

"Oh yeah. Easy to forget at the moment." He flashed her an easy-going smile, shoved out of bed, and padded toward the shower. With one eyebrow raised, he turned to her. "Join me?"

"I thought you'd never ask." She scrambled out of bed.

Two hours later the dishes were in the dishwasher, the kitchen cleaned up, and Brock held the front door open. "Since we are all a bit sore from our adventures yesterday, how about I give you all a tour of the countryside this bright sunny day? We can stop and play in a few tide pools in Birch Point Beach State Park, grab lunch— " he hesitated and glanced at his watch. "— or make that dinner at a great local restaurant I know and generally goof off."

"Sounds like a plan." Pepper and Lathen chorused.

She tapped her index finger to her lips. "I'd still like to see the Maine Lighthouse Museum. It's in Rockland. Right? Do we have time?"

"A girl after my own heart." He placed his hand over his heart for a beat. "Of course. May not get to see everything, but we can always come back." He glanced at their friends who nodded in agreement.

****

Once inside the museum, they opted for the self-tour. He glanced around at all the sparkling lighthouse lenses. "Can you believe most of these were collected by one man? Mr. Ken Black. He spent his entire life dedicated to the preservation of American's Lighthouse history."

"How did he have access to all of these artifacts?"

Gwen gawked at all the different items assembled in glass cases and lined on shelves.

"He became Commander in the United States Coast Guard and was responsible for the actual operation of many lighthouses. While an officer in charge of Coast Guard Station Rockland, he assembled the collection by obtaining permission from his district admiral, then visiting various stations and bases throughout the First Coast Guard District. By the time he retired his collection overflowed the Coast Guard Station in Rockland. Arrangements were made to loan the artifacts to the Shore Village Museum."

Pepper walked to a lantern exhibit. "If these lamps could talk."

"Another time we'll have to take the guided tour. There are heartwarming tales of keepers and families you should hear along with stories of bravery, heroism, romance and hardship associated with these lighthouses. Wish I could remember them all from my visits here." Pausing he pointed to the far wall.

"Check out some of these exhibits that highlight stories of valor while paying tribute to the US Coast Guard and the Life Saving Services." He moved to another display. "This one sheds light on the lady lightkeepers."

"Does Maine have the most lighthouses?" His buddy wanted to know.

"Maine may not have the most lighthouses, but we have the most historic ones in the nation," he said proudly.

"Gee, you're a walking encyclopedia on Lighthouses." Gwen chuckled.

"One of my favorite things growing up." He smiled

wistfully. "I was so in awe of their purpose—to protect and guide those who travel by sea along treacherous coastlines. Can you imagine if there were no lighthouses?" Glancing at his watch, he shook his head. "Where the heck does time go? We better be on our way."

****

Returning from their day trip, Gwen and Brock packed up their truck while Lathen and Pepper touched base with the rescue to determine how much longer they could be gone. After tossing their bags in the SUV, their friends padded up the steps to join Brock and her on the cabin's porch.

"We're all set to take off in the morning for Salem. How about the sunset hike on the other side of the ridge you promised us?" Lathen nudged his friend's shoulder.

"Lobster Cove can do without you two for a little longer?" she teased.

"Yep. Told them we have a snowy owl in Salem that needs our attention." Pepper smiled wide. "Best reason ever to extend a long weekend. Don't you think?"

"You betcha!" She stood, slipped her feet into her hiking sneakers and rested her arm on Brock's shoulder. "Ready to go check out the sunset?"

"I am." Brock eased out of the porch swing he'd shared with her. "This has been a fantastic reprieve from the real world. We need to do this more often."

"You're okay with our crashing your romantic getaway?" Pepper glanced from her long-time friend to Brock. Uncertainty flitted across her face and was gone in a nanosecond.

"Yep." She and Brock chorused. In truth, their

friend's arrival had eased her anxiety at being alone with Brock. They'd simply fell back into the relationship that began in Lobster Cove with a few new twists. She sighed.

Following the guys up to the rugged point, she leaned her head on Brock's shoulder while a fiery display of the bright yellow and orange sunset spread over the blue sky reflecting on the crashing ocean waves. What a fun time with her best friends. Work awaited tomorrow but she was excited to see Pepper's reaction to Brock's soon to be new house.

Brock wrapped his warm arms around her and she relaxed against him. The spectacular display faded to hues of burgundy and purple as the sun disappeared. It wasn't long until the waning full moon made its appearance washing everything in silver shadows.

As they made their way down the cliffs to the cabin, she enjoyed the peaceful feeling these days off had provided ready to meet the rest of the week with renewed vigor.

Chapter Fourteen
Back to Reality, Like It or Not

Storm clouds that had sat sulkily on the horizon all day yesterday made their appearance this morning with a cool mist and drizzle. The fog began rolling in and Brock was anxious to get on the road.

"Good thing we packed last night." Lathen slapped him on the shoulder. "Could be slow going today."

"You're right about that." Brock jumped into the truck and rolled the window down. Under the cover of the porch, Gwen and Pepper were discussing the logistics of accommodations once they arrived in Salem.

"Hey girls, gotta get a move on. You can make those decisions once we arrive at the Sanctuary. Got a lot of chores ahead of us before we report to work tomorrow." Quickly, he rolled the window back up and waited. Lathen gave him a thumbs-up as he climbed into the SUV.

Gwen hugged Pepper and made a run for the pickup as her friend did the same toward her vehicle.

Bounding into the truck, Gwen nearly lost her footing and flopped into the seat headfirst. The bottom of her sneakers wet and slick slipped on the metal side step of the truck. "Whew, nearly bit it." She grasped the handhold on the door's edge then glanced up as he covered a grin with his hand. "Brock Scutter wipe the grin off your face." Scrambling up into the seat, she gripped the wet armrest and closed the door harder than she intended then shoved the wet hair out of her face.

"Yes, ma'am." Try as he might he couldn't squelch the laughter that burbled up from his throat.

She narrowed her eyes and took a swipe at him. He fended it off with a fresh towel from the back seat. "Dry off, don't want you catching cold."

Relaxing into the seat, she toweled off her hair and snickered. "You're incorrigible. You know that?"

"So I've been told." He glanced in the rearview mirror to see the SUV's lights come on. His phone buzzed in his pocket again, he yanked it out, glanced at the screen and tossed it to her." That's the third time this morning."

"It's Bill. It looks like he's texted you twice and left a message." She glanced at Brock. "Want me to call him back? Wait, he just wants to know if you're still on schedule for the closing next Tuesday."

"Text him back. Yes. Provided everything is in order when we do the walkthrough on Saturday." He pulled out of the driveway and onto the street then glanced in her direction.

"Are you expecting a problem?" She licked her lips and fiddled with her backpack strap.

"No. I have a good feeling about the house. Want to make sure Pepper doesn't pick up on anything."

She nodded. "Smart idea."

The swish, swish of the windshield wipers cleared the window of drizzle and mist but did little as the fog rolled in thick as pea soup. He gripped the steering wheel so tight that his knuckles begin to ache. Finally, the fog lightened when he merged onto I-95S from US-

1.

Rain pattered on the windshield, but being able to see the road, mostly, dropped his stress level. He relaxed against the back of the seat and his grip on steering wheel loosened. "Are we setting up the turtle habitats and the owl's flight when we arrive?"

"Depends on the weather. But I'd sure like to. Kept the schedule light and the staffing heavy this afternoon in hopes of being able to do exactly that." She shifted in her seat. "How about we catch lunch on the way in, then work through the afternoon, get cleaned up and go out for a nice dinner. Unless of course you get called into an emergency at the clinic."

"Jacob won't do that to me." He ran his fingers through his hair rubbing at the back of his neck. "Unless it's the owl."

"We haven't heard a thing…so that's a good sign."

"Yeah, it is. Hopefully, we'll move her to your place tomorrow morning."

The rest of the trip was filled with discussion about the cabin, the beach, and the interesting things they'd learned. He looked forward to the family reunion his parents had promised, working less, and spending more time with Gwen. *No time like the present to change bad habits. Going to need to increase staff.*

In his mind, he went over the numbers from the last quarter and the income he'd projected for the third quarter. There was some wiggle room in there for additional staffing. He glanced in Gwen's direction surprised to find her staring at him.

"You haven't heard a word I've said for the past ten minutes." She pursed her lips. "Thinking about the clinic already?"

His face warmed. "Guilty. But in my defense, I was thinking about staffing so I can spend more time away from the clinic. This weekend was fantastic."

"Agreed. I was just bouncing ideas off you for setting up the owl's enclosure. When you didn't answer, I figured you…You know we really should give her a name. I feel kinda bad calling her owl all the time."

"I'll give it some thought. Don't think you need to be naming her after the circumstances that brought her to us."

"What do you mean?" She huffed.

"RoadTrip, Misfit. Need I say more?" He chuckled.

"How about Lucky. She's very lucky to be alive. When I think of all the unusual events that came together and saved her life— A trucker stopping after hitting her so close to the clinic. Seeing your lights in the clinic still on. Bringing her to the clinic. A vet, you, still there. The trucker had tools so you were able to cut her out of the grill and save her life. All of that happened in a matter of minutes. Didn't it?"

"Yes."

If that isn't divine intervention, I don't know what is. If anyone of those things hadn't happened, she wouldn't still be here."

"True." On the outskirts of town, he flipped on his blinker and turned into a familiar cafe. Lathen and Pepper followed him into the parking lot, took up two parking spaces beside him and rolled the window down. "Why are we stopping here?"

"Gwen thought we should get a bite to eat before embarking on the job at hand in the sanctuary. I know this place has great burgers and fries to die for."

They seated themselves and took a menu from the stand braced between the napkin holder and the wall. Gwen put hers back and glanced at Lathen. "Is there something you want to ask me?"

At that moment, the waitress stopped at the table and smiled warmly. "So what can I get for you?"

"Cheeseburger, fries and chocolate shake for us," he said nodding in Gwen's direction.

"We'll have the same, only make that one strawberry shake and one chocolate." Pepper stuffed the menus back in the wire stand.

Returning her attention to Lathen, Gwen shrugged one shoulder. "It's a talent. I can feel when someone has a burning question."

Surprise was etched on his face. "Actually, yes there is." He paused a beat. "How are Paul and Quintin really doing?" After another brief pause, he tapped his fingers on the table. "I promised myself I wouldn't butt in after you hired them. Except..."

"He can't stand it. Worse than an old mother hen about his guys," Pepper interjected with a chuckle. "I relayed your recent report to him before we left Lobster Cove. Still..."

"Oh, I understand completely. Paul is doing great. He suggested and implemented new software he was familiar with. Sam my security manager is thrilled. They worked together to tighten security which was what we needed. He fit in with the staff seamlessly." She smiled wide.

"We're very pleased. If you hadn't told me about Paul's PTSD, I'd never know. He handles himself well even in times of stress. The software installation was a bit rough. Our computers needed upgrades to run the system. There were a few bugs to work out, but he never missed a beat. Although at the end of the first week after the conversion, he did look a little worse for wear." She chuckled. "So did Sam."

"Great to hear." Lathen relaxed against the booth's seat.

"As for Quintin, at first he was a bit out of his element and it showed. As you know, he is uncomfortable around situations he can't control, and there is really no controlling the environment here. With new animals arriving, meeting their needs, and caring for the permanent residents, it's tough on any given day. However, Rocky our maintenance supervisor took him under his wing and within a couple of weeks found a routine that works. Quintin reports where he is needed, his job duties can drastically change from day to day."

"See I told you." Pepper smirked at him.

"He does well with the animals, pitch hits for Rocky in maintenance and does security rounds outside at times." He's a hard worker. Fits in more every day and enjoys the work. He even brought his wife and baby to see the Sanctuary on his day off. Gave them the full tour." She paused for a beat. "They'll both get a hefty raise at their ninety-day review."

"Wonderful. I'm relieved. Usually, I assign them to Lobster Cove before sending them out. But Pepper was sure you could handle them and you were in dire need."

"Sure was. Can't thank you enough. Heads up, I'll be hiring a few more hands around here. If you have anyone suited, please send them my way." Gwen licked her lips as the waitress stopped at their table, with steaming plates of burgers and fries. Another server followed with shakes and glasses of iced water.

After the meal, Lathen was quick to pick up the tab despite Brock's objections. Afterward, they all trouped out to the vehicles with renewed energy. The sun was trying to peek out from behind the clouds as Brock turned into the Salem Sanctuary parking lot. He rolled the window down and waved his friend on ahead to the road leading to the other habitats.

Quintin, Sam, and Paul strode out of the building that housed security and intercepted the SUV. After a moment, Sam pointed toward the reptile building and slapped the fender of the vehicle. Lathen pulled forward slowly. Paul returned to the building, Sam and Quintin followed behind the slow-moving SUV and trailer.

Gwen jumped out of the truck dodging a mud puddle and sprinted toward the men and the SUV.

Trinity came running from the opposite direction waving her hands in the air. "You are never going to believe this," she shouted. "The dog...Misfit... has slept on the porch to your cottage every night since you left. Wouldn't let the guys approach, it ran off, but... In fact he—I mean—she." She stopped mid-sentence and blinked at Gwen. "Do we know the gender?" Trinity sucked in a breath and continued. "The dog is on your porch right this very minute."

Gwen turned and motioned to him to hurry up. He rounded the front of the truck at a dead run and joined her. "What's up?"

"Misfit is on my front porch. She's slept there every night since we left." She pumped a fist in the air. "I knew it." Sprinting up the path to the cottage, he and Trinity in tow, she skidded to a stop behind a huge oak.

There on the porch in a ready-to-run stance was the dog, one ear perked forward, the other back, and head tilted to the side. Gwen motioned for them to stay put while she inched forward in a crouched position. When the dog sidled to the left, one foot on the step, she plopped down cross-legged and glanced away.

He couldn't believe his heart thundered in his chest as the scene played out in front of him. Aware of how much regaining this dog's trust meant to her, he was surprised to discover he was holding his breath. When Trinity shifted forward, he swung a restraining arm in front of her, never taking his eyes off Gwen. Voices in the distance grew silent.

The pup made its way toward her one step at a time tail slowly curving over its back. She slowly moved her hands to her knees then held one out in front of her. The creature backed away but didn't run. Misfit circled her then stopped behind her, took a few more steps and nudged her jacket pocket.

She let out a quiet laugh, reached into her pocket, took out a piece of beef jerky, let the dog sniff then take the jerky. It trotted off toward the other end of the cottage, paused then disappeared around the back. She got up, brushed her jeans off, pumped a fist in the air again, and hurried toward them.

"Did you see that? Did you?" She swung her arms around his neck, squeezed hard, and kissed him on the lips. "What a welcome back." The voices in the distance whooped and hollered as they got closer.

It looked like half the staff was walking up the path. Sam was the first to reach them. "Wow. Good job." He slapped her on the back. "Paul called us into security so we could watch what was happening on the monitors."

Pepper hugged Gwen. "Just like Ember at our place. You've gained her trust, won't be long now." She giggled and pointed toward the corner of the cottage. The dog was peering at them.

****

After all the excitement died down, the staff got to work unloading the materials, heated cubes, and habitats out of the SUV and trailer. They spent the rest of the afternoon, getting things set up, moving the portable flight into the aviary and relocating RoadTrip to her new digs. When the sun dipped behind the trees, it was decided to leave the rest of the relocations for tomorrow. "Let's order pizza. There's enough soda in the cottage for everyone. Thanks so much for all your help today." Gwen led the way.

"We'll reschedule our nice dinner with Pepper and Lathen for tomorrow night," she whispered to him. "If you're not too late at the clinic."

"I'll make sure I'm not. Barring emergencies."

She took out her cell phone and tapped the screen.

Several large pizzas were delivered. Gwen cleared off the table, pulled out stacks of plastic cups and paper plates. "Dig in everyone. Thank you so much for your efforts today and for keeping the thing running smoothly during my long weekend. I appreciate it."

Words of thanks flowed from everyone's lips as they gobbled down the pizza and guzzled the soda in record time.

Gwen wandered over to her big bay window overlooking the Sanctuary appearing deep in thought with her last piece of pizza and a cup of soda in her hands.

He watched her for a moment, then turned his attention to the aftermath of the impromptu pizza party. Boxes piled high next to the trash can, which overflowed with paper plates and cups. "Come on guys, help me tote all this out to the dumpster before you leave."

Grabbing the boxes, he headed for the trash as the others picked up the empty cups and dumped them in the garbage can. He picked up the container and opened the door to Misfit sitting patiently on the porch. She jumped up as he exited the cabin. "Hey girl, how about a pizza crust?" Slowly he set the container down, picked out a big piece of crust and carefully dropped it on the wooden surface.

By this time the dog had scurried down the steps and peered at him from the far corner of the cabin. Turning away he pushed open the door and called quietly. "Gwen, you might want to come out here." Then he made his way down the steps and over to the dumpster.

Gwen stepped out onto the porch. "What..." She glanced around and Misfit was creeping up the steps and toward the pizza crust. The dog glanced up at Gwen then took the pizza crust and turned her head toward him as he remained still at the dumpster. Gwen reached down and stroked the matted fur. "Sometime in the near future, you are going to need a trim and a bath." Misfit trotted to the far end of the porch, circled twice, and lay down still keeping her eye on him.

Raising the dumpster lid, he deposited the trash inside and quietly closed the cover. The dog never stirred. On the porch, Gwen nearly vibrated with excitement.

"She'll be inside with me anytime now. Part of the family." Smiling wide she slipped her arms around his waist as he climbed the stairs and they went inside where the group had watched the events from the window.

When everyone had said their goodbyes, Lathen and Pepper joined Gwen at the window. "Guess we better be going too. Got reservations at the Tree Top Motel on Main."

Snapped out of her reverie, Gwen whirled around. "You do no such thing. You'll stay here with me at the cottage. There's an extra bedroom."

The couple exchanged glances. "Yes, ma'am." Pepper gave her a sloppy salute. "I just thought…"

"Well, you thought wrong." Gwen grinned sheepishly at them. "Didn't mean to snap."

"No problem. I want to hear about the owl and everything anyway." Pepper stood. "We'll get our luggage out of the SUV." She took her husband's hand and tugged him toward the door. " Be right back."

He tried to stifle a jaw-popping yawn unsuccessfully. "I'm going to head home." He slid his arms around Gwen's waist. "Got a long day tomorrow." Waking up without her beside him was a depressing thought. It couldn't be helped, she had a full house and he didn't want to impose. *I'm just not sure she's ready to move in together, hell, not sure I am.*

"Why don't you just stay here tonight?" She turned to face him, brushing her lips across his.

"You've got company. I've got an early morning if I'm going to get out to make our dinner plans. Besides you and Pepper will be by early tomorrow to pick up Lucky, so she'll have time to settle in. Right?"

"S'pose so," she conceded.

He leaned over and kissed the corners of her mouth causing them to turn up in a half-smile. "After things settle down, we have a few things to work out."

She quirked an eyebrow her violet eyes sparkling. "Like what?"

"Living arrangements and life in general."

Slowly, unbuttoning three top buttons of his shirt, she pulled him to her and trailed kisses along his jawline. "Sounds serious."

"Not really, decisions to be made before we move into the house I'm buying."

Her eyes flew open and her jaw dropped. "Are you asking me to move in with you?"

"It's one of the topics we need to discuss." He kissed her. "Tonight, we both need to get to…"

Loud footsteps echoed on the porch and the front door banged open. "Don't mean to interrupt, but we're beat. Direct us to the bedroom and we'll disappear."

"That makes four of us. See you all in the morning." He released Gwen and sauntered toward the door. "Goodnight."

"Nite." Gwen kissed him at the door, peered to the end of the porch where Misfit remained curled up, then reluctantly turned her attention to her guests and pointed down the hall. "I only have one bathroom. So we'll have to take turns. Pepper, you know where the bedroom is."

"Lathen you go ahead, I want to talk to Gwen about a couple of things."

He groaned. "I suppose this means you two will be up all night talking and giggling like a couple teenagers."

Pepper flounced over to him and tousled his surfer blond hair with her fingers. "Don't you worry your pretty head. I'll join you soon enough." She winked at him.

"See you all tomorrow." Brock closed the door behind him. *One way or the other, she will be staying with me in the new house, our house.* A shiver of excitement ran down his spine. *Our house. What discoveries will we make in the coming week?*

Chapter Fifteen
Baffling Reoccurring Dreams—Emergency Magic
Saves the Day

Once again the dream had stolen her sleep. Gwen couldn't shake the feeling someone was trying to tell her something. Rolling over, she slapped the pillow over her head as the bright blue numbers on her clock read four-thirty in the morning. The faint aroma of freshly brewed coffee tickled her nose. *Good thing I set the timer on the coffee machine. I'm going to need the caffeine jolt this morning.* Her arm reached for the other side of the bed. She sighe*d. Empty.* Sitting up slowly, she stretched and swung her feet over the side of the bed and listened. Not a sound. Lathen and Pepper must still be asleep. *Lucky them.*

She pulled on a clean pair of jeans, her favorite purple pull-over, stuffed her socks in her sneakers and tiptoed down the stairs. Settling in one of the kitchen chairs, she pulled on her socks and shoes then poured a mug of the steaming liquid. Rain pattered on the window. She pushed open the glass letting in the fresh rain-washed morning breeze inhaling deeply.

Coffee smelled so good first thing in the morning. The first sip burnt her tongue and she cursed quietly. Padding to the front door, she checked to see if Misfit was still on the porch. The dog had relocated and was now curled up in front of the door. She eased the door open, grabbed a puppy biscuit from the box by the door and offered it to the dog. Misfit hesitated only a moment, then took the dog treat from her hand. Picking up the box, she backed into the room leaving the door open.

A couple of minutes with nose in the air sniffing, the pup trotted inside following her to the middle of the room where she'd placed the dog biscuit. After crunching the treat, the dog turned in a circle then strode to the door, settling next to the entrance on an old ragged rug, head up and eyes alert. Clapping her hands quietly, she returned to the kitchen.

The blueberry bagels were calling to her. She sliced one and dropped it in the toaster, put the schmear on the table with a knife and eased back into the chair. Head in her hands, she closed her eyes and tried to clarify the elements of the dream. Was there anything different about this one? Same painting in the unfamiliar dusty room. No familiar faces. The toaster popped and she nearly jumped out of her seat. When she reached for the bagel, there was movement in the entrance to the kitchen. She bobbled the bagel, nearly dropping it only to see a smiling Pepper in the tiny yellow sliver of dawn's light creeping across the room.

"Why are you sitting in the dark? Is that a blueberry bagel I smell?"

"Wasn't ready to officially start my day—yet. Yes, it's a blueberry bagel. Have one. "

Pepper snapped her fingers and slapped her palm to her forehead. "I forgot your strange habit. You've not figured out the day will start whether you turn on the light or not." She chuckled and put her hand on her friend's shoulder. "What's bothering you?"

"Of course I know that." Gwen snapped. "Sorry. Not been getting much sleep lately."

"Brock?"

"No, not really. There are some things we need to talk about but...this weekend was like we picked up where we left off during the holidays."

"That's a good thing. Right?" Pepper plopped down in the chair opposite Gwen then pointed across the room where Misfit still lay curled up.

She gave her friend a thumbs up then shook her head. Taking a bite of bagel, she pointed to the cabinet where the bagels were. "Help yourself."

In a flurry of activity, Pepper took out two bagels, poured a cup of coffee, popped one bagel in the toaster before returning to her chair. "I'll wait until Lathen comes down to toast his. Sometimes he likes them just plain." She cocked a brow and stared at Gwen expectantly. "Well...out with it."

Straightening the paper towel, she rested her bagel on the towel and took a sip of coffee. Unable to keep the dream to herself any longer, a long sigh escaped her lips. She took another long sip of her coffee considering what and how much to say. "I've had this reoccurring dream for weeks now. I can't figure out where I am. The only constant is the picture, a dusty room, and unfamiliar faces. This morning I woke up with a feeling someone or something was trying to tell me something. That was new."

"When did the dreams start?" Pepper spread schmear on her warm bagel and took a bite. She licked a bit of schmear from her upper lip. "Mmmmm. So good."

"Shortly after Brock took me over to the house he

is going to buy." She sipped her coffee watching the sunrise in all its glorious pinks, red, yellow and orange streaking across the dusky sky. Her hands cupped around her mug, thumb tracing the handle she took another sip.

"So is the setting inside the house?" Pepper took another keeping her eyes trained on Gwen.

"Don't see a house, only a room with boxes, chests, and a couple of old rocking chairs. Funny thing, everything is so dusty but the picture looks like it was recently painted. There are people milling around, not paying any attention to me, and I don't recognize anyone."

Pepper sat back in her chair just as the bright light flicked on. Gwen squealed, set her mug down with a jerk. Coffee sloshed over the sides of the mug as she attempted to cover her eyes. The dog bolted out the door at the noise.

"Don't have enough money to pay the electric bill?" Lathen asked amusement in his voice.

"Didn't want to wake anyone." She glanced sadly toward the entrance to the kitchen.

"You remember. Gwen believes if she doesn't turn the lights on the day won't start." Pepper grinned up at her husband. He bent down and kissed her.

"I didn't know that. Useful information if you ask me." He pointed to the bagel setting on the counter. "Mine?"

"Yep. The mug next to the coffee maker is for you too." Pepper said around another bite of blueberry bagel.

He popped it in the toaster, picked up both containers of schmear then took the lid off the strawberry. Gwen handed him the knife. "So what were you two whispering about?"

"Nothing," rushed out of Gwen's mouth.

Pepper narrowed her eyes at her friend and waggled her finger at her. "No secrets. Remember." Pepper turned her attention to Lathen. "Gwen's been having reoccurring dreams." She leaned back in her chair, balancing on the back two legs. "If you ask me, I'd say it's connected to Brock's new house."

"Why?" Lathen took a swig of coffee. Spread strawberry schmear on his bagel and straddled a chair between the two women. He rested his arms across the back of the chair, switching his gaze between them and took another drink of his coffee. "I thought you said this was one of the few older houses in Salem without haunting history."

"That's what the real estate agent told Brock. The guy is a friend of his, no reason to lie to him."

"He is a real estate agent." Lathen teased.

Setting her mug down harder than necessary as if to make a point, Pepper let the chair down on all four legs. "We need to visit this house sooner rather than later."

A stern expression crossed his normally friendly face. "Pepper, need I remind you we're guests in Gwen's home. The house is Brock's not ours. It's none of…"

Pepper waved her hand dismissively. "Sure it is. We've been friends too long and been through too much for me not to speak my mind or to sugar coat it."

"You're right. We planned to show you the house at the first opportunity. This weekend is what Brock said earlier. He's going to close on the house Tuesday unless you find or feel it's not a good idea. I have to say he has his heart set on this house. Even before it came on the market. He said something about a feeling he got each time he passed by the property."

"Wow. The plot thickens." Pepper grinned wide rubbing her hands together. "Love a good mystery."

"Even where there isn't one," she teased. "But I don't want to say anything else. I promised Brock. You should go into the house with an open mind." Pausing, she turned a pleading glance on Pepper. "Please."

"In other words, no more questions. After you have my curiosity peaked." Pepper hesitated a couple of beats. "How about we walk by the house? No harm doing that—Right?"

Lathen held out his hands, palms up as if keeping the women at bay. "Oh no. I want no part of this without Brock's permission. Besides, don't you girls have enough to do to get ready for the transfer of the owl and finish the installation of the new equipment?"

"Yeah, there is that," Gwen conceded.

Her phone vibrated across the table, she caught it as it nearly fell into her lap. Quickly she touched the screen and put the phone to her ear. "What's wrong?"

"Been a breach at the reptile house. Your feral dog attacked whoever attempted to enter through a broken window. The dog is on the ground whining. Should I call Dr. Brock?"

"Yes. We'll be right there." Shoving the phone in her pocket, she turned to her friends. "Breach at the reptile habitat. Misfit is hurt." Grabbing her rain slicker from the hook next to the kitchen door, she rushed out.

"Lathen grab our jackets." Pepper hollered over her shoulder and continued out the door. "What was the dog doing there?"

"I've no idea, but she needs our help. Paul is calling Brock. Better if we can transport Misfit, if necessary."

Outside, Pepper grabbed her friend's arm. "Hold up there Gwen. Anything you need from here?"

"Nope, everything we could possibly need is at the office or in the temp clinic." Jacket flapping in the breeze, she sprinted across the compound with her friends in hot pursuit.

Glass from the shattered window glinted on the damp ground. Spread across part of the ground was a blue tarp, Sam stood in front of the scene his arms spread wide. "I've called the police. There are footprints under the blue tarp." He jerked his chin to the left of the tarp. "Misfit is over there. Won't let anyone close. Be careful, boss."

She waved off his warning, hurried over and crouched near the dog. "What happened girl?" she crooned to the injured animal. "I know it hurts, let me take a look, and make you feel better."

From flat against its head, the dog's ears perked forward, it let out a low wine ending with a warning growl when Pepper approached. "By the way she is gasping for breath, I'd guess it's her ribs. I don't see any blood. Do you?" She turned her face up toward Pepper.

"Can't really get close enough." Pepper moved closer, drew in a deep breath and closed her eyes. After several minutes, she moved next to Gwen and the dog. "There, that's better." Misfit's eyes closed, her taut muscles relaxed, and breathing evened out though there was still a slight hitch. Pepper paused and glanced around. "Now what's going on here? Better if we can heal her here, rather than transport her to Brock's busy clinic."

"Wish I had your calming magic."

"You did the hard part. Communication with the creature is crucial so she'd understand there's nothing to fear from us. Especially with the progress you made with her this morning." With her back to the staff milling around, Pepper knelt down held her hands a couple of inches from the dog's fur, a lilac glow flowed from witch to canine.

Gwen held her breath hoping fervently there was nothing seriously wrong. Stroking the dog's head gently, she crooned to the pup. It's eyelids fluttered open, brown eyes clouded with pain stared up at her, then the lids closed again. Her cell phone shattered the hush surrounding them. She cursed under her breath and pulled the offending device from her pocket and glanced at the screen. "It's Brock," she hissed silencing the cell.

Pepper shook her head slowly. Without breaking her concentration, she whispered: "I've got this."

Gwen glanced up at Sam, who was hovering behind her and handed him her phone. In hushed tones she instructed him. "Call Brock back, explain the situation and tell him we won't need his intervention…yet. We'll fill him in later." She glanced meaningfully at Pepper.

Sam nodded and backed off shooing away the rest of the staff who had gathered, encouraging them to go about their duties. He touched the screen and walked toward the security office.

The wail of sirens in the distance had her glancing

wildly around. She couldn't let the officer see Pepper's magic. Catching the attention of Sally, a long-time trusted volunteer, she pointed toward the siren and waved a hand over the dog shaking her head vehemently.

Sally nodded in understanding, gave her boss a thumbs up, and trotted toward the parking lot.

Relieved, she turned her attention back to Misfit only to find Pepper sitting on the ground her hands propped behind her. The dog's head raised, wary eyes watching her every movement, then suddenly the pup's tail thumped the ground.

A weary smile turned up the corners of Pepper's mouth. "She'll be fine. I was able to mend the broken ribs, put them back in place, and repair muscle tears. She's going to be sore for a while. Nothing to be done about that but pain meds and muscle relaxants may help."

"Thanks so much." Gwen hugged her good friend then stiffened. "Where's your hubby?"

"Distracting a few of your staff so we don't have to explain what just happened."

"Oh, I—that thought didn't cross my mind. Glad it did yours."

"Occupational hazard." Pepper snickered. "Would you look at that. A breakthrough."

Misfit had rolled over and stood on her wobbly legs. A second later she plopped down putting her head in Gwen's lap. She sighed. "None of this would have happened to the dog had it not been for me."

"Don't play the blame game. The dog was fated to be part of your life for a reason. Don't question it. Move forward. Remember the magic storm? You couldn't understand why it triggered such strong anti-witch sentiment in a town that thrives on it. Looking back, we now understand. Lobster Cove was in my future. Salem Sanctuary has thrived thanks in part to my dear departed Aunt Ashling. Everything has come full circle." Pepper stood, wiped the dirt from her behind and fisted her hands on her hips leveling her gaze at Gwen. "Now what are you going to do about Brock?" A snort escaped her lips, and she pointed. "Speak of the devil. My work's done here. I'm going to find my husband before he gets into trouble." Pepper flounced off in the direction of the security office.

"But wait." She huffed out a breath as her friend disappeared. Assisting Misfit to her feet, she stood up. Brock stopped momentarily at the police cruiser, exchanged words with the officer and Sally. Then he strode straight for her and the dog. Bracing herself for a scolding, she was surprised when his arms slid around her and held tight. A low growl sounded from Misfit.

"It's okay girl." Gwen leaned down and stroked the dog's fur. "He's a friend."

He raised an eyebrow. "A friend, huh? Let me recap my morning. I came in early to a waiting room full of emergencies. Jacob was barely treading water. I get a phone call on my personal cell informing me there'd been a break-in at the Salem Sanctuary. Sam or maybe it was Paul, hell I don't know, told me the dog had been hurt. He couldn't tell me how bad. Only that you may be bringing the dog in. He hung up before I could ask if everyone else was all right. So I waited. Nothing. Not one word."

"Sorry. I told Sam to call you back. In all the confusion I guess it didn't get done."

"It did. But, I was worried when you didn't answer your cell. Sam called back and his story was full of holes as if he deliberately left out details. When I asked him to elaborate, he indicated you'd fill me in later. I finished up with my patient, flew out the door of the clinic, but paused long enough to tell Jacob there was an emergency at the sanctuary. Well…for you later is now. What the hell happened? Why is Sally detaining the officer?"

"My fault. I didn't want him to see Pepper's healing magic with Misfit, so I sent Sally to buy some time. Pepper couldn't stop and I couldn't let him see her working on the dog." She collapsed against his muscular chest and buried her head under his chin. "Can't anything ever go smoothly?"

He caressed her back and rested his cheek against the top of her head. "You're in wildlife rescue and rehab. You know the answer to that."

"I do. But I don't have to like it." She sniffed.

"Wait a minute. Pepper healed the dog?"

Nodding, she gazed up at him. When their eyes met, that familiar zing of awareness shot through her. Suddenly, her heart pounded, pulse raced and her legs might as well been wet noodles. *Pull yourself together woman. Who am I kidding? My knight in shining armor is standing right in front of me. All I have to do is, what, admit to being fully and completely head over heels in love with the man and live happily ever after? Yeah right. Magic, witches, werewolves, maybe even vampires exist. But fairy tales— those are for kids who didn't know any better. Let your guard down, whomp,* she waved her arm around nearly hitting Brock, *real-life smacks you to the ground.* She pushed against his chest. *Not going to happen to me.*

He reached for her shoulders and held her firm. "What's wrong? Send mixed messages much?" A mischievous twinkle sparked in his eyes.

Footsteps in the gravel sounded behind them. "Excuse me." The officer had finally escaped Sally's grasp and stood behind them. "I need to talk to you. There was a break-in?" His gaze fell on the shattered glass scattered on the ground below the window.

For the first time, she noticed blood on one of the shards of glass. She glanced at Misfit at her side leaning against her leg. Pepper hadn't mentioned any cuts or abrasions on the skin or stain on the deep mahogany fur. Had she missed something?"

Pepper sprinted out to where Gwen stood. "I did not. If there's blood, it's the perps." Her friend peered from the officer to her then back.

She hated when Pepper figured out what she was thinking then answered her. It was disconcerting, to say the least. Bringing her attention back to the officer, she pointed toward the security building. "You'll need to check the surveillance feed and talk with my security officers, they're the ones that alerted me. My friends and I arrived after the fact."

"And like I told you in the parking lot, I arrived after you." Brock smiled at the officer.

The officer leaned down and bagged the piece of glass with the blood on it. "We can eliminate the dog?"

"Yes, sir," she answered after giving Pepper a sideways glance. "Speaking of the dog, I need to get her back to my cottage where she can recuperate. She'll hate to be locked in, but I see no other choice."

"I'll need to see the security video and get a copy."

He rocked back on his heels. "Also need statements from each of you before I leave."

She bristled. "Dog first. Then I've got to check on the rest of the residents. Make sure none of the turtles are missing or…"

"You give the statement here, or down at the station." The officer said curtly, then blew out a breath.

Ignoring the officer, she bent down, crooned to Misfit, helped the dog to her feet, then walked slowly, pausing to wait for the dog to follow her back to the cottage. They slipped inside, and she encouraged the dog to ease onto the ragged rug. "I'm sorry, but you have to stay here." *There goes all the trust we built up.* Quickly closing the door, she turned and nearly ran into the officer who'd apparently followed her along with the rest of the group.

She stiffened and raised an eyebrow. "Are you forgetting who the victim is here, officer— " Tilting her head, she peered at his name tag then at his face. "Murphy." Fingering the phone in her pocket, she tugged it out and scrolled down the screen of names.

Murphy took off his hat and slapped it against his pants leg. When he ran his fingers through his thinning brown hair and replaced his hat he glanced at her sheepishly. "I mean, let's check on your turtles. Then take a look at the surveillance and see if we can piece together what happened." He nodded at her. "Lead the way."

Without a word, she turned on her heel and led the little group to the reptile enclosure.

Chapter Sixteen

Haunted Dreams, Magic Discovered—Things May Not Be as They Appear

Letting the door whoosh shut behind him, Brock waved to the security guard and made his way through the vet clinic. The first rays of sun filtered through the windows and spread across the clinic's in-patient room floor. Sipping his coffee, he climbed on the stool in front of the owl's enclosure. "Well, today's the day Lucky." The bird fixed its yellow eyes on him, ruffled its feathers as best it could, and flipped it's one relatively good wing.

Last night, he'd called the trucker and told him that the bird would be moving to her permanent home at Salem Sanctuary today. The transport enclosure was ready. Lucky had gulped down breakfast and now blinked more slowly.

Tempted to get the owl out and into her travel cage, he reconsidered. It would be best to wait for Pepper and Gwen to arrive with their calming and telepathic talents. Less stress on the bird knowing what was going to happen. While he'd learned to communicate with the animals in his care, he couldn't hold a candle to Gwen's abilities.

Gypsy magic, that's what Pepper called it. She would know. He remembered well the scathing discussion she'd directed at him when he refused to believe he could communicate with the animals as well as she could. Still, he'd learned a lot from Pepper and Gwen.

Turning his phone over in his pocket, he glanced at the clock. Not enough time to call, Dylan, his sister in Lobster Cove. Never enough time. Did she have the same latent talent he did? Was she aware of Gypsy magic? Witnessing first hand her ability to calm injured creatures when he'd assisted in her veterinary clinic last year during the holidays. He smiled. The same holidays he'd met Gwen and discovered magic. At that time, it never occurred to him there was more to it than just understanding animal behavior and body language. Now a whole lot of things were different.

Deep in thought, he finished the coffee picked up on the way in this morning and absently tossed the cup in the trash. A clanking sound brought his attention to the bird. Big yellow eyes stared at him unblinking. The owl grabbed the enclosure door with its beak and rattled it back and forth.

"You ready to get out?" When he reached for the gate, outside the sound of an engine and crunch of tires rolling to a stop in front of the clinic diverted his attention.

"Gwen and company are here," the security guard's voice echoed down the empty hall. *Wouldn't he ever learn to use the intercom?* He reached over and tapped the intercom button. "Thanks. Let them in."

"Will do." Again the words bounced off the walls. The security guard's chair groaned when he got up and his rubber-soled shoes squeaked on the floor as he made his way to the door. Jangling keys and the click of a lock preceded his greeting.

Brock shook his head and glanced back at the owl. She shook the gate more impatiently.

Thunderstruck, he peered a the owl. "You know they are here for you? Don't you?"

Blinking owlishly, the bird uncertainly took a step back from the door and waited.

Out of a supply cabinet, he pulled out leather gauntlets and tugged them on. He released the latch and carefully toweled the owl transferring her to the travel crate for the ride to the sanctuary.

Three sets of footsteps echoed on the polished tile floor. Pepper and Gwen peeked around the door to the in-patient area. Gwen padded across the floor and leisurely brushed her lips across his. "She ready to go?" she turned her attention to Lucky. "What a good bird you are," she cooed to the bird.

He waggled a finger at her. "She knew you were coming. Starting rattling the door with her beak. She's never done anything like that."

Pepper shrugged and Gwen grinned. "We tried communicating with Lucky on our way here." Then she handed her friend a twenty. "You win. Didn't think it was possible without being in close contact with the animal."

Pepper took the twenty and stuffed it in her pocket. "Ye of little faith."

Lathen snickered. "You're lucky. Brock was observing the bird or your little experiment wouldn't have worked. No witnesses."

The door to the clinic opened, and Delta's voice floated through the reception area as she greeted the security guard. "Morning. Gwen here to pick up the owl already?"

A muffled voice answered her.

He glanced at his watch. "Better get Lucky loaded up before the clinic opens for business. I've a couple of routine patients early. If the owl settles in at the sanctuary this afternoon, I could give you a tour of the house."

"Sounds good." Gwen agreed as the others nodded.

"Bill is chomping at the bit to get the papers signed. Already has the inspection completed. The house passed with flying colors. The title is free and clear of problems."

"Of course." Gwen sent a meaningful glance in Pepper's direction.

Shoving his hands in his front pockets, he glared at her. "We agreed to let Pepper and Lathen make up their own minds regarding the house."

She held up her hands in a gesture of surrender. "I didn't say a word to Pepper that could sway her opinion."

Pepper held up her right hand then nodded solemnly. A slight twitch to her lips, made him feel Gwen's statement wasn't exactly true.

He switched his attention to Lathen, but before he could open his mouth his friend picked up the bird's travel enclosure.

"Time to go." Lathen hurried out the door Pepper held open for him.

"We'll meet you at the house around two this afternoon, provided there are no unforeseen problems with Lucky." Gwen smiled sweetly then stood on tiptoe and brushed her lips across his.

When she leaned away, he snatched her around the waist. "On no, you don't." Pulling her to him, he kissed her hungrily.

"Come on guys. Get a room." Pepper giggled.

Undaunted by Pepper's comments, he continued the kiss a few moments longer then released her. "That's better, don't you think?"

Her cheeks pinked. Silent for a beat, she wrapped her arms around his neck, trailed kisses from his throat to his jawline ending with a kiss to the corner of his lips. "Until tonight," she whispered in a sultry voice, winked at him, then flounced out the door slightly behind Pepper and Lathen.

The owl's file and duplicate he'd made for Gwen was still sitting on the counter. He picked the duplicate up and sprinted after them. "Don't you want the release and medical records?"

She whirled around and snatched the file out of his hand. "Of course." She listened intently to the instructions he gave her concerning the owl and promised to call if there were any problems. "See you this afternoon." Climbing into the backseat, she blew him a kiss as he closed the door.

Lathen loaded the owl into the back of the SUV, strapped the enclosure down, and closed the door.

****

The first to arrive, he cut the engine, pulled out his cell phone and tapped in a number. The call went directly to voice mail. "Hey Bill, I'm at the house. Wanted to do one more tour of the premises before tomorrow's closing." He ended the call and leaned back in his seat. About ten minutes later Pepper's SUV pulled up behind his pickup. Jumping out of the truck he met the group behind her vehicle. "Everything went good with Lucky?"

"Sure did. The staff had her enclosure ready. We opened her travel crate next to the specially built platform and Lucky climbed right up on it. She ruffled her feathers then let out a couple of deep-throated hoots in succession, waited a couple of minutes, then stared at me clicking her beak." She snickered.

"You're lucky she didn't hiss or whistle at you. She's done that a few times at the clinic when she didn't get her way."

Gwen laughed. "Pepper interpreted the clicking to mean the bird was hungry. We fed her and left her to explore while we observed via the camera Paul set up to help us keep tabs her." Gwen pulled out her phone and leaned her head against him while she scrolled through pictures on the screen. Swiping through a few more, she stopped and handed the phone to him.

"See there are the wide intertwining perches and platforms set up for her to get around." She swiped some more and tapped the video of the bird cautiously moving from perch to platform, resting and continuing on. "Wait for it." She pointed at the screen. The owl's talons gripped the perch tight and then the bird tentatively flapped its wing a few times, stopped, stretched its legs, flexing talons, gripped the perch again, and flapped harder several times. Proudly she glanced at him.

"Didn't Pepper and Lathen do a great job designing the enclosure? The staff had no problem putting it all together. Lucky seems to like it."

"She's trying to strengthen her good wing. That's great."

"It is. The bird's a survivor." Pepper switched her attention from him and grinned at her husband. "Kinda like the one you built for Kaylee, only she has more mobility with two wings."

"Yeah, I doubt the owl will ever fly again." Sadly, he shook his head and glanced at the video.

"Never say never." Gwen grinned at Pepper. "They said Kaylee wouldn't survive and if she did, she'd be terribly disabled. You've seen her at Pepper's place. There's little she can't do."

"Soars like an osprey." Pepper giggled. "Catches her own fish in the ocean when we let her," Pepper said proudly.

Gwen hip bumped Pepper and laughed. "That's because she is an osprey."

"Ladies and gentlemen, shall we?" Brock motioned toward the house jangling the keys.

"We're ready, lead the way." Pepper eyed the house, then bounced up the path to the front porch. "Beautiful house." She cocked her head to look at the small gray stone gargoyles adorning each end of the structure. She backed up and pointed to the one perched at the top of the house. "Wow."

Gwen did a double-take at the creatures. "Those weren't there last time we were here."

"I know. They appeared just before we left on our long weekend." Brock shrugged. "Figured the owners found them, didn't want the creatures, and left them for us. Bill said the owners cleared everything they wanted out of the house when he gave them the earnest money and signed the contract after the inspection."

He unlocked the door. It swung wide open with a loud, long *creak*. Doing a double-take at the door, he glanced at Gwen. *Funny it didn't creak when we were here previously.* Waving his hand, he motioned everyone inside.

Pepper stepped through the entrance, gasped, and sucked in a breath. When she grabbed Lathen's arm and pointed. He let out a low whistle.

His hand rested on the dragon head newel post as he grinned wide. "She's something, isn't she? Her body forms the handrail and her tail curls up at the end and forms the last baluster upstairs."

"Wow. The craftsmanship is phenomenal." Lathen gingerly ran his hand over the dragon head and up the handrail. "Thought maybe the carved scales over her body would be rough, but they're smooth." He shook his head. "That's an ability I'd love to learn."

"Wait until you see the crown moldings and carving in the door panels." Gwen blurted out. "It's all surreal." She sprinted up the first four steps and turned to see her friend still standing in the doorway, her arms wrapped around herself.

The men followed Gwen's gaze. Lathen moved to Pepper. "What is it?"

"A lot of love and protection was built and woven into this house. It couldn't stop…" Pepper shook her head and blinked. Her gaze met Lathen's and concern clouded his eyes. "Why are you all staring at me?"

Brock surveyed the group. "Is there something you want to tell us?"

"First off, your real estate agent is dead wrong. This house may not have an official witch's historical record according to Salem's registry. But it definitely was built and owned by magical practitioners until their bloodline ran out. Which would explain why…"

"It's haunted." Brock's face fell. "That's one thing I don't want to deal with. Apparently, the owners lied."

"Now don't go off all half-cocked." Gwen rested her hand on Brock's arm. "Let's hear Pepper out. After all she's the one with the power to see and feel what happened in this house."

"It's possible that the family didn't want their history known to date back as far as the late 1700s. Even though the witch trials were over, it was still a dangerous time for witches. Covens still met in secret. Heck in some places today they continue to meet in secret." She hesitated.

"Out with it." Brock rubbed the back of his neck.

"You said this house was built in the 1700s?

"That's what the title work claims. Is that also a deception?"

Pepper scrunched up her face, then chewed on her bottom lip."Probably… It's not so much a deception as an omission by the original family that owned the property. Flames destroyed the original house a year or so after it was built. Not sure when it happened. A replica of the old house was rebuilt on the same plot of land, and in the same place."

"I'm sure glad you arrived before I signed the papers to purchase the house." The door slammed shut and the shutters banged outside. "What the hell?" He glanced out the window. There wasn't a breath of air stirring the leaves on the trees or anything else for that matter.

Chapter Seventeen
What Magic Wants, Magic Gets—A Secret Untold

Gwen stood in awe for a long moment, then peered at her friend hoping for an explanation.

Ignoring the commotion, Pepper continued, "Why? The house wants you to buy it. There's no danger or malevolence on the home's part or such magic woven within. It's a great fit for you and... ah... your emerging magic."

He cocked a brow in question. "The house is telling you all this?"

"Well, sort of. Feelings conveyed. Long ago whispers of magic practitioners leaving messages in the house for the magic to continue. Apparently, you are the first interested buyer in many years with magic in your blood."

"Come on, long ago whispers. What's that mean? Exactly?"

"It means that I'm not proficient in ancient Gaelic. The messages left magically in these walls are in Gaelic. I can only partially decipher them because of the old-fashioned language barrier." Pepper waved her hand dismissively. "But the house's meaning is clear. It wants you to buy it."

"Didn't you say you felt a pull when you walked by the house long before it came on the market?" Gwen tucked a wayward strand of hair behind her ear.

He frowned at her. "I thought we weren't going to taint Pepper's opinion."

A musical laugh bubbled out of Pepper's throat. "Little late for that, the house outed itself. I don't see any reason for you to change your mind. It's not haunted, only infused with magic reawakened." She waved her arm dismissively. "Now give us the tour." She reached over and flipped the light switch. The crystal chandelier flickered on. An array of rainbow colors spread across the ceiling.

"How is that possible? There is no…" Brock scratched his chin and watched the shifting light.

"Don't know. Magic?" Pepper dissolved into a fit of giggles and started up the stairs. "Come on, Gwen show me those door panels you were going on about." Pepper ran her fingers lightly over the dragon banister. She stopped dead in her tracks. "Oh my." Transfixed on the third step of the winding staircase, her eyes glazed over and she murmured a few strange words.

She reached for Pepper's shoulder, only to be intercepted by Lathen who took hold of her hand and shook his head. "Leave her be."

A few seconds later, her best friend blinked and glanced around. "You are absolutely not going to believe this."

Someone turned the door handle and tried to shake the door. "Brock are you in there? I think the door is stuck." Bill's voice boomed from outside the door. "It didn't do this when I walked the property with the inspector."

Brock sucked in a breath and easily opened the door. "You're getting weak in your old age."

Bill strode inside. Stopped, closed the door, and

turned the handle again. The door *creaked* but opened without a problem. The real estate agent paused and scratched his head. "Well, we can get someone to check it out in case there is a—problem with the wood or…"

"Don't worry about it. What can I do for you?"

The real estate agent rested his briefcase on the nearest table and took out several pieces of paper. "I stopped by your clinic, they told me you were going to the house. Thought I'd catch you and go over the inspection, the items listed the family plan to leave with the house or I'll have them donated to charity." He held the paper out.

Brock pursed his lips and frowned. "Can't we do this later? I wanted to show the house to our friends.

"You're a tough guy to catch. The closing is tomorrow and…"

"Apparently there are some omissions on the title. Like it burnt down shortly after it was built and an exact replica built in the same place." Brock scrubbed his hand over his face. "Wonder what else they failed to disclose?"

Bill rocked back on his heels. "You're right there was no mention in the title work. Does it make a difference to you? I could see if they'll drop the price when confronted with the facts. By the way, how'd you find out? Are you sure your info is accurate?"

"Positive." Brock took the papers from Bill. "Tell you what, I'll review these this evening and bring them to the closing with me. If I have any questions or change my mind about the purchase, I'll call you."

"Wait. Are you considering backing out because of a tiny omission that happened long ago? If your information is even correct." Bill raised an eyebrow.

"It is Salem, and… But no—" Brock glanced at Gwen. "I'm still planning on going through with the purchase." He opened the door and waited for Bill to exit. After he closed the door, the strangest sensation swept through the house. "Did you feel that?"

Wide-eyed, Gwen nodded and switched her gaze to Pepper. "Did the house just sigh?"

Pepper's forehead creased. "I've never known a house to show emotions, but it would appear this is a first. I'd have to say yes." Her gaze swept over her husband and landed squarely on Brock. "You know I've been familiar with magic all my life, but in the past couple of weeks, I've seen and experienced things I wouldn't have believed possible. But…Gypsy magic has to be different than the run of the mill witch's magic." She snickered. "Or maybe it's what happens when the magic is dormant for years with the buildup of power." Shrugging, she glanced up the staircase and caressed the banister. "Are you going to give us a tour or just stand there?"

"What happened when you touched the banister the first time?" Brock blurted.

"I'll save that for after the tour." Pepper climbed the stairs to the top, turned waited for them to catch up.

She led Pepper and Lathen down the hall pointing out the carving on each door and the matching woodwork in the rooms. At the end of the hall, a door popped open.

"Wasn't that locked last time we were here?" Brock asked standing in the doorway a set of spiral stairs led upward.

"Yes, it was." Gwen hesitantly agreed with him.

"What do you know." Lathen peered over Brock's

shoulder. "From the outside, this floor appears to be the top floor. Where could those stairs lead?"

"To the attic, of course." Gwen pushed through the men and tilted her head to stare at the wrought iron staircase. She took hold of the banister and quick as a wink negotiated the narrow stairs. At the top, she called down, "It's a small attic. Must have been used as an artist's studio. There is a fairly large window in the end. You should be able to see it from the outside."

She brushed the cobwebs from the oil lamp sitting on a small table next to the slanting wall, careful not to hit her head as she straightened and moved more toward the center of the room that formed the peak of the roof. Pausing in front of the window, she sneezed. Taking a paper towel out of her pocket, she cleaned a spot on the dusty window to look outside.

Brock raced up behind her then stood dumbfounded at the top of the stairs. "There is no way this should be here. I've studied the outside of the house for months." He scratched his head.

Footsteps sounded on the metal stairs as Pepper and Lathen slowly made their way up the steps and joined their friends. Lathen let out a low whistle and moved closer to the window. "I have to agree with you bro, this window is not visible from the outside. Yet, it must get wonderful morning sun from the east." He ran his fingers over the corner of the dust-covered window sill, wiped his hand on his jeans, and moved to the other side of the room to investigate an old steamer trunk.

"A magically disguised room. How exciting." Pepper whispered conspiratorially scooting next to Gwen who still stood at the window.

"There seems to be more to this house than I

bargained for." Brock squinted at the peak of the roof.

"In Salem, there always is," Pepper agreed.

"Would you look at this." Gwen returned to the little table, reached out and touched the palette of dried, cracked paints covered in dust. The palette was not far from an easel located to catch the morning sun. A deteriorating cloth covered a large canvas. Carefully flipping up the cover to reveal a painting, she sucked in a breath—*It was the painting in my dreams.*

"What's wrong?" In a whisper of movement, Pepper was at her side.

"I—I've seen this picture before," she stammered quietly. "And look, not a speck of dust on either the painting or the easel. Running her fingers along the edges of the approximately three foot by five foot painting, she paused and glanced at her clean fingers.

"Of course you have, this painting looks like the downstairs in this house." Pepper paused to tilt her head surveying the painting from different angles. "Don't you think? See the dragon staircase?"

Gwen ran her fingers over the painting's surface and her fingertips disappeared into the painting. She yelped. Yanked her hand to her chest, then held it out, and wiggled her fingers. "What the hell? Did you see that?"

Pepper stood, her mouth hanging open for a beat then nodded. "Did you feel anything inside the painting? Like objects?"

"I don't know. Yanked it out so fast," she whispered.

"What are you girls up to?" Brock leaned a shoulder on the framework of the roof beams that extended floor to ceiling in an A-Frame configuration.

Lathen looked up from his exam of the steamer trunk and peered at the women.

She and Pepper stared at each other for a beat then switched their attention to the men.

"You two look like you've seen a ghost," Lathen joked.

"Not exactly," she said hesitatingly. "You are not going to believe…"

Pepper interrupted. "Can you believe all this great stuff up here. An artist must have lived here at one time. No malevolent spirits here, but this house has a magic history. It might be fun to discover its past. If you are comfortable with that?" Pepper raised an eyebrow then shrugged. "Unless you are ready to walk away from the sale."

Brock narrowed his eyes at her. "I'm not going to sign on the dotted line until we've discovered why the owners were less than honest with us. But I'm not walking away…yet."

Pepper grinned. "It's possible they're not aware. If they have no magic, it's just a house. Your magic called to the house…and it answered. Now you're going to punish the house for something you started, knowingly or not?" Pepper raised a brow and held Brock's gaze.

"Hey punish is a harsh word and not one used for inanimate objects." The front door slammed shut, Brock hesitated for a beat. "I could have sworn I closed that door." He started down the stairs and stopped. "I have a right to know what I'm getting into. I do love the house. But…in addition to the other things, how is it this enormous room isn't visible to the outside, especially with that fairly large window?"

"Magically disguised. Like I told you," Pepper said

impatiently.

He shook his head and his stomach growled loudly. "We'll discuss this over dinner. I'm starved. There's a great burger place just down the street. Handmade milkshakes."

"Hmmm…I second that idea." Lathen raised a hand then lowered it to drape an arm across Pepper's shoulders. She smiled up at him and started down the stairs.

Gwen still feeling shell shocked followed the others down the stairs. At the bottom, she pulled her phone out of her pocket. "I want to check on Lucky and make sure there are no problems at the Sanctuary. It's been so weird dealing with break-ins that I'm a little on edge."

She shook her head. "Can't figure out why we are the target. None of our inhabitants could be used in the pet trade. They're disabled. Thanks to that exact trade. If that's really the reason."

"Great idea. Touch base with them on the way to dinner." Brock opened the front door and waited for everyone to exit. He peeked inside once more, then carefully closed and locked the door. Resting his hand on her lower back, he guided her to the truck. "Meet you at the burger place down the block," he called to their friends.

Gwen slid Pepper a questioning glance then clambered into the truck.

Pepper winked at her and jumped into the SUV beside her husband. "See you there."

Chapter Eighteen
Gypsy Magic Calls, But Will They Answer?

Brock requested an isolated table in the corner and the waitress left menus with them. After perusing the menu for a few minutes, Lathen asked, "Is everyone ready to order?" They nodded, and Brock waved the waitress over to take their orders.

Gwen disconnected the call she'd made to the Sanctuary and tucked her phone back in her pocket. "I'm happy to announce that Lucky is settled in, eating and putting everyone on notice that she owns her enclosure. Clicking her beak in displeasure when someone moves to close."

Pepper laughed. "Not usually the case with a bird in a new environment. You may have your hands full with an ornery owl of that size."

"Probably behaving like that because she expects everyone to communicate with her as we do." Gwen gave a dismissive wave of her hand. "When they don't she's going to try to get the upper hand."

Her best friend shrugged. "Time will tell."

Carrying a small tray, their waitress stopped by the table with drinks. "Food will be out in a few." She smiled and flitted off.

"How about changing the subject for a minute?" Brock stirred his thick chocolate shake, spooned up a bite, slid it in his mouth, and then leveled his gaze at

Pepper. "Answer me one thing. Is there any reason I shouldn't buy this house?"

Pepper chewed on her bottom lip for a moment, then turned her glass of lemonade around and around in her hand. The condensation trailed down the glass on to the napkin forming a damp ring. "Not exactly. I would advise a bit more investigation into its background. Gwen and I could check the library and online after dinner while you review the paperwork Bill gave you. By the way, have you been in the house after dark?"

"Come to think of it, no. Our schedules haven't allowed it. Is there a reason we should be there after dark? You said it wasn't haunted. Right?"

"It would be wise to do a little investigation after dark before you sign the papers." Pepper took a sip of her lemonade eying her friend's rich chocolate malt. "Gwen and I will stop by the library right after dinner then meet you two at the house say around eight?"

The waitress brought their food on a big tray and set the plates in front of them. "Everything look all right?" She checked her order pad. When the others nodded, she left the table.

"Okay. We'll review the papers at my apartment and swing by the house afterward. Fair enough?" Brock scrubbed his hand over his face. "You girls will stay out of trouble. Right?"

His friend choked on his sip of beer, then sputtered, "You do remember who you are talking to?"

Pepper gave him the stink eye, then smiled at Brock.

"Of course," Gwen said innocently wiping her sweaty hands on her pants. *I should level with Brock about the painting. But why did Pepper interrupt when I was about to tell him? Better talk to Pepper first.* She took a bite of her cheeseburger and chewed thoughtfully then washed it down with a sip of her chocolate malt.

After dinner, the couples parted ways. Once the women were inside Pepper's SUV, she turned to her friend. "Why didn't you want me to tell the guys about the painting? Is that why you interrupted me?"

"Because there's more you're not telling me. About the dream? Was the painting in it?"

She sighed. "Yes, and a feeling that the painting means something. In my dream, I see flames, an older man shaking a young woman. She stomps on his foot and escapes then more flames. So when we learned the original house burnt down and this one was built exactly in the same place, I have to wonder if…"

"Did the people say anything?"

"Not that I could understand. He was being belligerent and she wasn't backing down. Which was weird for the time frame of their dress."

"What do you mean?"

"The man and woman were dressed as if they were from the past. Maybe late 1600 to early 1700s." She waved her hand in dismissal. "Maybe my subconscious is working overtime with what we've learned about the house. Sorting it out, making the pieces fit."

"But you just learned the house burnt down, the dreams were before."

"Yesss…" Drawing out the word, she paused searching her friend's eyes. "Pepper am I losing it?"

"No." She chortled. "I believe someone is trying to tell you something. What I can't figure out is why you—not Brock?"

"Oh, I can answer that. Brock is still coming to terms with the whole magic world. Thanks to you, I'm already there and have been for years."

"You could be right." Pepper bobbed her head up and down, flipped her blinker on and turned into the library parking lot. Except for a few cars parked on the fringe, the lot was empty. "What time does the library close these days?"

She glanced at her watch. "We've got little over an hour to do our research."

"Plenty of time. We'll photograph the info we need. Faster than taking notes. I'll start with the newspapers and see how far back they go." Pepper slung her backpack over her shoulder and shut the SUV door.

After rifling through her backpack for pen and paper, she clambered out the door and patted her pocket to make sure her phone was still there. "I believe the first newspapers printed in Boston was 1690. So maybe we'll get lucky."

"Maybe…But might be more info in the legal papers written during the witch hunts."

After an hour with very little luck, she and Pepper decided to return to the house. When they arrived, there was no sign of the men, but the front door was unlocked.

"I know Brock locked the door when we left." She hesitantly pushed the door open and flipped on the light. "Is it trespassing or B&E if someone you know has a key and permission to enter?" Giggling nervously, she glanced at Pepper.

"Of course not. Besides, the guys will be here any minute." Pepper pushed past her and rushed upstairs. "I want to take a look at the painting again."

"You would." She frowned and followed her friend through the door at the end of the hallway and up the spiral staircase.

When Pepper touched her hand to the painting, it was rough paint on a canvas, no give, and nothing more. Her friend looked inquiringly at her. "What did you do that allowed your fingers to pass through the painting?"

"I don't know. Maybe I imagined it." She reached tentatively toward the painting. Her heartbeat a tattoo in her chest and she swallowed hard. She tried again, her fingers brushed over the painting. Nothing. Suddenly her hand sank through the painting bumping into something soft. She closed her fingers around the object and withdrew her hand. Resting in her palm was a cloth doll. Turning it over in her hand, she saw the name John Hathorne scribbled on the backside. She sniffed and sneezed as the fragrance of ancient herbs wafted through the air.

"A poppet for keeping hostile forces at bay. Or to control? Protection…maybe? Rosemary, Sage, Chamomile, Hyssop, Patchouli and PennyRoyal are a few I can identify—an unusual combination." Pepper took the cloth doll from Gwen. "I know that name…" She put her index finger to her lips and frowned, then snapped her fingers and shook her index finger at Gwen. "He was a notorious judge in the Salem Witch Trials."

Heavy footsteps sounded at the bottom of the stairs. "We better put this back and tell the guys. This house may not be on Salem's historical registry, but it was owned by a family of witches."

Carefully, Gwen took the poppet from Pepper and eased her hand into the painting. A vortex sucked her arm then her entire body into the painting swirls of red, blue, and yellow swam around her then she was falling. She gulped in air as her stomach flipped threatening to spill its contents into the void. Her throat hurt from screaming, yet there was no sound. Something hard hit her backside, then it was quiet, she blinked and rubbed her eyes. Finding herself sitting in a rocking chair that squeaked announcing her arrival, she straightened and several pairs of eyes peered at her with interest. The room was familiar— it was the living room of Brock's soon-to-be house, only the furnishings were quite different. The dragon staircase…

Before she could grasp what was happening a swirling portal of colors opened up in the center of the room. With a whoosh Pepper unceremoniously landed in the middle of the hardwood floor with a thud.

Pepper jumped up and brushed herself and stared at Gwen. "Another fine mess you've gotten us into. I nearly didn't catch a hold of your magic trail into the painting." She paused and glanced around. "Where the hell are we?" Pepper switched her attention to the three women and two men observing them from wooden chairs scattered around the room. "Hey, this is Brock's house…but it isn't. Oh no…" Her hand flew to her mouth as she sidled over and positioned herself to the side of Gwen's chair.

"What?"

"Judging by the clothes these people are wearing, and the decor, the painting seems to have sucked us back in time," Pepper whispered eying the group sitting before them.

"Friend or foe?" she whispered back. Clearing her throat, she stood. "Is there a reason you have summoned us here?"

Slowly the youngest of the group, a girl looking to be in her late teens got to her feet. "You are our only hope to correct the grave injustice done to our family."

"How do you figure?"

The teen's long skirt rustled as she wiped her hands on her white apron and held out her hand. "I'm Beth Colson." At the scathing look, the older woman gave the girl her face reddened. "Elizabeth Colson but my friends call me Beth."

"Okay Beth, why or better how are we here?" Gwen asked with more bravado than she felt, hoping these people were more friend than foe.

"We didn't carelessly burn down our house. Judge Hathorne did as a warning. He's a bad person for more reasons than most know."

Pepper's shoulders relaxed as she studied the girl. "History reflects that he was a cruel zealot unable to show mercy. They referred to him as the "Hanging Judge" using his bench to commit murder. That's a pretty bad reputation."

"Well deserved. But he…" the girl glanced back to the others. When the older woman nodded encouragingly the girl blurted, "He burned down our house because I saw and heard him casting spells. He was a witch."

"You've got to be kidding. Are we talking about the same John Hathorne that persecuted all the witches in the Salem Witch Trials?" Pepper brushed off bits of dust from her jeans.

"The very same. He never allowed witnesses or the

accused to clear their names before he pronounced them guilty of witchcraft. No one suspects. He'll kill me if he gets that chance. My grandmother, mother, and my aunt have all been accused of witchcraft."

The two older women nodded sadly.

"I suspect mother and my aunt will be arrested soon. This night, a warrant will be issued for me. But I'll disappear before they catch me. Before I go, I want to set the record straight."

"What proof do you have?" Gwen asked.

Beth walked over and gently took Pepper's and Gwen's hands and closed her eyes.

Immediately a scene played out in Gwen's mind of a man standing in front of a wooden table. Candles burned brightly as he poured over a large book open on the table. The man raised his arms and tossed something into a bowl on the surface.

A shadow rose out of the pages of the book and floated toward the door. A loud knock caused the man to jump and spin around to face the sound. Gwen involuntarily sucked in a breath as Pepper gasped. The man in the room was Judge John Hathorne. The scene faded from her mind and Beth dropped their hands.

Gwen blinked and scrubbed her hand over her face. "Did you see?"

"I did. Sneaky bastard!" Pepper fisted her hands on her hips and glanced at the teenager. "No one else knew?"

"No, ma'am. Not alive." Beth walked to the dragon newel post and forced the cap off with nails on chalkboard sound and withdrew one sheet of newspaper with the headline 'Tryal's of Evil'. She handed it to Gwen. The article suggested that a person of influence would prosecute an accused witch to cover his own guilt. Her gaze lifted from the paper to Beth. "Who wrote this?"

"A man I shared my vision with. He was also a witch and suspected. His home burned with him inside before the article came to light. I was given a copy in case of his demise. After his death, I feared for my life and family so grandmother let the dragon keep our secret. Time has come to let the secret out."

"Why us? Why now? Surely we aren't the first magic practitioners to procure the house? Heck, I'm just learning my magic and Brock, well he's the one purchasing the house, isn't sure where he stands."

"Gypsy magic is strong in some." Beth peered unwaveringly at Gwen. "You are the first that weren't our kin. A stranger finding such a document would be more believable than one who's lineage bears the witchcraft burden." The young girl took the paper from her and carefully rolled it up and returned the document to its hiding place. "Our time is running out and the house knows it."

"Are you saying the newspaper is still in the dragon?" Gwen's voice rose in disbelief. "Wait— What? You've been waiting a long time. Is there an expiration date on righting a wrong?"

The girl nodded solemnly. "Awaiting discovery. A protection spell has preserved the staircase since the original house was built, burnt and rebuilt. Until the truth is known we can't rest. The man used his status as a judge to commit murder to cover his secret. And knowing I knew his secret, had proof, somehow he was able to cast a spell limiting my ability to reveal the truth. I can feel it."

"Wait… there's no such thing," Pepper argued.

Beth raised an eyebrow. "Modern-day witches and magic wielders are not nearly as strong as in my time. Magic is no longer passed down from generation to generation for fear of discovery or maybe even disbelief." She shrugged. "All I know is what I feel as my memory fades of the incident. If we fail, my family is doomed to walk this earth forever, never allowed to go into the light." A big tear rolled down the girl's brave face.

Chapter Nineteen
Disappearance and Panic, Magic Reigns

Brock tossed his briefcase with the purchase papers in the back seat and slid behind the wheel. "Glad that's done. I hate paperwork."

"You're in the wrong business then." Lathen snorted and settled into the passenger seat. "You sure about all of this?"

He arched a brow. "What do you mean by that?"

"I mean we haven't heard what the girls discovered yet."

"Oh, just because the documents are signed, doesn't mean I have to give them to Bill. I was referring to your paperwork comment."

"Patient files, prescriptions, running your business, mounds of paperwork is what I was talking about, not the house documents." His friend snickered.

"Oh. That's what I have receptionists and vet techs for." He laughed. "But you're right the rules and regs for complying with the vet board can be paperwork intensive, but computerized filing makes it easier." He pulled up behind Gwen's SUV. "Looks like the girls made it here before us."

"This may not bode well for their research on your house." Lathen shuddered.

"Or there was nothing to find," he said brightly. Shoving open the truck door, he jumped to the ground and jogged up the sidewalk, pausing to let his friend catch up. "Well, they're here and left the door wide open. That's not like Gwen." Pensively, he entered the house and closed the door firmly. "Gwen—Pepper—where are you?"

Silence greeted him. They searched the entire downstairs, peeked out the back door, closed it behind them, then walked around the back and side yards.

"Gee, funny I hadn't noticed this shed in the far corner of the property. Especially, since we checked the fence around the entire property." He sprinted to the shed and opened the door. "A lot of nice garden tools but no Gwen or Pepper."

Returning to the house, Lathen opened the back door. "Maybe they're upstairs." His friend bounded up the stairs calling out to the women and opening each door.

"I'll go on to the attic stairs and see if they are up there. That painting seems to intrigue them," he said on a chuckle. "Meet you up there."

"Sure thing. I'll call out if I find them."

He pushed through the door and negotiated the spiral staircase. The attic was empty. The cloth that hung over the painting was flipped over. *I know Gwen flipped the cover over the painting before we left the last time we were up here.* He shrugged, gave the painting one quick glance and returned the cloth over the painting. At the bottom of the attic stairs, he met Lathen.

"No sign of them anywhere. Except both their backpacks are laying at the top of the stairs next to the first door on the right." Lathen held up the women's packs.

He pulled out his phone. "I think we better call the police. Something isn't right." His phone rang as he was about to touch the number for the police.

"Brock here," he answered distracted.

A distraught but calm voice greeted him."Dr. Scutter, Misfit is missing."

"But we left her in the cott— "

"You did sir. Thirty minutes ago, she raised such a fuss, howling, and barking that we figured she needed out to do her duty or to be fed. Trinity walked to the cottage and opened the door. The dog bolted right out knocking her to the ground. If we don't find that dog, Gwen will have our heads not to mention our jobs."

Unable to stand still, he paced while talking to Paul at the sanctuary. *I don't have time for this.* "Slow down Paul. Where have you searched for the dog?"

"Everywhere on the grounds. And…"

He blew out a breath. "I'm handling a situation here right now. I'll get back to you—"

Downstairs the door banged open and thundering paws raced up the stairs. Misfit blew right him and up the spiral stairs into the attic. "Don't worry Paul, Misfit just showed up at the house. I'll handle it from here." He disconnected the call and sprinted up the stairs with his friend close behind him.

The dog stood in front of the painting, pawing at the easel and howling plaintively. They exchanged glances.

Lathen was the first to speak. "The dog knows something we don't. Better take a good look at the painting." He walked around behind the painting.

After flipping the cloth up, Brock bent down to examine the painting. After a couple of minutes, he let out a low whistle. "You need to come over here and look at this." Pointing at the painting, he said, "The scene depicted here has changed. I don't remember people being seated around the room the first time I looked at the painting. Do you?"

"Nooo… But I didn't look that close."

"Holy shit. Would you look at that? If I didn't know better, I'd say the woman in the rocking chair is Gwen and Pepper is sprawled on the floor."

"What the hell." Lathen shoved Brock out of the way, took his phone out of his pocket and turned on the flashlight. "How in the hell did they get…"

"Did someone or something trap them inside the picture?" His voice reflected sheer panic. He picked up the painting and shook it, then felt like a fool. *Get a grip man.*

"I'm pretty sure that won't help. Pepper claims to have heard of secreting things inside a painting with magic. Or a painting capturing the essessence of someone. But in reality…Not so much…at least I hope not." Lathen stared forlornly at the painting.

All the while, Misfit continued to howl and bite at the painting.

"What do we do?" Brock asked urgently.

"Nothing we can do. Pepper is a talented, powerful witch, if they are in there, she'll figure out how to get them out," Lathen said confidently.

A vortex of colors spun around the painting growing in size until it engulfed the entire painting, easel, and floor surrounding the items. They took several steps back as Pepper and Gwen flew out of the whirling portal and landed sprawled on the floor with a *thud*. Clouds of dust rose from the floor as the colors faded. The easel rocked back and forth on the floor then settled, the painting resting on it unharmed. Misfit rushed through his legs and licked Gwen's face.

He and Lathen rushed to Pepper and Gwen. He took Gwen's hand and pulled her up from the floor and into his arms. "What in the hell happened?"

Lathen muttered the same words as he held Pepper. "You got a lot of s'plaining to do."

"You're absolutely not going to believe what happened." Gwen paused and glanced down at Misfit. "How did she get here?"

"It was the damndest thing. I got a call from Paul in a panic. Misfit was raising such a fuss at the cottage that Trinity went to see what was wrong. When she opened the door, the dog flattened her and took off. They couldn't find Misfit anywhere. As I was on the phone with him, Misfit showed up here, ran straight to the painting and started howling. It's a wonder the neighbors didn't complain. Now it's your turn. What the hell happened?"

Gwen and Pepper took turns explaining their experience from when Gwen's hand first slipped into the painting and pulled out a poppet to later being sucked into the painting and the information Beth relayed to them. Conveniently, they left out the part about the newspaper.

Gwen bolted across the floor, down the spiral stairs, down the second-floor stairs and screeched to a halt beside the dragon's head. When she began to tug on it, Brock came up behind her and put his hand across her arm restraining her actions. "We can't destroy property that doesn't belong to us…. And at this rate may never belong to us."

"Like hell, I can't. Watch me." She twisted and tugged. This time the dragon head came off with a *pop* knocking her back a step or two into his chest. Scurrying back to the newel post, she reached inside and carefully pulled out the sheet of newspaper triumphantly. "Beth was right. It's still here."

"It certainly is." Pepper breathed. "Now what?"

She carefully handed the brittle yellowing paper to him. Lathen looked over his shoulder. As the men read the article, she and Pepper exchanged glances.

"I'm not exactly sure." Gwen breathed. Maybe Salem's historical society. Isn't it an independent organization dedicated to the study, promotion, and preservation for Salem's history for the benefit of the community and its visitors?"

"Except if you're a real witch, then you're run out of town." Pepper protested hands on hips.

"Still a little bitter huh? Don't blame you. But fate had your back." Gwen smiled and jerked her chin at Lathen, then tapped a finger to her lips. "The place for it would be the Salem Witch Museum, but how do we go about arranging it? Especially when the contents will upend all that is known about the Judge."

"First of all, it will have to be authenticated. That could be difficult. A timeline to publication would help." He squinted attempting to read the date, then handed the paper back to Gwen and looped an arm around her shoulder. "Can't make out the publication date."

"That's because it wasn't. The author was killed before it went to print. But he gave Beth a copy the night before in case something happened to him. Beth said there were rumblings and rumors along that line before it was written."

"So it never was published. Gonna make it hard to authenticate under those circumstances." Lathen shook his head.

"The Judge had such a bad reputation, maybe it could go a long way to explaining his actions. I mean using the bench to commit murder...that's a pretty strong statement. Hell, if I remember my history correctly, his great-great-grandson renowned writer Nathaniel Hawthorne was so ashamed at his ancestor's actions that Nathaniel changed the spelling of his last name from Hathorne to Hawthorne to dissociate himself from the Judge."

Gwen leaned against him. "Any chance you know someone who could help us?" She batted her long dark eyelashes at him. "Beth and her family are counting on us."

He brushed a couple of strands of blue and green hair out of her face and kissed her nose. "Maybe. Let me make a couple of phone calls." Taking only a few steps, he paused and looked at his watch. "It's getting late, I should notify Bill I'm going to postpone the closing."

"NO!" Gwen and Pepper blurted in unison.

"We...huh...you were meant to own and occupy this house. That much is clear from all that we have learned today. There was no deceit on the part of the owners. They're non-magical people and didn't have a clue."

The front door opened and slammed closed as if to accentuate the women's statement.

Hesitating for a moment, he stared at his phone, then snapped his fingers. "I know who to contact.

Maybe he can see us early tomorrow. Meanwhile, the safest place for that newspaper is right back where you found it. If what you—excuse me—Beth says is true, there are spells protecting it."

"What about the closing? Once word gets out about what we found… notoriety might be a problem." Gwen tucked the paper back into the newel post and replaced the dragon's head.

"True." He scrolled through his phone, touched a number, and put the phone to his ear as someone knocked on the door. He squeezed her shoulder and released her as his brow wrinkled and he walked toward the door. As he eased it open, Bill bustled through the door.

"Damn man, don't you answer your phone anymore?" The real estate agent glanced at the others in the room and lowered his voice. "Didn't know you had company."

"Well, good evening to you too. Of course, I answer my phone." He glanced at his recent calls log and his face heated. "Looks like my phone got switched to silent. Sorry." Continuing to scroll through his call log, he breathed a sigh of relief. "No missed calls from the clinic." He shook his head. "Don't know how it happened. I'm usually so careful. Motioning toward his guests, he said, "Pepper, Lathen, this is Bill, my real estate agent."

Bill gave an acknowledging nod to them. "Never mind that. The title company had an early morning cancellation and wanted to know if we wanted it. Since I couldn't reach you, I took it hoping it would work out."

Clapping Bill on the back, he grinned. "Good for

you. What time?"

"Seven-thirty tomorrow morning."

"Perfect. I'll be there."

Slightly taken aback, Bill kicked at the pieces of sawdust below the newel post. "Cleaners didn't do a very good job. Want me to call 'em back?"

"Nope. I'll handle it. Mind if I keep the keys?"

"Would it matter if I did?" Bill chuckled. "When do you plan to move in?"

"Not really. I plan to start moving some things tomorrow. Any problem with that?"

"There is the three day right of rescission."

"I'll waive it."

"Okay. I best be off. See you tomorrow bright and early." Bill clasped his hand, then nodded in Pepper and Lathen's direction. "Nice to meet you. The real estate agent winked at Gwen. "Good to see you again."

"Likewise. Nite Bill." Gwen stood beside Brock as he closed the door.

"That was downright weird. I was about to call him and poof, there he is at my door. We needed an early morning closing, and we got it." He hesitated for a couple of beats. "I need to buy lottery tickets."

Gwen glanced down at Misfit snoozing next to the bottom of the stairs. "Guess we better get back to the Sanctuary and make sure all is well. No phone calls. That bodes even better. And I'm really beat. Been an unbelievable day."

"I hate to bring it up, but we have to head back to Lobster Cove in a few days. Checked in with them this morning and everything is fine, but can only imagine paperwork piling up. We hadn't planned to be gone this long."

"Building supplies are being delivered next week, so I need to be on hand for that." Lathen grinned. "We're adding an addition to the bird enclosure and Kaylee insists hers needs a remodel."

"No… He thinks her enclosure is too small for her to fly around. Even though she gets outside flight time most days, even during the winter." Pepper poked him in the chest to accentuate the statement.

Lathen laughed. "Gotta keep the women in my life happy. Even the feathered and furred ones. Tonk and I have to stick together. You remember Tonk, the wolf pup that came to us after being hit by a car?"

"Yes. Poor little pup," Gwen said.

"He's a really large wolf now, still walks with a limp, but it doesn't slow him down one bit."

"Great to hear. I remember my sis, Dylan had her doubts when she first saw him. Pretty messed up."

"Brock, why don't you come on back to the cottage with us. We'll do rounds in the morning and you can check on Lucky. Attend your closing and we'll maybe meet with your expert after that?" Gwen peered hopefully up into his eyes.

"Too late to call him now, but he's an early riser, so we should be able to work something out." He wrapped an arm around her waist and pulled her to him. "As to the invitation, I'm all in." Leaning down he took her mouth with his and made his intentions quite clear.

Lathen cleared his throat. "Need to wait 'til we get to the cottage."

Pepper giggled. "Gwen you have been holding out on me."

Gwen pulled away and snickered. "Well, the vet's out of the bag now if it wasn't before."

Chapter Twenty
Night Visions and Business as Usual

A thin orange line along the horizon warned that dawn was near. Gwen put the coffee on, took cinnamons rolls she'd made last week out of the freezer, and popped them in the microwave. Misfit paced to be let out as she filled the dog's food bowl. "Not going out alone anymore girl." She took the leash from the hook by the door and slipped a sweater over her shoulders. "Come on, let's go." Turning the security light on, she scanned the area behind her cottage then stepped outside. The rain in the wee hours of the morning had left the path in the back yard wet with puddles in places. She inhaled deeply and enjoyed the fresh rain-washed air.

Misfit still limped a bit from her altercation, but happily plodded through the puddles, sniffed over the grassy area, did her business and glanced pleadingly up at Gwen. "Nope. Can't let you roam. We'll go back and get breakfast. It's a busy day ahead." The dog lowered its head and her tail drooped, as she trudged back to the cottage. "It's not that bad. You have a comfortable place to sleep, food on a regular basis, and someone who cares for you." Chuckling she opened the door, waited for Misfit to plod through the door, and followed her in.

Brock stood in the middle of the kitchen, a mug of

steaming liquid in one hand, a cinnamon roll in the other. "I've got to stay over more often if this is the kind of treatment I get." He waggled his eyebrows and took another bite of the roll.

After releasing Misfit, she took her sweater off, hung it and the leash on the hook next to the door, then walked over to him.

Setting his mug and cinnamon roll on the counter, he gathered her into his arms. Holding her snugly, he leaned over and brushed his lips gently over hers. "Good morning my love," he murmured against her lips. Raising his mouth from hers, he gazed into her eyes.

A fleeting thought had her wondering if the eyes were really a window into one's soul. But she was distracted. The touch of his lips was a delicious sensation she reveled in. Standing on tiptoe, she parted her lips to meet his kiss demanding more. He didn't disappoint. Crushing her to him, he pressed his mouth to hers hungrily. A groan escaped his lips and he gently traced her lips with the tip of his tongue then lifted his head. "No time. We'll have to continue this tonight." Eyes smoldering, a seductive smile crossed his lips. "I'll make it worth your while. I promise."

She licked her lips tasting the remnants of frosting and cinnamon. It was delightful. "I'll hold you to it." She handed him his mug, roll, and a napkin. "So what's on today's agenda?"

"I want to check-in at the clinic before going to the closing. Then we'll see how my day shakes out. Hopefully, I can reach Butch and see what we can discover about the newspaper."

"You going to have him come to the house?"

"Yep. Don't think it wise to remove the paper from the house at this time. I want you, Pepper and Lathen there when he arrives. While I trust Pepper's instincts in that there's nothing malevolent going on, I'm just not sure what to expect from the house."

"I understand. We'll be ready when you are."

"Good. Want to take a quick peek at Lucky, then I gotta go." He kissed her again, this time his kiss was as tender and light as the summer breeze.

His kiss sent new spirals of ecstasy through her as he looped his arm around her shoulder and walked to the aviary. Lucky's large yellow eyes blinked sleepily at them. Soft hoots floated in the air as she ruffled her feathers and turned her back to them.

"Guess she's not ready to get up."

"Looks to me like she spent most of the night stalking her food bowl." She laughed pointing to the empty bowl turned upside down in the middle of the enclosure.

"Didn't you lock the food bowl down?"

"Yes, but for an owl with plenty of time on her hands, it doesn't take long to disengage the bowl, we've discovered. Easier to just toss her food to her during the day. At night, we leave a few scraps in the bowl since she's diurnal—active hunting both day and night."

"I'd say she's doing fine. We'll leave her alone for now." He flipped through her chart. "She's gaining weight. No mention of problems, so we'll leave a thorough exam for later in the week."

"Sounds like a plan." They walked hand in hand to the cottage, where he kissed her again then took the path to the parking lot. She stood in the cottage doorway blew him a kiss, which he reached out and pretended to catch, as he got into his truck. With a wave, he drove away.

Closing the door quietly, she returned to the kitchen, poured a glass of orange juice, took a cinnamon roll from the microwave and eased into a chair at the table. Early morning sounds of birds greeting the day with their chirps, buzzing of insects, and the waking rhetoric of sanctuary inhabitants were a balm to her psyche. Opting out of her usual coffee after yesterday's adventures, she sipped on orange juice her nerves still a little jangled.

The full ramifications of yesterday hadn't completely registered until sometime during the night when she'd been jarred awake by Beth's face in her dreams. *I spent fricking part of yesterday in the seventeenth century, with a family of witches. Holy shit. Did Pepper have a similar experience in the wee hours this morning?*

The pipes clanked as someone ran water in the other part of the cottage. Footsteps in the hallway, told her Lathen and Pepper were up. *Maybe I'll get my answer shortly.*

Pepper bounded into the kitchen and back-peddled to a stop before the coffee maker. She grabbed a mug and filled it to the brim with the rich liquid. Breathing deeply, she hesitated and took a sip. "Hot." She blew across the top of her mug and smiled as her husband sauntered into the room.

"What I night I had. Beth's face popped into my dreams and floated there amid a wonderful dream of pleasure and... Oh well never mind. But it did kill the vibe." Glancing around, she pinned Gwen with her stare. "Brock already gone?" Pointing to the remaining half-frozen cinnamon rolls, she asked, "You make those?"

"Yep. On both counts. He wanted to stop by the clinic before going to the closing. Then he'll try to reach his contact, Butch, after that. I made the rolls last week and froze them in batches of six. Help yourself. Warm 'em up in the microwave." She took a bite of her roll and chewed while Pepper plopped the rolls onto a napkin and popped them into the microwave. "Beth entered my dreams last night also."

"To be expected after being whisked into the seventeenth century and back. Not to mention the circumstances Beth and her family are in. Our subconscious worked overtime. Unless Beth has the ability to enter the dream world." Pepper shrugged. "Which is doubtful. She'd already relayed her message, now it's a waiting game." After the rolls were heated, Pepper handed one to Lathen and took one for herself. Biting into the ooey-gooey confection, she closed her eyes. "Mmmm... you make the best cinnamon rolls. I've used your recipe, but they never turn out as good. You holding back on me girl?"

"Nooo...I wrote the recipe down from memory, I don't always use a recipe, so sometimes things change." She made pinching motions with her fingers then shrugged. "A pinch of this, a little more of that and make sure you warm the yeast. Don't let it sit too long."

"Have to watch you make them sometime. So I can get it right. We love these things." She held up the roll and took a big bite, then licked the frosting off her fingers.

Lathen sat down at the table with his coffee and roll. He took a bite then pulled his phone out and checked the messages. "Nothing pressing, Alec has it handled. Though I'm not sure he'd tell me if he didn't unless it was something he and Mike couldn't take care of."

"Want to do rounds with me? I'd like the two of you to see RoadTrip and her buddies." She pushed up from the chair, rinsed her dishes, and put them in the dishwasher.

"Sure." Pepper jumped up and added her dishes to the washer. "Never saw the point of washing the dishes before you put them in the dishwasher." At Gwen's dour look, she ran them under the water and replaced them in the washer. "Just say'n."

She laughed. "You're probably right."

. "Ladies. I'm going to make a quick phone call then I'll catch up with you." He grabbed Pepper around the waist and pulled her to him. "Now you behave yourself." He kissed her on the cheek and sent Gwen a stern look. "That includes you. No more incidents like yesterday. Lost nearly ten years off mine and Brock's lives."

"Got it." The women chorused and scooted out the back door.

"After yesterday's escapades, is Brock still okay with buying the house?" Pepper paused for a beat to glance at Gwen.

"Yeah. He has faith in your abilities. What most concerns him are any malevolent spirits. After a hard day at the clinic, the last thing he wants to deal with in his own home is problems of the supernatural kind."

"Boy, I hear that. Home is our sanctuary."

Arriving at the reptile habitat, she tugged on the door and found it was locked. Paul's voice came from an intercom by the door. "Hey Gwen, I'll buzz you in." A click sounded and she pulled on the door again. "Since when do we have automatic locks on the habitat?" She asked before walking inside.

"Since someone keeps messing with them. Quintin and I added a few upgrades since the last episode. Bars on the windows, a security door, alarm, and video feed so we can see who's coming and going. The windows still open for fresh air."

"Not to mention the new intercom system," Quintin added.

"We put that together with the extra parts we found. Not a big deal. Stop by security when you're through there. We can give you a tour. Sam approved it all and most of the parts came from Rocky's stash of spare parts. That guy is a packrat, I'm telling you," Paul said in an amused voice.

Quintin's chuckle came over the speaker. "You can say that again."

Inside she made her way across the floor to RoadTrip's enclosure. Her bowl was full of greens and fresh water flowed over a mini waterfall at the end of her sandy area. The turtle turned her head and looked up with her good eye and scooted toward Gwen. "Hey girl, how are you today?" She stroked RT's shell for a moment. When she touched RoadTrip's feet she promptly drew them into her shell. "Quick to respond these days. Good job."

The intercom squawked again and the door banged open, the warm summer breeze circulated around the room. Lathen appeared behind Pepper.

She winked at him and turned her attention back to the turtle. "Wow, she is quite tame for all she's been through." Pepper leaned over and gave the turtle a visual exam.

"Yeah, spent quite a bit of time with her getting her to eat, exercise, and to take meds. Coaxing that jaw open is nearly impossible. Keeping her head out to put salve in her eye was nearly as bad." Shaking her head, she moved to a larger enclosure with more sand and lots of hiding places. "This is our nursery for the baby Desert Tortoises. Brock hopes most of them can be returned to the wild eventually. So we make sure their needs are taken care of, but keep our distance." Closing the top on the nursery, she motioned them across the room to enclosures lined up along the wall. These are our other Wood Turtles. This one will eventually share a habitat with RoadTrip, once RT and Red Blaze are deemed healthy. The other two, we haven't named yet, will also share an enclosure once we're sure there are no lingering infections. As you know, we're licensed for a breeding program, but never had an occasion to consider it."

"I'd be interested to see what develops. Keep me in the loop." Pepper grinned.

"Will do." She led them out of the reptile habitat, glanced at her watch, and sauntered toward the aviary compound. "We'll check on Lucky next." Peering in the side window, Lucky was already eying the door with suspicion from her flight. Tugging the door open, the group was greeted with a loud hiss from the owl.

Upon recognizing the individuals, she hooted and clicked her beak, turning her head to the food fridge. "Gee know how we rate." Gwen picked up Lucky's chart and checked her feeding schedule. "Nice try, you were just fed an hour ago." Picking up the target stick, she donned leather gauntlets and approached the bird. Touching Lucky's good wing, the owl lifted its wing and extended it for examination.

She passed the stick to Pepper and crept closer to Lucky. Cautiously she touched the owl's feet and the bird raised each one in turn. But when she took the stick from Pepper and touched the injured wing, Lucky screeched loud and long and sidled away clearly displeased.

"I guess she's done with the two of you." Lathen laughed.

Pepper shot him an evil eye then addressed her best friend, "You've been working with her a lot and it shows."

"Well, actually Brock started, and I took over while she was at the clinic. Trying to exam an uncooperative owl as large as this one is more stressful to all. Better to take time to do a little training and make exams easier and less stressful.. Especially with our talents." She grinned and polished her nails against her shirt. "Makes training almost easy." Having crossed over to the fridge, she took out a tidbit and tossed it to Lucky who caught and gobbled it down.

"No wonder she looks for food when you appear." Pepper teased.

"She did a good job doing as we asked. She deserved a treat." Her phone chimed in her pocket indicating a message. *Hmmm... I don't remember the phone ringing.* She checked her phone's volume level and found she must have accidently switched it to silent.

Chapter Twenty-One
A New Twist to an Old Legacy

"Hey, Gwen! I'm just leaving the closing. All went as planned. Can you meet me at the house in say thirty minutes?"

"Sure. I was wrapping up a tour for Pepper and Lathen. All's well here too. I had a message from the DOW and now we are playing telephone tag. You didn't by chance hear from them?"

"Nope. See ya soon." He ended the call, strode to his truck and got in. Leaning back against the seat he took a long breath then released it slowly. What a whirlwind his life had become. He considered those yellow sticky notes Delta had purchased. It depicted two devils chasing one another with a caption "One damn thing after another."

A laugh bubbled up deep in his throat. He let it go and laughed until tears formed in his eyes. Not usually given to fits of laughter it felt good. He looked around hoping no one saw him. They didn't. Starting the truck he turned onto Main and headed for the house—his house. *Would it be their house in the future? Of course, it would.*

A satisfying feeling settled in his gut. Maybe domestic life was for him after all. His sister Dylan made it work and she was a country vet, making house calls and traveling a good part of her time. Yet, her family seemed to adapt quite well. He snickered. They did seem to really appreciate having her home for several weeks when she got sick last year and he covered for her.

In his mind, it was the trip to Lobster Cove where fate seemed to intervene in his life for the first time. Well, at least the first time he'd recognized it. Gwen was the best thing that had ever happened to him. Her friends, Lathen and Pepper, now his, were another case of fate sticking its nose in his life. Magic…had not been in his vocabulary until recently. Let alone using it to refer to his vet practice, his life, and love. Now, nothing would surprise him.

Pulling in behind a dark expensive-looking SUV unfamiliar to him, he killed the engine and sat for a moment. *Must be Butch's. Didn't know he got a new vehicle.* Normally he would have jumped out and dived right into whatever awaited him, but recent experience had made him cautious. Two people waited inside the vehicle. Neither made a move to open their doors as he drove up and cut the engine. *Strange.* As he reached for the door handle, Gwen's SUV glided up behind his and stopped. She jumped out, along with Pepper and Lathen, Misfit trotted beside Gwen.

He opened the door in time to hop out and catch Gwen around the waist. "About time you got here."

She giggled. "Don't think you've been here much longer than us. Who's in the SUV? Butch?"

"S'pose so."

As if on cue, the passenger side of the vehicle opened and Butch swung out. A woman dressed in a business suit slipped out of the driver's side and removed her sunglasses. Butch waited behind the vehicle for her then walked toward him.

"Brock. This is the house you closed on?"

"Yep."

"Wow, didn't know it was on the market. I've had my eye on it for a while, along with several others I know of. Lucky you."

"Thanks." His attention moved to Butch's companion. Immediately it appeared as if the woman stood sizing him up swinging her sunglasses round and round slowly by the bow.

Butch motioned toward the woman. "Anyway…Martha here is an expert in old paper. Figured you wouldn't mind if I brought her along since she was available this morning."

"Newspapers to be exact." The short stocky woman tucked her glasses in her coat pocket and extended her hand toward Brock. "Nice to meet you—"

"Brock. These are my friends Gwen, Pepper, and Lathen. Pepper and Lathen own a wildlife rescue and rehab center in Lobster Cove. They're here visiting Gwen, who owns the Salem Sanctuary."

Greetings were exchanged. He motioned everyone into the house. Misfit, hung back checking out the strangers before trotting into the house. She positioned herself a few feet from the door, out of the way, her gaze fixed on Gwen.

Martha and Butch's eyes rounded as they entered the house and stared at the dragon staircase.

"Beautiful isn't it?" He caressed the banister then continued into what he considered the family room with its huge stone fireplace. Doing a double-take, he was surprised the firebox was set with kindling and logs ready to be started. *Who…How…Nevermind. Too warm this morning for a fire.* For a moment he saw how it could or would be.

A cozy crackling fire. He and Gwen cuddled together on the couch facing the fireplace a big bowl of popcorn between them. A toddler with jet black hair hanging onto the arm of the couch waving an arm for balance and reaching for the popcorn. Whoa— Wait— He shook his head and concentrated on the here and now. "Make yourselves comfortable. Not much to offer you since I closed on the house this morning and haven't started to move in yet."

"That's fine." The woman remained standing. "I'd like to see this newspaper Butch told me about. From the late 1690s or early 1700s? Not many newspapers around during that time. It would be quite a find. Where did you say you discovered it?"

Gwen glanced uneasily at him.

"Martha," Butch said companionably barely hiding his impatience with her. "I'd like to take a look at the woodwork in this house if you don't mind." He swiveled his head to get a better look upstairs. "Had my eye on this house for a long time."

"Well, time is money in my world,' she huffed. "But we'll have a look."

It was unusual for Butch to rein in a business associate. He was ordinarily an easy-going person. "I'd be happy to show you the second story real quick. There are impressive carvings etched into the door panels and molding inside the bedrooms. Follow me."

The minute his guests cleared the second-floor landing, he glanced down at Gwen who was quickly removing the dragon's head. He directed them to the end of the hall before pointing out the door panels, then opened the door to one of the rooms indicating the molding matched the panels on the doors.

"Unbelievable," Martha breathed. "How much do you know about the history of this house?"

"Not much. We are in the process of researching the home's history. So far nothing documented as unusual." He shrugged. "You know spirits, ghosts, that type of thing. Apparently, the structure burned down shortly after it was built, leaving only the staircase and fireplace intact. It was rebuilt on exactly the same spot incorporating the staircase and stone fireplace."

When he returned to the main level, Gwen had the yellowed sheet of newspaper spread out on the coffee table. The dragon's head had been returned to its rightful place. "Here it is. We found it hidden in the house. The previous owners didn't know anything about it." Brock pointed to the paper.

"We did a bit of research on the time period and found only a couple of newspapers that printed information on the witch trials. It appeared to be a very dangerous profession—journalism back then." Gwen grimaced. "Don't remember the names of the brave ones that documented the news." She rubbed her temples and closed her eyes for a moment.

"Hell, it's a dangerous profession now, especially if you rile someone or are on the wrong side of an issue. Not sure the reporters or news anchors now days are as unbiased as they should be. But I don't want to open that can of worms." Pepper waved her hand in dismissal.

Martha carefully took the corner of the paper between her thumb and index finger, rubbed lightly, turned it over, then returned it to the table. "Certainly looks and feels authentic. Even the inkblots…" she trailed off.

"I can't make out the person's name who wrote it. In your research, did you find anything to indicate it had been circulated? But… it would be an unpopular view. Though, I've read accounts of rumors of such things about the Judge. None stuck of course."

"According to what we did find, the person who wrote this died before it was published in a house fire of questionable origin." Gwen shifted from foot to foot uncomfortably.

Taking out her phone, she took pictures of the paper and a close up of the smudged name of the person who wrote it. "Very interesting and unusual. Looks like the last name could be Mather."

"So exactly what is your area of expertise?" Brock rocked back on his heels with one hand shoved in his pocket.

"Documentation of the Salem Witch Trials, and early attempts at newspaper accounts in the new world. I'm a historian with an interest in the Salem Witch Trials." Martha sighed. "I'm the tenth generation great grand-daughter of Abigail Hobbs. She was a teenager during the trials and couldn't keep her mouth shut. Accounts say she pled guilty to witchcraft but not before she accused several others including John Proctor and Minister Burroughs, a well-respected member of the community. She was responsible for accusations that climbed up the social hierarchy."

"Wow. Abigail was portrayed as a spitfire in those times." Pepper grinned.

The woman's cheeks pinked. "Abigail was a colorful character. Her father William Hobbs and her step-mother Deliverance Hobbs were also accused of witchcraft. To make a long story short, she was among those named in the Act for Reversal of Attainder by the Massachusetts Great and General Court, October 17, 1711. So you see, I have scholarly and personal reasons for my interest."

"Are you familiar with Elizabeth Colson?" Gwen asked cautiously.

"Yes, yes, of course. She was about the same age as Abigail during that time. In fact, I suspect they may have known each other. Her family was accused of witchcraft. Her mother and grandmother were jailed. Her mother was released but her grandmother died in jail. Elizabeth was never arrested. She disappeared and was believed to have resurfaced in 1704, married Adam Hart if memory serves and had three children. Anyway, I'll do some checking and get back to you." Martha put her sunglasses back on and walked toward the door. "What's your end deal with this paper?"

"If in fact, it's authentic, we'd like it to be added as a possible alternate situation to the Judge. We all know nothing was black and white back then. Except what influential people wanted others to believe. Maybe put the paper in Salem's Witch Museum. Let people make up their own minds if he was or wasn't? Could explain a lot toward his behavior," he suggested.

"You'd be interested to know that somehow Elizabeth and her family are, uh, were tied to this house." Gwen glanced nonchalantly at the woman.

Martha raised an eyebrow then stared at Gwen over her glasses. "Really? I don't suppose you'd let me take the paper with me?"

He cleared his throat. "No. I feel safer if it's left

with us."

"Where exactly did you find it?"

"In was secreted below the dragon's head in the newel post. We were checking the staircase for safety issues and the head seemed loose." He hesitated for a beat. *Never was a good liar.*

"Imagine our surprise when it popped off and inside was the paper," Gwen finished sidling closer to him.

He slid an arm around her waist and squeezed lightly thankful for the support.

"And you say this staircase was left standing when the rest of the house burnt to the ground?" Martha asked incredulously.

"Yes, it and the stone fireplace." He motioned toward the wall where the fireplace covered nearly the entire wall.

"Must have been some kind of magic to make that happen." She ran her fingers up and down the wood several times. "Well preserved. Don't you think? Gotta run. Coming, Butch? We'll be in touch."

"Right behind you." Butch grinned at him. "Quite the find."

"So it would appear." The men shook hands and he closed the door behind Martha and Butch.

"Well, that was a tangle." Gwen leaned heavily again him. "You really shouldn't weave tales. It's not your strong suit." She giggled.

"Thanks for bailing me out." He rubbed his hand up and down her arm.

"Wow, this isn't at all what we expected when we came for a visit. What a fun time we've had. But all things must come to an end. We need to return to

Lobster Cove. Got a text there's problems with the supply delivery and the contractor is complaining about his time schedule. But…" Pepper rolled her eyes and hip-checked Gwen. "You two have to keep us apprised of what happens here. I hate to leave before Beth's situation is settled. But duty calls. You understand."

"I do. We brought the situation to light, but I don't think it's enough to release Beth and her family. Do you?"

"It's a start. More than they had to begin with." Lathen glanced around. "Brock, you going to bring that painting down here? Maybe hang it on the wall?"

"Until Beth and her family commandeered us into their world, it was an ordinary visit planned with a peek at Brock's new house." Gwen smiled. "When you think about it, this has been a wild ride."

"Oh, Gwen nothing is ordinary when we get together." Pepper chortled. "Been that way since we met years ago. Doubt it's going to change now."

"Not sure." He leaned his head on top of Gwen's. "Funny you should mention that Lathen, I was considering doing exactly that. It would look good hanging on the wall opposite the fireplace, don't you think?" Staring at the blank wall, he walked over and knocked lightly looking for a stud that would hold the weight of the painting. Finding an area he thought would work, he took a pen out of his pocket and made a mark on the wall. "Are you two leaving in the morning then? Before the heavy lifting of moving day arrives."

Lathen grinned at him and nodded. "Exactly."

Pepper added, "Yes. Unfortunately. Don't get me wrong, I love my center. But this is so exciting." Pepper spread her arms wide. "A little bit of satisfaction to out a witch as wicked as Judge John Hathorne."

"You're just trying to get back at Salem's good old boys for outing you." Gwen snickered.

"Maybe, but it all turned out as it was meant be." Pepper tugged on the door. It didn't budge.

"Awww come on. Let us go. Brock and Gwen have it handled." Pepper stood hands on hips staring at the door. "Besides, we'll be back."

Lathen took hold of the door handle and yanked. Nothing but a groan of old wood. He glanced at Pepper, then switched to Brock and Gwen. "A little help."

"I bought the house and waived the right of rescission. I'll be moved in within the week." He raised an eyebrow then gave Gwen a sideways glance. "What more do you want?" Raising his arms up, he let them fall to his side. *I can't believe I am conversing with a house.* "Maybe you're supposed to acknowledge your plan to stick around." Brock chuckled as Pepper and Lathen peered at each other then at Gwen.

"Okay, okay, okay. I'll be around here when I'm not at the sanctuary or at my cottage. I do have obligations you know." Gwen's tone of voice had Misfit getting up from her station beside the door with a low growl. "Now see what you've done. Pissed off the dog."

The door lock clicked loudly. Gwen reached for the door and easily pulled it open. Misfit bolted outside followed by Pepper and Lathen, then he and Gwen bringing up the rear.

Gwen tossed the keys to her SUV to Lathen. "I'm going to stay here a while longer. Brock can bring me home later."

"Sure no problem. We gotta pack. See you when

you get there." Lathen fobbed the car door open and waited for Pepper to climb inside. "You might want to get a handle on that house of yours." Lathen snickered sprinting around to the driver's side door.

"Very funny. Your better half is the one who insisted I buy the property." He shot back good-naturedly.

"Nooo…you called me. Simply put, you had magic envy. I live on enchanted land. You had to get yourself an enchanted house." Pepper roared with laughter as she waved and Lathen turned the SUV toward the road. "Of course that was before you realized the hidden Gypsy magic in your family's cabin in Puffin Cove." Pepper's laughter wafted in the night breeze until they were almost out of sight.

Gwen sat down on the porch and pulled him down beside her. "You okay with the events of the past few days?" She twisted around so her eyes met his. Misfit trotted up the steps and circled twice before settling next to her.

"Yeah, not anywhere near the shock at Pepper's cabin over the holidays. Speaking of holidays…"

Chapter Twenty-Two

Will the Poacher Problem Be Resolved Amid the Sanctuary Decisions?

She glanced over at him perplexed. "Holidays are nearly four months away. Don't you think we have enough other things going on without considering the holidays?" Holding up her fingers, she began to tick off the loose ends to date. "Beth and her family, authentication of the paper, poachers outcome, moving into your house, the painting, turtles, owl— "

"And the list goes on." He interrupted chuckling. "Not those holidays, the end of summer celebration and gala. How about I take you on a real date?"

"So all our outings up until now were pretend dates?" She crossed her arms over her chest and stuck her lip out in a pout.

Laughing he shook his head. "I mean one that doesn't include injured animals, poachers, bewitched time-travel paintings, Gypsy magic cabins, or whatever else we've encountered in the past few months. A date like most couples enjoy."

"What fun is that?" She deliberately ran the tip of her tongue around her moist lips knowing her actions would get his attention. Still holding the pout he'd termed cute on other occasions.

With his fingertip, he tilted her chin up, brushed his lips over hers and murmured, "Tease. I suggest we

Tena Stetler

adjourn to my apartment."

"Ohhh I love that idea." She turned toward him, slipping one leg over his and straddled him deepening the kiss while wrapping her arms around his neck.

"Oh to hell with the apartment, there is a perfectly good couch in this newly purchased home." He eased his hands under her butt cheeks and stood. She wrapped her legs around his waist and wiggled against him.

"Now that's a great idea." She breathed a kiss on the pulsing hollow at his throat and trailed her lips along his jawline to the soft area below his ear.

He reached toward the door. It flew open wide and closed behind the dog who trotted in behind them. Easing her down on the sofa, he unzipped her jeans and pulled them off her legs, followed by her panties tossing them on the end of the couch. Standing between her legs, he stripped off his pants and briefs then tugged his shirt over his head flinging it on the floor.

"Don't mind if the house…." She giggled letting her gaze wander over the hard male body erect before her. "Wow, I love this view." As he leaned down to pull her t-shirt off, she reached out and stroked his length eliciting a low groan from him as he arched against her hand.

"Nope, the house is mine and it might as well get used to us doing what couples do." When he released the catch on her bra, her breasts spilled in his hands. Kneading each one, his mouth closed over first one teasing the nipple with the tip of his tongue then licked his way to the other. She arched against him and he let out a little hum.

Trailing kisses along the side of her breast, he licked his way to her belly button caressing it with the tip of his tongue. Moaning she didn't know what to do with her hands as he spread her legs wider with his shoulders, his warm breath caressing her hot quivering center. One finger then two slipped inside her as his tongue worked its magic on her tiny bundle of nerves.

Unable to hold back any longer she screamed his name as she crashed over the edge of ecstasy. He worked his magic until she was completely spent. Her breath coming in gasps and her legs felt like gelatin as he leaned away.

He grinned up at her positioning himself at her opening. "Liked that did you? Let's see if I can bring you to another screaming climax." He chuckled and pushed inside slowly. She writhed against him, grabbing his hips, trying to pull him in, wanting more, needing all of him. Now.

But he wasn't inclined to accommodate her. He continued his slow undulations until he was fully seated inside her. Unhurriedly, he stroked in and out as he teased her center with his fingers until she pulsed around him and screamed his name again over and over. "That's what I like to hear from my woman."

Unable to hold on any longer, he buried himself deep inside riding out wave after wave of pleasure. Finally, he rested his cheek on her breast for a moment sucking a nipple into his mouth before rolling to his side taking her with him and still inside. He took her mouth, his tongue thrust inside and danced alongside hers for a long moment. When he opened his eyes, she was staring at him.

Her lips turned up in a lazy smile. "So this is the way you like your women?"

"No, you are misquoting me. I said, woman. And

yes it is—if you mean naked and well satisfied."

She glanced at their clothes lying in a heap on the floor. "What about you? I too like my partner naked and well satisfied."

"Well you're in luck I fit your description. Only I'm looking forward to taking you in the shower before escorting you home." A seductive laugh rumbled up in his throat. "I made sure the utilities were turned on this morning. Though I admit this is not what I had planned."

****

She hugged Pepper as Lathen loaded the vehicle. "I'm going to miss you. Thanks so much for coming and sharing our adventure thus far." Her eyes glistened and a wayward tear rolled down her cheek. She viciously wiped it away with the back of her hand. Pepper, her extended family, Lathen, and his pack were all she had for family.

Lathen's family spent the holidays in Lobster Cove. *That was where I met Brock. How my world has changed as Pepper predicted.* Her friend's voice brought her back to the present.

"You be sure to keep us up-to-date on Beth and her family. I have no doubt you'll have them into the light in no time. BUT… if you need me, don't hesitate to call." Pepper sniffed and hugged her best friend. "We'll be back soon. Or you could always come to Lobster Cove."

"We're all set." Lathen grinned walking up the path to the cottage.

Gwen quickly moved from Pepper to Lathen wrapping him in a tight bear hug.

"Hey what's all this?" Lathen rocked back then

wrapped his arms around her patting her back. "We're only a few hours away." Leaning her back by the shoulders, he smiled that understanding smile of his that crinkled the corners of his eyes then waggled his eyebrows. "And we are leaving you in good hands." His gaze shifted to Brock.

"I know." She sniffled. "It's so much fun having you all around. Never a dull moment."

"You mean shirking your duties to spend time with us." Pepper snorted.

"Hey right back at you." Gwen laughed feeling better. She soft punched Lathen in the shoulder and gave Pepper a quick final hug.

Standing in the doorway watching the scene unfold, Brock joined the group. "I for one, see right through your hasty retreat home. It's called moving day." He gave Pepper a quick hug and grasped Lathen's hand in a strong shake. "We'll see you soon."

"Bet on it." Lathen returned to the vehicle and held the door open while Pepper crawled inside. Shutting the door, he sprinted to the driver's side and jumped in. Windows down, the couple waved as the SUV bumped down the drive to the main road turning toward the highway home.

Standing arm in arm on the cottage porch, both waved as their friends' vehicle disappeared out of sight. Misfit snuffled around where the SUV had been parked then bolted up the porch steps and circled twice on her blanket in the corner before settling down.

"Don't get too comfortable girl, we still have to do rounds checking on the residents." She peered up at Brock. "You want to join us, check on Lucky before you leave for the clinic?" she asked hopefully.

He glanced at his watch. "Actually, I'm only going to call in at the clinic. Today the movers are coming."

"Wow, I didn't realize you'd already scheduled the move."

"Why pay more rent when I have a house of my own?" He chuckled. "Today was the only day in the next three weeks the moving company had free. Even then I had to call in a favor from the man who owns the company."

"Need any help?"

"I'd love to have your help. But you've been gone so much from the Sanctuary, I don't want to intrude." A door banged open. Brock looked across the Sanctuary. Paul strode purposely toward them.

She met him at the bottom of the porch stairs. "What's up?"

"While you were out last night, I got a call from Officer Murphy. Dept. Of Wildlife caught the guy who tried to break in a few days back. Seems he was actually doubled crossed by his own partner. He was under the impression that we were holding not only the injured turtles but the several healthy ones they bagged. When in fact, it appears his partner had taken the bag with the healthy ones to the buyer the night they were almost caught in the woods."

He shook his head disgustedly. "Such dirtbags. Anyway, when the officer told him there were no healthy ones, the guy rolled over on his partner. They are searching for him now, hoping to get info on his buyer. Maybe even rescue the healthy turtles before they are sold."

"Great news." She clapped her hands together. "So we don't have to worry about him coming back. That's a relief."

Paul waffled his hand back and forth. "Well until they catch the other guy, don't want to let our guard down. Apparently, this is a fairly large operation. The joint task force of the police and DOW plan to take 'em all down. That's kinda where we come in."

"How so?" She peered up at him questioningly.

"Any rescued creatures discovered they'd like to bring here for doc's examination to make sure they aren't too stressed to be released. Or if they are, place them here to rest and recuperate until they are able to be released." He took his hat off his head, rubbed the back of his neck and replaced the hat. "I said they'd have to talk to you and doc but that I'd relay the message."

"Message received." Brock looked thoughtful for a beat. "Any idea of the time frame?"

"Nope. I'd guess they have to capture the partner and get him to talk." Paul turned his attention to her. "Believe Trinity told the staff to prepare for new arrivals. I told her about the call since you weren't here. I hope that was all right."

"Of course. Trinity has full authority in my absence. Thank you for handling the situation, Paul. You did good. Of course, we'll take the animals." Pride welled up inside her at the growth and abilities of her staff.

"Count me in too." Brock clapped Paul on the shoulder.

A shy smile played around the corner of Paul's mouth as he kicked at the dirt with the toe of his boot. "Didn't see any reason to bother you two since you had company, especially when there wasn't a situation, yet."

"Perfect. Anything else need my attention?" She shaded her eyes with her hand and glanced toward the aviary where Trinity's office was located.

"Trinity wants to see you after rounds, but that's it as far as I know." Paul paused for a beat. "If that's all, I'd best get back to the office."

"I'll tell Trinity when I see her. But just so you know, after rounds and if nothing needs my attention, I'll be helping Brock at his new house. He's moving in today."

Paul switched his attention to Brock. "Congrats on the new house."

"Thank you." Brock slipped his arm around her. "Shall we check on everyone?"

"Yep, sooner it's done, the sooner we get you moved in." She whistled for Misfit. "Barring any complications here." When the dog trotted over, she reached down and rubbed the mutt's ears. "Let's go."

Inside the aviary, Lucky greeted them with a happy hoot and a strong wing flap. The other wing quivered at her side as she stretched it out and down then pulled it back into place.

"Would you look at that." Gwen moved closer. "How's your wing today?" She reached out to support it as the wing sagged lower than the other. Lucky was quick to nip a warning. "You know Pepper made Kaylee flap both wings for her dinner."

"I wasn't sure Lucky would ever control the muscles in that wing, but… I could be wrong." He picked up the target stick and touched the wing. Lucky screeched positioning the wing away and snapped her beak at the stick.

"I've got a plan. If I can find Kaylee's old physical

therapy file, we can use those exercises to rehab Lucky." She sprinted through the aviary, past Trinity sitting at her desk and into the archived files cabinet. The dog raced along behind her.

"What you looking for?" Trinity pushed up from the desk and walked over to her. "I organized those files alphabetically and by year over the last few months."

"Kaylee's rehab files. Lucky stretched her bad wing down and brought it back up to her side. You know what that means?" Gwen asked excitedly.

"Not a clue." Trinity shook her head, glancing at Brock as he entered the room.

"Lucky has muscle control in that wing. With constant exercise and strengthening motions, she could one day fly again. Pepper documented Kaylee's progress and exercises in her file, that should be archived here somewhere." She rifled through the first cabinet's top two drawers.

"All of Pepper's files are in the red cabinet." Trinity walked over and pulled open the bottom drawer, flipped through several files then held up a dog-eared pink file triumphantly. "Is this what you're looking for?"

Gwen snatched the file from her assistant and flipped through the graphs, diagrams, and notes. "Yep. This is it. We are going to implement these exercises as soon as I talk with Pepper." She took her phone out of her backpack.

"Hold on now." Brock walked up behind her and put a hand over her arm. "Let's finish checking on the residents. Give Pepper a call on the way to the house. If I know you, and I do, you'll want to oversee Lucky's rehab personally."

"For that, I need a plan and…"

"I need to have a few minutes of your time before you leave." Trinity padded over to her desk and picked up a stack of envelopes. "I need approvals, signatures on these checks, and requisition forms for the grants from Pepper. Paul told you about Murphy and the DOW?" She settled into the chair and brought up several spreadsheets on the computer screen.

"Yes. You acted exactly as I would have. Excellent job. Prepare all the extra space we have in the event we need it all. If not, we're that much further ahead next time." She skirted around Trinity's desk to review the spreadsheets.

Pointing to each one in turn then shuffling the windows, Trinity said. "These are what need to be replaced right away. These items can wait. And this is our wish list before winter sets in. The budget you set out for this quarter has an overage that will cover most of the items and half the wish list. Since Pepper and Lathen donated all the items they brought for the turtles and Lucky, we're way under the projected expenses."

"Wonderful." She returned to the front of Trinity's desk and sat in a chair facing her employee. "By the way, I have a volunteer, Rita, coming in to help out with the paperwork and anything else you want her to do. Her iguana was one of Brock's patients. She's really good with animals too. A win win in my book. She'll start college locally but can volunteer weekends, summer, spring and fall breaks. Rita mentioned a Veterinary Technician Program in addition to a business degree."

Trinity's eyes sparkled as she made eye contact.

"Sounds like she'll be a great fit."

"Wow, been talking to Rita, huh?" Brock fidgeted at the door. Misfit plopped down beside him and huffed out a breath.

She nodded then held her index finger up. "Just one more thing and we'll go." Returning her attention to her assistant, she leaned back in the chair and tented her fingers. "You happy here?"

Surprise etched on Trinity's face. "Of course."

"Any chance you would consider going full time? It would be a salaried position, so no more overtime. With the sanctuary growing by leaps and bounds, things are changing."

"Understood and I'd love to go full-time. What would the salary be?"

"That's something I'd have to work out. A little pressed for time at the moment. But I can guarantee it would be a fair amount with benefits such as paid vacation and health insurance."

"Sounds wonderful. I'm not going anywhere." Trinity grinned from ear to ear leaning back in her chair.

"Great. I'm going to be gone for the rest of the day. But if you need me, I'm only a phone call away." She shoved out of the chair and sauntered toward the door.

"I heard. Brock bought a new house." Trinity turned to Brock. "Congrats."

"Word sure travels fast around here." He opened the door for Gwen.

As she passed by him, she whispered. "That's because Trinity and Paul are an item. Isn't it great?"

He turned to her, eyes wide. "Really? You're kidding. I never would have thought." He looked over his shoulder at Trinity, who gave a little wave before turning her attention back to the computer monitor.

"Don't say anything. They think it's their secret." She chuckled. He closed the door behind her.

They walked hand in hand to the reptile habitat and checked on the turtles. RT was sunning herself. The other Wood Turtles were under the leaf covers provided. The Desert Tortoises were crawling around the perimeter of their enclosure.

"Looks like the Desert Tortoises will be ready to return to the wild soon." He leaned over and watched them climb over each other while one dug a hole.

"Yeah, hate to see 'em go, especially with fall coming."

"Have you given any more thought to a breeding program? Seems a great idea since you have two males and two females. They are a threatened species. With these little ones, it will be sixteen years or so before you have to worry about babies. There may even be government grants you could apply for."

"I'm still considering it. Charlotte, one of our veterinary interns, is researching it for me and doing a feasibility study. When I get the information from her, I'll go over it with you. I'm licensed, so no problem there."

He helped her into the truck, kissed her lips, and closed the door. Misfit paced at the side of the truck and whined. "Don't worry girl. Come on. "He opened the back door and lifted the dog into the back seat. "Away we go."

She pulled out her phone and dialed Pepper. After discussing the pros and cons of working up a rehab program for Lucky, she and Pepper agreed on a course of action to be implemented immediately. "I'll keep you informed as to our progress." She hung up the phone and smiled. "Think your owl may just fly again."

"Fantastic." He pulled up in front of the house. "Okay if I drop you off while I run to my apartment to get the movers started?"

"Sure."

Reaching into the console, he pulled out a sheet of paper. "This is a list of the furnishings and items left behind by the previous owner. I'm going to give them to charity."

She took the list. "The phone number at the top is the charity?"

"Yep. I'll call them on my way to the apartment and let them know you are waiting at the house for them. Wasn't sure how this was going to shake out, so I called the charity yesterday to give 'em a heads up and instructions. I'd call today with an arrival time and the address. I really appreciate your help. "

"No problem. Hopefully, we'll have all charitable donations gone before the movers arrive with your stuff." She cocked her head toward him. "Do you have much?"

"Nope. The necessities, that's about it. I've spent most of my time getting the clinic up and running…until you came along."

Twisting in her seat, she glanced at him. "Strange our relationship has gotten serious, and I've never been to your apartment."

"You're dedicated to your job too. The cottage feels more like home than my apartment."

"The trip to your family cabin kinda brought our relationship to the next level." She smiled dreamily.

"Loved that trip. No responsibilities, No interruptions. Mystery…magic."

A snort of laughter burst from his lips. "Unless you consider Pepper and Lathen popping in on us."

She shrugged one shoulder. "They're family and don't count."

He snorted again. "Probably best not to inform Pepper she doesn't count." Chuckling he parked in front of the house and cut the engine.

"You're right about that. But you know what I meant." She shoved at his shoulder, then pushed the door open and stepped outside. Misfit clambered over the front seat and jumped out of the door. Gwen caught her and scolded. "It's a long way to the ground from this truck. You could have gotten hurt. Don't do that again." The dog cocked her head, swiveled one ear, then trotted up the path to the house unconcerned.

"I can give the charity a call and have them come on over."

"Thank you." He came around the truck and caught her up in a hug.

Though they were in a crunch for time, she settled against him, enjoying the feel of his arms around her. He brushed a gentle kiss across her lips. She reveled in the velvety warmth of his kiss. The pit of her stomach went into a wild swirl of desire, then he raised his mouth from hers reluctantly.

"It's going to be a long day and we'd better get started. We'll continue where we left off tonight?"

"You can bet on it." Standing on tiptoe she touched her lips to his once more then turned and sauntered toward the door. It swung open. "Guess I don't need a key." She waved him on. "I got this."

Chapter Twenty-Three
End of Summer Gala and a Welcome Decision

It had been a couple of days since Brock got all moved in and settled in his new house. Gwen helped him hang the painting on the wall opposite the stone fireplace high enough to thwart touching. No use chancing another time-travel escapade. It looked great there, but she could see subtle changes in it from time to time while they moved Brock's furniture, computer, and personal items inside.

She could feel the anxiety building for Beth and her family. How long before it would be too late? She'd made headway, planting the seed that the Judge was a witch. But it wasn't enough. Authenticate the article, Beth and her family should be free.

As far as Brock was concerned, he admitted the changes and feeling some unrest around the painting. But he shrugged it off, saying the house magic and all was his now and he'd learn to deal with it.

The Sanctuary kept her busy so she hadn't returned since their romp in the bedroom in the wee hours of the morning. Today, she raced around the cottage making sure her dress was ready, shoes and bag matched. She was already forty-five minutes late after losing track of time during Lucky's rehab. The bird was doing very well. She would fly again.

A quiet knock on the door had her cursing as she

attempted to zip up her dress. After getting the cantankerous apparatus in place, she yanked open the door to Trinity.

"I thought you were still here." Her assistant glanced at her watch then over at Misfit curled up on the rug in the corner of the room. "She staying here? I can tell the guys she's here alone and to monitor the camera around your house often."

"I haven't decided yet. I may take her with me and leave her in the SUV for a few hours. Aren't you going to the gala?"

A wistful expression crossed Trinity's face. "No... too many people." She sighed.

"Since when don't you like people? You were the belle of the ball last year."

"Things change."

For a few minutes, she debated with herself. Interfering in her employees' personal lives wasn't her business. But, Paul was going to need nudging along and since Lathen wasn't here to do it... Wait... *I've got it.* "That's too bad. No date?"

"Something like that." Trinity glanced at her watch again. "You're going to be so late." She snickered. "Now get going. Don't worry about me." She raised her hand in a wave and walked out the door, turning only once. "Leave now." Her assistant warned.

She toed her shoes on, grabbed her bag, and started out the door. Better to leave the dog in the cottage than leave her cooped up in the SUV. "Misfit, you stay here and be good. Understand?"

The dog huffed, got up, circled the rug, and plopped back down with her back to Gwen.

"Fine." She closed the door and sprinted to the

SUV. Once inside, she dug in her evening bag for her phone. *God, I hate these little bags*. Finally, she dumped it out on the seat and grabbed her phone and called the Sanctuary's security office.

"Hey, boss lady." Paul's deep voice resounded through the phone.

"Hi Paul. I've left Misfit at the cottage alone. Please keep an eye on her. I shouldn't be too late."

"You got it. I'll make sure the next shift is aware just in case you are running late."

"Thanks." Next, she touched the numbers to Lathen, put the phone on speaker, and turned down the driveway toward town.

He picked up on the first ring. "Everything all right, Gwen?"

"Yeah, but I have a favor to ask." She explained the budding relationship between Paul and Trinity. The problem with the gala and asked Lathen to give Paul a little encouragement and nudge toward attending social events.

"No kidding, Paul and Trinity. Never would have guessed." He snorted into the phone. "She's well aware he's got baggage?"

"He's come so far. It's time he takes the next steps if this is going to work between them. She's a social butterfly."

"Then she's with the wrong man," Lathen said flatly. "But… since Pepper is glaring at me, having overheard our conversation, I'll make a call." He sighed.

She exacted a promise he wouldn't repeat what she'd told him to anyone exempting Pepper and disconnected the call.

Arriving at the community center just as another car pulled out of a parking place close to the door, she pumped her fist. "Yes." Sprinting in the door, she waved to several people she knew on the way through the double doors, then searched the crowd. Her face crumpled.

Brock was leaning in close and laughing with a tall good looking woman with miles of long blonde hair. The woman was hanging on his every word. Her hand rested around his waist. Hurt spiraled through her, then the green-eyed monster raised its ugly head. She whirled around to leave through the same doors she'd just come in. Tears threatened to spill down her cheeks, she blinked them back. *Should have known he's too good to be true.* She took a deep breath. *Not going down that rabbit hole. The woman is probably a customer at the clinic or a business associate. After all, Brock is active in community affairs.*

She straightened her shoulders, not the unsure woman around men she'd been before Brock. Pasting on a smile, she forced herself to put one foot in front of the other toward where they were standing.

Halfway there, Martha grabbed her arm. With a raised eyebrow, she leaned in and whispered. "By the end of the evening, I should have some good news for you and Brock." The woman floated off as another man standing next to Butch beckoned her from across the room. "Enjoy yourself tonight."

The knot in her stomach tightened as she continued on toward Brock and the woman. Well aware he could have had any woman he wanted here or in Puffin Cove. That he chose her did little to calm her swirling stomach. Her cheeks warmed at jumping to a hasty conclusion. The closer she got, the more uncomfortable Brock appeared. Relief spread across her tense body. His back still to her, he gracefully took the blonde's hand from around his waist, turned and smiled. She was close enough to hear the conversation now.

"Nice to see you again. But I need to find my date. She's running a bit behind." He clasped her hands together, gently pushing her away. Her arms fell to her sides.

With a haughty eyebrow raised, the blonde caressed his arm. "If you were my date, you can bet, I'd be early and at your side all night."

Ignoring the remark, he spun around and right into Gwen's raised arms. "There you are." He bent down and kissed her long and hard. "I was beginning to worry."

With an arched eyebrow, she slid a quick glance from him to the other woman. "I could see that."

He groaned and leaned in whispering against her ear, "Not what it appeared. That's Trudy Arlington. A real estate heiress. Her daddy owns…a lot of commercial property and businesses in Salem. She's been a thorn in my side since I moved to town. But I can't afford to make enemies where she's concerned as well connected in Salem social circles as she is. Especially now where the situation with the paper is concerned. She or her daddy is on every committee in Salem."

"I'm well acquainted with Mr. Arlington. He's the one that threatened the Salem Sanctuary if I didn't let Pepper go after the magic storm. He's not to be trusted."

"The apple doesn't fall far from the tree." He

caressed her shoulders easing her away and his eyes lit with appreciation. "You look absolutely ravishing tonight."

"Thank you. Sorry, I'm late. I lost track of time during Lucky's training then Trinity stopped by…"

"But you're here now, that's all that matters." Nuzzling her neck, he inhaled deeply then kissed her cheek. "You wore my favorite fragrance. May I have this dance?" He slipped an arm around her waist guiding her onto the dance floor. The music was slow and the lights dimmed. She wrapped her arms around his neck, resting her cheek against his broad chest, and let him lead her across the floor.

Feeling a little like Cinderella at the ball, she could hardly believe this was happening to her. It had been an extremely long time since she'd attended the gala. Previously, there'd been no time for frivolous things like galas and dates with handsome men. But Pepper's inheritance and generosity toward the sanctuary had changed everything.

As far as the handsome man, that's where feeling like Cinderella came in. Brock was everything she'd ever dreamed of and he cared about wildlife. Her passion. She sighed as the music came to an end and looked up into his smoldering blue/green eyes. *Yep, this was heaven.*

He brushed his lips across hers and murmured. "I'm going to get us something to drink." The lights brightened and the music ramped up. Twining his fingers in hers they ambled over to the table where trays of finger foods were arranged. He caught a waiter with a silver tray of fluted glasses filled with amber sparkling liquid. He took two and handed one to her.

The bubbles tickled her nose as she took a sip.

"Oh good, I caught you two together. The historical committee and a representative from the chamber want to take a look at your document." Martha's enthusium was reflected in her bright smile.

"We can arrange that Monday evening around seven if that would work for everyone." He took a sip of wine.

Pausing for a moment, Martha wrinkled her nose. "Any chance for an afternoon appointment?"

He shook his head. "I'm at the clinic during the day." Grimacing he shrugged. "Unless you want to do it on a weekend."

Martha gave her a hopeful glance. "How about Gwen?"

"Unfortunately, Salem Sanctuary keeps me busy during the day. But I'm free tomorrow afternoon. Anyone available on Sunday? How about you Brock?"

He frowned at her. "Planned on spending the day with you after checking on Lucky, but we could meet with them for an hour tomorrow afternoon around two."

Martha smiled wide. "Perfect. Two o'clock tomorrow afternoon it is. I'll tell everyone." She glided across the floor and was caught up into the arms of another man and whisked onto the dance floor.

"The sooner we get this off our plate, the sooner I can quit worrying about Beth and her family. Wandering the earth because you can't go into the light must be terrible." The band struck up a lively tune about the Devil in Georgia. "This is one of my favorite songs." She tugged him onto the dance floor. After a couple of fast tunes, the lights dimmed and the band struck up a slow tune about can't help falling in love.

He held her close as they moved slowly around the dance floor. In an amazingly on key, smooth baritone voice, he crooned the words to the song quietly in her ear. She melted into him, head resting on his chest until the song ended.

"You have an amazing voice." She glanced up into his sparkling eyes.

"Thank you. I spent a few years singing in college. But the spotlight wasn't my thing." He bumped into a burly man and turned to excuse himself only to find the trucker who'd saved Lucky. "Wow, imagine meeting you here." He made the introductions. "Gwen is working with Lucky daily, the owl may fly again."

"That's great. I'm glad everything worked out. Fate is funny sometimes." The trucker remarked turning back to the woman on his arm and with a wave, he was swallowed up by the crowd.

"Quite a successful gala. Don't remember the one last year being this large." Brock stopped to survey the room, then took her hand ambling toward the group beckoning them to a table. Butch, Martha and several others Gwen recognized as council members, including Mr. Arlington were seated. Her stomach roiled. But luckily his daughter was nowhere to be seen. *Thank goodness for little favors.*

Small talk turned to questions concerning the newspaper article and its contents. A friendly debate over if such accusations were plausible. Surprisingly, Martha informed them it was quite possible. Rumors circulated in the Judge's time, but anyone claiming proof disappeared or was charged as a witch. The fact that Brock's house was originally owned by the Colson family impressed the group.

Gwen glanced up, sucked in a breath then smiled elbowing Brock in the ribs lightly. "Look who just walked in." She nodded in the entrance's direction. Returning her attention to the group, she smiled. "We've been neglecting our other friends. Please excuse us, see you all tomorrow afternoon."

Brock shifted his gaze in time to see Paul hold the door open for Trinity. She took his offered arm and they paused inside the community center ballroom.

"I don't believe it." Brock grinned and motioned them over. She discreetly took a picture of the couple with her phone and texted it to Pepper.

"Hi guys. Didn't think you were going to make it." Gwen's lips twitched.

"We can't stay long. I have an early shift in the morning. Trinity wanted to put in an appearance and I figured why not." Paul shifted from one foot to the other, nervously scanning the room. A bead of perspiration formed on his forehead.

"Wonderful." Brock snagged four fluted glasses of wine from a waiter and handed two to Paul and one to Gwen. He raised his glass. "To the end of Summer and the beginning of the bewitching fall festivities."

"Yep." Paul raised a glass touching his to the others. The glasses sang as their rims touched. The band started the next set with a lively tune. Trinity glanced at Paul who sighed, took her hand, and whisked her out onto the dance floor. His limp hardly noticeable.

"That cats out of the bag," she chirped cheerfully.

"What's your policy about employees dating each other?" Brock asked.

"No policy until one becomes necessary. They are both adults and private people. I don't see them causing a stir." She put a hand over her mouth to stifle a yawn. "I've had enough fun for one night."

"Me too. How about I escort you home."

"Sounds good. You can stay the night, check on Lucky, and make the rounds before we go over to your place. Misfit will need to come with us. Don't want to leave her alone again. Hopefully, she behaved herself this evening. Though she was displeased at being left, she was tired and curled up on her blanket as I left."

****

A quick breakfast and they sauntered toward the aviary where Lucky was housed. Misfit raced around them in circles. Upon entering her habitat, the owl blinked her large yellow eyes and directed her attention to the pouch Gwen carried. "Good morning girl. How about we show Brock the reason you made me late for the gala." She slipped her right arm into the leather gauntlet and raised her arm.

The bird stretched one wing out then the other, fluffed her feathers, and settled her wings in place. The injured one still hung lower than the other. Taking a small fish out of her pouch, she stood approximately three feet from Lucky. The owl leaned forward as far as she could without losing her balance in an attempt to reach the tasty morsel.

Gwen took another step back. "Come on Lucky, you can do it." Wiggling the fish, she held the food shoulder height.

Lucky bounced on her talons, flapped her wings carefully, paused momentarily, then ducked down and launched herself at Gwen, wings flapping furiously. The owl landed precariously on her arm, regained her balance, tucked her wings and snatched the fish from

Gwen's grip tearing it apart and gobbling it down as if she was starved.

"Gee you'd think we never feed you." She laughed returning the owl to her perch and turned to Brock.

"Wow. I'd never have believed it if I hadn't seen her with my own eyes. She's controlling that injured wing better than I ever thought possible. You're a miracle worker." He grinned broadly.

She took another fish out of the pouch. "One more time girl." Holding the fish out like before, she encouraged the bird to fly. Lucky bounced, flapped and launched herself at Gwen again. This time with no hesitation. "Good girl Lucky." After the bird consumed her food, Gwen put the owl on the perch, tossed her another fish then dumped the remaining contents of her pouch in a bowl at the end of the long branch closest to her perch. "She doesn't like to eat from the bowl. But if she gets hungry enough, she'll eat. Besides, our vet intern, Charlotte will be in and toss her meat later this evening and get her to exercise her wings."

"Shall we go then?"

"Yep." She stepped outside the aviary and whistled for Misfit. The dog came barreling around the corner of the building, skidding to a stop a foot from them and dropped a squeaky toy.

"Where did you find that?" Gingerly, she picked up the well-worn toy. "Well, finders keepers, I guess." She tossed the toy toward the truck. Misfit chased after it then with the toy in her mouth waited by the vehicle.

"Now how did she know we were taking my truck?"

She shrugged. "Guess we're more predictable than we thought."

Chapter Twenty-Four

A Phone Call and a Surprise Revelation Gets the Job Done

Brock's phone buzzed in his pocket as the doorbell rang precisely at two in the afternoon.

"I'll get the door." Gwen sprinted down the stairs from the second floor where she was putting things away in the master bathroom with Misfit on her heels. She flung open the door to Martha, Butch and several people she'd seen at the gala. "Come on in. Brock just got a phone call, so he'll be a minute. Make yourselves comfortable." Motioning them into what Brock had dubbed the family room with its full wall stone fireplace.

Misfit eyed the newcomers suspiciously giving them a wide berth, then finally settled down curling up on a rug below the painting. Gwen glanced at the dog then at the painting on the opposite wall before he went into the study and closed the door.

With the phone to his ear, he eased down in the high back leather chair behind the desk. "Good afternoon...No it's evening in Ireland." He chuckled. "To what do I owe the pleasure of your call?"

"Son, we are in the US now and will be at the family cabin in Puffin Cove by the weekend. Oh, by the way, you're on speakerphone. We're planning a family get together before the snow flies up there. What's your schedule look like?"

"I have a full calendar this coming week and am on call next weekend. After that maybe. Not sure what Gwen's schedule is like. What are you thinking?"

"We're planning a long weekend, maybe four days of fun in the autumn sun. Dylan and Molly are available in two weekends, which seems to fit with yours. Haven't reached your brother, Jeremiah— as usual, but we are determined to include him this time. As you discovered we have a few things to discuss."

"Oh, like what?" He asked innocently.

"The Gypsy magic that isn't so hidden anymore." His mother chortled. "We should have leveled with your kids before now. Obviously, we weren't as good at judging who had what talents as we thought. Could you imagine if your brother would have appeared at the cabin instead of you?"

"He'd have gone into shock, as I was."

"Yes, but fate saw to it to introduce you to magic wielders before you went to the cabin. Therefore avoiding a full-on meltdown."

His father cleared his throat. "You're being overdramatic, Kate."

"I'm not and you know it, Shamus. Anyway, how's the wonderful woman you're seeing? Don't wait too long to put a ring on that finger. She's for you."

"Mom, playing matchmaker doesn't become you." He chided. "And Gwen is fine. She's helping get the house all set up and livable."

"What house?" his mother shot back.

"Oh, guess in all the chaos around here, I failed to mention that I bought a house here in Salem. Can't wait for you to see it."

"After the get together, we'll be there." His father tried to shush his mother, then warned, "Here it comes."

"Oh, Shamus stop it. Son, is it haunted? Was it a witch's house? Is it on the historic registry? Don't tell me you bought one of those new houses being built west of town. You didn't even tell us you were shopping for a house. Does Gwen love it?"

"It's a house. The rest you'll see when you get here." He laughed knowing full well his reply would drive his mother crazy. *Turn about is fair play since she never warned me about the cabin.*

His father tried to get the conversation back on track to spite his mother's objections. "We'll plan the get together for two weekends from now for four days. Saturday-Tuesday. Will that work?"

"What about Jeremiah?"

"We'll take care of him and his new bride."

"Oh, I see you are going to spring this on her too? Unfair tactics Mom."

A light knock sounded on the study door. "Guys, I gotta go. Members of the Salem Historical Committee and the town council arrived at the same time you called. Can't keep them waiting any longer."

"Wait… what are they doing at your house? What are you not telling us?" his mother blustered.

"Not a thing, Mom. Call me to confirm when you've talked to Jeremiah. I haven't even met his bride. What's her name?"

"Morgan," His father said over his mother's fussing. "We'll be in touch. Oh, don't forget to extend an invitation to our family get together to Gwen's friends, the witch, and her husband." On that note, his father disconnected the call.

Grinning from ear to ear, he strode across the room. *It wasn't often I'm able to get the best of Mom. But this time...* He swatted at the air. *Gotcha!* When he opened the door, Gwen stood hands on hips glaring at him.

"It's about time." She studied him for a moment. "You look like the cat that ate the canary. What's gives?"

"Sorry about that. I'll tell you later. Time to get this business over with since all the powers that be in Salem are congregated here." He slung an arm over Gwen's shoulder and swaggered into the family room. Gwen glanced at him questioningly.

"Gwen explained everything," Martha began waving her hand over the document resting on the coffee table. "I checked my sources and you are correct, this belonged to the Colson family. Did you know that my tenth generation great-grandmother, Abigail Hobbs, was arrested for witchcraft with Giles Corey, Mary Warren, and Bridget Bishop?" She waved her hand dismissively sending a covert wink in Gwen's direction. "With that kind of ancestry, you can find out almost anything about what happened in Salem during the witch trials."

"Gee wished we'd known you before we spun our wheels at the library researching this house," Gwen teased.

His brow furrowed and his lips set in a thin line as he shifted his gaze between Gwen and Martha. Even Butch had a shit-eating grin spread over his face. "Is there something I should know?" he asked hesitantly.

"Hell yes. We've authenticated the document and

want to put it in The Witch Museum as soon as possible to have it on display for the Halloween season." The heads of the other people in the room nodded emphatically. "How do you wish to proceed?"

"Uh…I'm not sure." Brock exchanged glances with Gwen.

"Martha, can we see you in the study for a moment?"

"Of course dear." She peered at the others in the room. "I think we're done here. You'll be notified as soon as we work out the details of turning over the document to The Witch Museum."

Mr. Arlington cleared his throat. "Shouldn't we be in on the negations?"

"I've got it from here. We don't need you mucking up the arrangements." Martha raised an eyebrow. "As we discussed earlier, you've got a history with Ms. Gwen Taylor and Salem Sanctuary. It's not a good one. Let's not let that influence this important discovery."

Mr. Arlington frowned then sent Gwen a scathing look before following the others to the door. He paused. "If you need…"

"I won't. Be on your way." Martha made shooing motions with her hands. Butch's lips twitched as he stood beside her.

With a harrumph, he closed the door behind him none too lightly.

"Okay. Someone tell me what just happened." Gwen glanced at Martha.

"Well, you aren't the only one who talks with ghosts or spirits. Though I've never had occasion to travel to the past. That must have been quite a shock."

"What? How could you know?" Gwen stammered

peering at Brock. "I didn't tell her a thing."

"Nope, a little ghost told me. Now can we get on to arrangements for The Witch Museum to take possession of the newspaper?"

"About that." Brock cleared his throat. "How about we make a replica to be placed in The Witch Museum and leave the original in the location that has protected it from destruction since the 1700s?"

"It's not going to be popular with the relatives of Judge John Hathorne or other historians." Gwen blanched.

"You let me worry about that. I have the credentials to back up my findings. I believe other historians will flock to see the document. "She polished her nails on the lapel of her suit coat. "This will cause a ripple through the scholars. Maybe even ruffle some feathers." Martha appeared giddy at the prospect. Turning thoughtful once again, she said, "I agree with you, keeping the original safe, and putting a replica on display at The Witch Museum is a good idea. But, there will be those who will require to see the original. Are you amenable to making such arrangements when necessary?"

"I believe so. One stipulation. The document doesn't leave this house." Brock jumped when the screen door banged as if the house had put an emphasis on that statement.

Martha's head swiveled around. "Oh don't worry." She said seeming to the house. "We'll protect your precious newspaper."

"You knew all along?" Gwen stared in amazement.

"Of course. Magic speaks to magic. This house is quite the find Mr. Scutter. I don't suppose you'd consider selling it?"

"Nope. I had my eye on this house long before it came on the market. I believe fate had a hand in my purchasing it." A faint hum could be heard throughout the house.

Gwen smiled and whispered to him. "Your house purrs."

Martha shrugged. "Well, it was worth a try. I know someone who will produce a perfect replica of the document. All you have to do it make it available when necessary. We'll make an appointment. Now we really have to be going." She glanced at Butch who looked at his watch and nodded.

"Fair enough." He glanced at Butch. "Thank you, my friend. You are a man of many talents."

"As are you." Butch reached for the door, only to have it swing open. The crisp autumn breeze rustled the falling leaves as Martha and Butch stepped out onto the porch. "Fall is in the air."

"That it is." He slung an arm around Gwen as they stood on the top of the stairs and waved while their acquaintances got into the car and drove away.

She turned her face up to peer at him. "Who was on the phone?"

"My parents. They're back stateside and planning the family get together the weekend after next at the cabin. Will that work with your schedule?"

"But I'm not family," She argued.

"We'll have to see about that. But for now, they consider you family. Oh, and we need to contact Pepper and Lathen. Mom and Dad would like them to come also. After all, they are your family."

"And your friends." The sun dropped below the

horizon. Fingers of red, yellow and orange streaked across the blue sky. They walked into the house and closed the door. A white mist filled the room. Gwen gripped his hand tight. "Now what?" A sheet of brittle yellowed paper drifted to the floor. She picked it up nudging him in the side as she read.

Gwen and friends.

First, let me ask for forgiveness in the way we rudely commandeered you into our century. Thank you so much for helping us. We will be leaving this plane of existence soon. But wanted to let you know how grateful we are and let you know we are all going into the light. Enjoy the house, it is truly yours now. Love Beth.

Gwen looked to the painting but the chairs were all empty and no one was standing by the fireplace. The mist thickened and took the shape of Beth, her mother, father, and aunt. Beth reached out and hugged Gwen. "Give Pepper our thanks and love too." A bright light shone near the second story landing. "It's time to go. Again. Thank you so much." In the blink of an eye, the mist disappeared and the light swallowed up the shapes.

"I didn't think things could get any weirder, but…that was strange." Gwen wiped a tear from her eye. "Glad to see them off." She took her phone out of her pocket. "I need to call Pepper and bring her up to date on the happenings." She paused for a couple of beats. "So far."

"Don't forget to invite them to the family get together at the cabin, two weeks from Saturday. We'll be there through Tuesday according to Mom."

"Will do." She settled onto the couch, feet tucked up under her.

He was too wound to settle down. Stepping out

onto the porch, he ambled around the property. It was the first time he'd spent much time in the backyard. The wooden fence needed repair in a few places to be dog proof. Speaking of dogs, he glanced around and found Misfit wandering along behind him. "Cooped up too long in the house? Decided to join me for a while?" He reached down and scratched the pup behind the ears. For a moment, he fingered his phone in his pocket, then pulled it out and scrolled to a number he'd not called in a while. Staring at the number for a beat, he touched the call icon and put the phone to his ear.

A male voice answered after only one ring. "Brock? What's wrong?"

"Not a thing bro. Time I checked in on you. Heard you got married. Why didn't I get an invitation?"

His brother cleared his throat. "It was kinda a spur of the moment type of thing. I knew Mom and Dad were in Ireland, Dylan, Molly, and Riva are so busy with their families. And you dude, live and breathe that vet clinic you took over."

"Spur of the moment wedding? Dude, that's forever. You didn't…"

"Of course not. We'd been seeing each other for a couple of years and the time seemed right. Morgan's sister, the only family she has, is out of the country on some kind of charitable mission. It was just a ceremony with the judge at the courthouse. Figured we'd celebrate when the family gathered. I was right."

"You're a hard person to catch. Mom and Dad were trying to get a hold of you today. Have you talked to them?"

"Yeah. Morgan and I will be at the cabin weekend after next. Have any idea what's going on? They haven't called a pow-wow in many moons." Jeremiah chuckled.

"No clue. Guess they thought it was time to get the family together. Maybe to meet Morgan?"

"I'm not buying that. Mom said you have a serious relationship too now. Tell me about Gwen. That's her name, right? Runs or owns some kind of wildlife sanctuary in Salem where you're the staff vet? Figures that's the only way you'd meet a woman, through work."

"Wow. Know an awful lot about my circumstances. While I know nothing about yours. Still working for the law firm? Is that where you met Morgan?"

"Yeah, sort of. I bought out my partner and hired an intern, Morgan. We're a two lawyer firm now with a small staff and take only the cases we want. Had to get off the hamster wheel. Life's too short."

"Never thought I'd hear those words from my workaholic brother. But I hear ya."

"Look who's calling the kettle black." He laughed. A sound he hadn't heard from his brother in a long time. "Looking forward to catching up with everyone. Mom said you were at the cabin a few weeks ago. Is it still the same?"

"Kinda. Took Gwen to visit the lighthouse and Owls Head."

His brother let out a low whistle. "I guess you've settled down. Took her to the cabin. Huh?"

"Yeah, she's a special woman." The back door banged open, the porch light came on, and Gwen wandered toward him, her long patchwork skirt blowing in the breeze. With a wave of his hand, he motioned her to him embracing her. "Well, Jer I gotta get going. Wanted to make sure you would make it to the family gathering. Look forward to seeing you and meeting Morgan."

"Same here and meeting Gwen. See ya soon."

He ended the call and brought his lips down on hers. "I missed you," he murmured against her mouth pressing his chest against her warm soft breasts.

"What? I was only inside talking with Pepper for a little while. They'll clear their schedule and join the gathering." She melted against him wrapping her arms around him. "Why don't we go inside and…"

"My thoughts exactly." He whistled for Misfit and swept Gwen up in his arms, breathed a kiss at her neck as he carried her to the house.

Chapter Twenty-Five
Business as Usual Until…

Gwen was so busy with Lucky and the other creatures at the Sanctuary that two weeks passed at the speed of light. Trinity had taken over most of the administrative work, now that she was full time and she was training Rita. The girl was a great fit and asset to the Sanctuary. She was happy to let Trinity have those duties, giving her more time with the animals, and doing things she loved.

Since the gala and the newspaper being housed at The Witch Museum, things between her and Brock had taken a serious turn. At least that was the way it felt. Was she ready to settle down with him? She'd never given it much consideration until recently. Things were moving fast and she was surprised to find she was okay with it. While she looked forward to meeting Brock's mom and dad as well as his siblings, a little trepidation niggled at the back of her mind. "Come on Misfit time for rounds. But you can't come into Lucky's aviary." The dog trotted up to her and cocked her head.

"You need to stay out here." She pointed to the landing in front of the aviary. The dog circled twice and settled down to the left of the entrance. Pulling the door open, she slipped into Lucky's aviary and cooed to the owl. "Ready for PT?" The owls head whipped around, bright yellow eyes locked on her as she slid her hand into the gauntlet and picked up the pouch. She stuffed it full of the bird's favorite treats and turned her attention to the owl lightly stroking its wings until the bird clicked its beak and shoved her hand away in warning. "Okay, okay, come on you know the drill." Backing several feet away, she held the food out. Lucky stretched her wings out waiting for Gwen to praise her. "Nice stretch, now come on...you can do it." The bird did a couple of test wing flaps, leaned way forward then flew the distance to her landing gracefully on the leather gauntlet. "Good girl." Releasing the meat into Lucky's beak, she raised her arm signaling the bird to return to the perch. The next thirty minutes were spent with Lucky target training and strengthening exercises.

"Excuse me." Trinity stuck her head in the door as Gwen was finishing up. "Are you leaving for a few days?"

"Yes. Charlotte will be working with Lucky daily while I'm gone, provided the owl doesn't give her too much static." She removed the gauntlets and placed them in a drawer out of Lucky's reach. She'd already lost a pair to the owl who apparently found it quite entertaining to tear them to shreds. Giving the bird's wing one last caress, she strode toward the door. "I was about to come tell you."

Her assistant backed away and nodded. "Just checking. Anything special you need me to do while you're gone?"

Once outside Lucky's enclosure, she leaned on the door running through her head all the little things that needed to be done while she was gone. "Nope, you're handling all the paperwork and most administrative duties. I appreciate that. Charlotte and Lindy will check on the welfare of the creatures. Sam and Paul have security running like clockwork. This Sanctuary runs quite well, whether I'm here or not. If something comes up, you know how to reach me. But you can handle most things until I get back. Right?" She smiled encouragingly at Trinity knowing her assistant was still a bit nervous about being left in charge.

"I hope so."

Gwen raised an eyebrow. "Really?"

Trinity straightened. "Yes, everything will be fine. So you're going to meet Brock's parents—and family."

She took a deep breath and blew it out slowly. "Yep. I hope they like me."

"What's not to like? You own and operate the most awesome sanctuary in the state. As far as Brock is concerned the sun rises and sets in you." She slapped her hand over her mouth.

"Where'd you hear that?" Gwen grinned.

"Oh…Guys talk. I might have overheard…" She waved her hand in dismissal as her cheeks pinked. "Besides, I can see it when you're together."

"Okay. Anyway, his opinion is only one."

Trinity put her hands on her hips and stared at her boss. "His is the one that counts."

She snickered. "There are still his mom, dad, two sisters, and brother. Thank goodness I already met Dylan. She's the vet in Lobster Cove and is tight with Pepper. We're good." She wiped her sweaty hands on her jeans.

Trinity studied her boss. "Wow. You're really nervous."

"A little I guess. Everything is moving so fast. I just got used to being a couple. Helping him get settled in a new house, that's a long story for another time. Now his whole family."

"Oh, yeah, Paul mentioned something about a Halloween party house warming. Believe it or not, he appears to be looking forward to it."

"Good for him—and you. I hadn't heard a thing about a house warming. Although Halloween would be the perfect setting," she mused. "Not surprising he hasn't mentioned it. We've been so busy with work, I've barely seen Brock." As if on cue, inside her pocket, her phone played the tune she'd selected for Brock. "Speak of the devil." She couldn't help but smile. She held up an index finger, then tapped the screen. "Hi you."

"Hey, miss me?" His deep voice flowed through the phone. "I'm going to be able to scoot out of here an hour early. Any chance you could be ready in say—ninety minutes?"

Adrenaline shot through her and she sucked in a breath. "Sure. Though I'm still not sure what to do with Misfit. I suppose the staff could keep an eye on her. But being left alone in the house might be a problem."

He snorted. "Already handled. Talked to Mom and Dad, they said to bring her along."

"You think of everything." She relaxed a little.

"It's my job." He chuckled. "You and that dog are becoming inseparable. I remember when you were happy if she showed up at your cottage."

"She has trust issues. Not her fault. Lucky on the other hand will be fine with Charlotte and Lindy. Although she will try to intimidate them. But the girls don't react to that type of behavior." She snickered. "They'll also supervise the volunteers caring for the rest of our residents."

"Great. See you in a few. Love you." The words rolled off his tongue without hesitation.

"Me too." She disconnected the phone holding it to her chest for a minute more. That wasn't the first time he'd said those three wonderful but scary words. Still it made her queasy inside. That little four-letter word made her mouth go dry, butterflies zoom inside her belly and her heart beat nearly out of her chest. *I gotta get a grip.*

Slipping the phone back in her pocket she noticed Trinity standing there staring at her quizzically. She pointed to the phone. "Brock, he's on his way here to pick me up. We're leaving early. Misfit will come with us so you don't have to worry about her."

"She's not a…" The far off ring of a phone caught her assistant's attention. "I better get that. Have fun and don't worry about a thing. We've got this." Trinity turned and sprinted down the hall to her office addition connected to the aviary.

I have no doubt you can handle this, but can I handle Brock's family? Oh, stop it. I've got this. She hurried back to the cottage, flung open the door, and called out, "Misfit. Misfit." The dog was nowhere to be found. Standing on the porch she called again. Her phone buzzed. Puzzled, she looked at the screen, touched the answer icon.

Paul's voice boomed over the receiver. "Misfit was over here at security. We've sent her on her way when you called."

The dog was becoming quite the social butterfly and ambassador for the Sanctuary. "Thanks. I see her." Inside the cabin, she gathered up the suitcase she'd packed earlier. Added Mistfit's bowls, the container of food, a few toys, leashes, and treats in a bag of her own and set everything next to the door. The dog thundered inside, skidded to a halt beside the bags and sniffed, then turned and stared at her.

"We're going on a road trip. I expect you to be on your best behavior. You're going to have a blast."

Misfit wiggled her tail uncertainly listening intently to Gwen's cheerful, upbeat voice.

Gravel crunched under vehicle tires as Brock parked the truck in front of the cottage and hopped out. The dog nosed the screen door open and ran to greet him. "Hey, girl." He stopped and scratched behind her ears, ruffling the scruff around her neck.

Gwen stood in the doorway with the luggage lined on the porch. "We're all ready to go."

He bounded up the stairs grabbed her around the waist and swung her around.

She squealed. "Put me down."

Laughing, he whirled her around once more before lowering her to her feet and planting a smacking kiss on her lips. "We are going to have so much fun. Pepper and Lathen are caravaning with Dylan and her family. Should be at the cabin later tonight."

"How exciting. Wait 'til Pepper hears about Lucky's progress. We need to document the procedure used on Kaylee and Lucky, put it on the Salem's Sanctuary's website and Lobster Cove's Rescue and Rehab Center's website for other wildlife rehabs to try it out."

"Great idea. How to do video examples with Lucky would be fantastic. You can do exactly that when we return. Right now, we're off." With the bags piled on top of the wheeled suitcase, he whistled for Misfit and jogged to the pickup towing the suitcase behind. He paused and peered at her still standing on the porch fiddling with the door lock. "Something wrong?"

"No. I'll be right there."

He opened the truck door and helped the dog into the back seat. Stowed the gear in the bed and he closed the hard tonneau cover and locked it.

Tossing her keys in the backpack, she sprinted down the steps and out to the pickup. He met her at the passenger side door. "Spill it."

Eyes wide feigning innocence, she cried, "What? Let's go."

"Not until you tell me what is going on in that pretty little head of yours." He took her by the shoulders and held her tight. "Did something happen today?"

"No. I'm fine," she insisted.

"And I'm jolly Saint Nick. Now out with it."

She chewed on her bottom lip. "Okay, maybe I'm a little nervous about meeting your family. After all, they wield a lot of ancient Gypsy magic. I'm just…"

He threw his head back and roared with laughter. "Is that all? Honey, they are going to love you. If for no other reason than I finally found someone I could spend the rest of my life with."

She sucked in a breath and her eyes flew open wide. "Really? You sure about that?" She was barely able to get the words out and still be her flippant self.

He paused a moment as if considering. "Of course. What do you think is happening between us?" He drew her close and kissed her lingering for a few seconds. "Nevermind, we'll figure it all out later. As far as magic is concerned, thanks to Pepper you're an old hand. If anyone should be intimidated, it would be me. Up until Pepper blindsided me at her center and our recent visit to the cabin, I had no idea magic existed let alone in my own family. Can you imagine what Jeremiah's reaction is going to be? Not to mention his new wife? Babe, you've got nothing to worry about."

Those words echoed around in her head causing her pulse to race. *What do you think is happening between us?* She hadn't given that much thought. *Our whirlwind romance just became a category five storm. Surprisingly, I'm all right with that. I hope.*

Inside the truck, Misfit whined and pawed at the window, finally barking her displeasure at being confined.

"See even your pup is anxious to be on the road." Still smiling, he helped her into the truck, gave her butt a caress and kissed her again while fastening the seatbelt.

She returned the kiss with wild abandon, wrapping her arms around his neck. Some of the anxiety abated as she melted into him.

He eased away. "You keep this up and we'll have to go back into the cabin, which will result in us arriving even later. Believe me, my family is going to love you. Quit worrying." He closed her door. Returning to the driver's side, he climbed into the cab and started the engine. "Puffin Cove, here we come."

On the little over three hour drive to his family's cabin, her nerves calmed, she brought him up-to-date on the Desert Tortoises and Charlotte's positive report on breeding them. The Wood Turtles relocation to the communal habitat and they were adjusting well. No problems with the rest of the residents. "Let's hope it stays that way while we're gone."

"No reason it won't. You're going to have to get used to taking time off and having a personal life outside the Sanctuary."

"Says the man who checks his phone several times an hour when he's away from the clinic." She smirked.

"Touché." Passing by the wooden sign welcoming them to Puffin Cove, he slowly drove through the town stopping to wave at familiar people on the street, then turned onto the gravel road to the cabin. Lathen's truck was parked behind an unfamiliar vehicle. He pulled in and parked next to the truck. "Looks like they beat us here." He turned to glance at her only to find she'd hopped out of the truck and had the back passenger door open with Misfit leashed and down on the ground.

Pepper rushed out the front door with who she supposed was Brock's parents, Kate and Shamus. She sucked in a breath, straightened and glanced down at the dog whose tail wagged sporadically while she stood at alert in front of Gwen. Brock came up behind her and put a reassuring arm around her waist.

"It's fine, they'll love you. Take Misfit off protection mode."

"What? Oh, yeah." She reached down, scratched the dog's ears and whispered. "It's all right. Friends."

Chapter Twenty-Six
Family Reunion and Gypsy Magic Revealed

To Brock's relief, the dog's posture relaxed. In truth, he didn't know what to expect. They'd always been a close-knit family. But recently, with his parents across the pond, his brother getting married without a big wedding and all family members meeting the bride to be, things were changing. He scrubbed his hand across his face. *Lots of things are changing.* He blew out a breath and caught sight of his smiling parents rushing from the cabin behind Pepper. That woman had more energy than any one person should be allowed.

Pepper pounded up the path and launched herself enveloping them in a hug. "Great to see you again." She turned to him then switched to Gwen with a quick wink. "What a fantastic family. You're a lucky gal."

"Thanks. I think."

"I know that look. Quit worrying. They couldn't wait to meet you. Seems our Brock was a bit of a player until you tamed him."

Gwen shot her a warning glance.

Her friend's eyes sparkled as her bubbly voice seemed to ease Gwen's insecurities. "Hey, their words not mine. Don't shoot the messenger. Smile girl. You got this." Pepper released Gwen making room for Brock's parents.

His dad, a tall man with dark hair streaked with

gray and his mom, a short plump woman, with silver hair that cascaded to the middle of her back reached the group, gave him a hug and glanced at Gwen. "This must the woman who finally snared our son." His father smiled wide with satisfaction.

"Dad don't start." They'd been after him to settle down with a nice girl since he graduated from vet school and bought the clinic. His mother sent plenty of women in his direction. None remotely interesting. Most looking for husband material. Once they discovered his work schedule and dedication to his clinic, they disengaged rather quickly. Then along came Gwen.

A smile spread across his face at the thought of her. Together they'd negotiated the dating waters their schedules allowed, learned to take time off to enjoy life rather than live, breathe, and eat work. *Yep, now I'm ready to take the next steps. I just hope she is. Kinda blind-sided her at the cottage. I hadn't meant to blurt my feelings...well hell it's done and I don't regret it.* His mother's lilting voice interrupted his musings.

"Shamus." His mother frowned and hip-checked her husband. "You promised." Kate reached for Gwen and pulled her into a hug. "So happy to finally meet you. Dylan has told us so much about you. Got a little Gypsy spark we hear." Kate gave her a squeeze then released her hold.

"So it seems." Gwen smoothed the wrinkles from her shirt caused by the long car ride and licked her lips sidling closer to Brock.

His father raised his arms in a gesture of surrender. "Me! Gypsy magic before we get into the house? Jeremiah isn't even here yet." His dad laughed out loud his dark eyes shining as he turned his attention to Brock. "Son, I was merely stating the obvious."

His mother pretended to pout. "She knows. Been here before with our son." She clasped her son's hand. "Come on, come on. We have a feast fit for royalty."

"Because we are." His father chuckled. "Who do we have here?" He jerked his chin toward Misfit.

The dog stood steadfastly beside Gwen. Misfit's gaze swept the group, but no defensive posture present. Pepper ruffled the dog's fur with her fingers then ambled toward the house where Lathen was waiting on the porch.

Gwen's feet appeared stuck in place. He squeezed her arm gently and nodded to the dog. "Misfit is Gwen's recent rescue."

His voice seemed to bring Gwen out of her thoughts. "Oh sorry. Yes, Misfit is a new addition to our family…ah…my family." She shifted from foot to foot the corner of her mouth turned up in a shy grin.

"You had it right the first time. Our family." He slung his arm around her shoulder and encouraged her forward. "I'm starved. Aren't you?"

"Yes. I am." Gwen slid her arm around his waist her body softened against him.

Misfit sniffed at Kate and Shamus's shoes before taking the lead toward the front door.

"Wait. I need to get Misfit's food and bowls out of the truck. She's probably thirsty after the road trip."

"All ready done." His mother smiled knowingly at him. "Everything is in your room at the top of the stairs as usual. Dog's bag is in the living room, her bowls filled with water and food. The cabin loves guests of all kinds."

Walking up to the cabin, a warm welcome home feeling washed over him. *Well, now that's different.* The scene inside was utter chaos. Molly's three boys and Riva's two were running through the cabin at top speed. Dylan's boy and girl, younger than the rest, were standing behind their father, Lance, watching the activity with huge rounded eyes.

When Misfit trotted into the cabin, she barked at all the excitement wagging her tail uncertainly, and her gaze flitted from the children to Gwen.

"It's okay girl." The expression on Gwen's face belayed her uneasiness.

He waded into the fray and made the introductions to sisters Molly and her husband Talbert, Riva and her husband Caleb, including Dylan and her husband Lance. Gwen extended her hand shaking hands in greeting to everyone. Dylan smiled and sent her a reassuring wink.

"I'll round up the wild ones a bit later after they've expended their excess energy and we'll do introductions."

"Smart." Molly and Riva chorused ushering their boys out the back door.

Gwen relaxed against him, leaned down with hands resting on her knees and peered at Dylan's kids still hiding behind their parents. "It's a bit overwhelming isn't it?" She offered her hand to the little girl. "I'm Gwen. Remember seeing me in Lobster Cove?"

The little girl of about four years old nodded. "You played video's for us."

"I sure did." She crouched down eye level with the child.

"My name's Candy." The little girl took a step

forward, twisted around and pointed her tiny finger to the boy standing beside her. "He's my brother, Corbin."

"Nice to meet you, Candy." She shook the little girl's hand then reached toward Corbin. He scooted farther back tucking his face behind his dad.

"He's shy," Candy announced importantly. "He'll warm up to you after a while."

Dylan laughed and sent a sideways glance to Lance before switching her attention to Gwen. "She's heard us say that before."

Gwen leaned sideways smiling at Corbin. "It's nice to meet you also." She straightened. "Cute kids."

"Thank you. Their cousins always overwhelm them when we get together. Probably because we don't do it often enough." Dylan laughed.

"Can I pet your dog?" Candy's big eyes shifted from Misfit to Gwen then to Dylan.

Gwen observed Misfit for a moment. "I don't know. Maybe we should ask her." She introduced Misfit to Candy. The dog wagged her tail and leaned in toward the little girl. "Looks like she's all right with it. Go slow."

"Mom always says no sudden movements." Candy hesitantly put her hand out for Misfit to sniff, then touched the top of her head gently. "Your fur is so soft." Her hand drifted down the dog's back. "You're beautiful." The girl's big brown eyes, swiveled up to meet Gwen's "Why'd you name her Misfit?"

"At the time she came to us, she was afraid of people. Didn't fit in with the rest of the residents at my rescue. So the description stuck as her name."

"She has a turtle named RoadTrip too." Brock offered. "What she sees in the creature is the name she gives it."

The little girl thought for a beat then giggled switching her gaze to her mom. "Is that why you called me Candy? Because I'm so sweet." The dimples in her cheeks deepened. She was the spitting image of her mom.

Dylan ruffled her daughter's hair and chuckled. "Something like that."

"Come on. Food's getting cold," his father called from the dining room. "Your mom's got a buffet set up in the kitchen. The kids' table is set up out on the porch. Grab a plate, fill it, and join us. Drinks are in here. Iced drinks in the cooler, coffee on the table, hot water, and tea bags on the side table next to the wall." He strode to the back door and pushed it open. "Boys if you want to eat, get in here, and wash your hands."

Molly and Riva joined their father at the door. "Any food fights break out, and you'll all remain inside for the remainder of the visit. Understood?" Riva said in a no-nonsense voice. Molly reiterated the statement. The boys trooped in, took turns washing their hands as their mothers filled plates, and carried them outside.

He and Gwen made their way through the mountain of food to choose from filling their plates. His brother, Jeremiah and a petite woman with huge hazel eyes burst through the front door which slammed after them causing his brother to do a double-take.

Shrugging out of his jacket, Jeremiah took his wife's coat and hung them on the hooks by the door. "Sorry, we're late. Traffic was a bitch, a client was late, and an emergency at the law firm had to be handled before I could leave."

With a raised eyebrow, his father squeezed

Jeremiah's shoulder. "All that matters is you're here now." Shamus hugged the petite woman standing next to his son. "Welcome Morgan." Introductions were made and instructions to the food repeated.

After everyone was seated around the large polished oak dining table, Shamus cleared his throat. "Suppose you all are wondering why, after all this time, we required the family to gather at our cabin."

"The thought did cross our minds." Jeremiah glanced around the table at his siblings' faces. "Figured you wanted everyone to meet Morgan since informal get togethers have been difficult with all of our schedules." He slid a glance at Gwen.

"Believe it or not, Jeremiah not everything is about you." She laughed softly. "Though I'm sure everyone is glad to meet Morgan," his mother said gently. "And we're all happy to welcome Gwen to the family. But…"

"I'm afraid your mother and I have been remiss in filling you kids in on the family heritage. Bad things can and do occur when that type of information is omitted. Which brings us to an incident that happened while your mother and I were in Ireland. The family castle that's been in the care of cousins for a long time fell into disrepair. Foreclosure was threatened and the property could have fallen to those who don't understand our family heritage or…" He hesitated for a couple beats staring steadily at Jeremiah then Morgan. He sucked in a breath. "Gypsy Magic."

"I thought you were seriously going to tell us something important. Had me going for a bit." Jeremiah snorted.

Morgan's eyes went wide when Shamus didn't even crack a smile. "You're serious?"

"Yes. The situation here came to light when Brock and Gwen used the cabin a while back for a long weekend getaway. In Ireland, we nearly lost the castle to an unscrupulous warlock and a maleficent ghost. Thank the stars your mother and I were there with quick thinking, financial creativity, and assistance from friends in a local coven, the castle remains with the Scutter family. We'll be returning to Ireland to oversee repairs to bring the castle back to its original glory. And to make sure the inhabitants, human or spirits are those we welcome."

Brock let out a low whistle. "How did that happen?"

"As with our immediate family, your mother and I thought we knew who would inherit the family talents." His father sighed. "We were wrong and the cabin let us know. That situation is about to be corrected." Shamus stared directly into Jeremiah's eyes.

Brock noted the color in his brother's face was quickly draining away. He cleared his throat and started to say something only to have his father cut him off.

"With the cousins at the castle, they had no idea Gypsy magic existed, let alone ran in our family, nor that Fae blood ran through our veins."

Gwen glanced around the table, then sent Pepper a sly smile.

Jeremiah raised his hands in the air as if he could stop the onslaught of words from his father's mouth. "Now just wait one minute. Are you telling me? No wait, you expect me to believe that we as a family have the ability to wield magic? If you've brought us here as some kind of joke…"

"Oh, I assure you brother. This is no joke. This

land, the cabin, and the boathouse are enchanted with powerful Fae protection magic twined with our own Gypsy magic. As Dad alluded to earlier, Gwen and I found out first hand a few weeks ago on our visit here. Neither Molly, Riva, nor Dylan were of any help until I reached out to Mom and Dad." He glared at each sister in turn and pointed a finger. "You all knew."

Dylan raised her hands in a gesture of surrender. "Leave me out of this. I was as shocked as you were our family had a magic history. I did benefit from the knowledge magic existed from working with Pepper."

"Yeah, right. That's why you sent me to Pepper's with the little owl without warning me." He pointed an accusing finger at her. "Tell me you don't communicate with the animals under your care."

Dylan shrugged. "It's a talent any vet should have."

"Yeah right. Anyway, back to our heritage. Mom and Dad gave me a roundabout answer and assured me that upon their return stateside, all would be revealed. Meanwhile, our best friends—" he nodded in Pepper and Lathen's direction. "—informed us what they thought was happening. The explanation fit. Of course, I'd been indoctrinated into the belief that magic was real while I was in Lobster Cove helping Dylan out and where I met Gwen."

He grinned at her, lacing his fingers with hers. *What a lucky turn of events my going to Lobster Cove to help Dylan.* He sighed. Jeremiah's raised voice and his parents determined reply brought him back to the situation at hand.

"This is a lot to drop in my lap, especially in front of Morgan. My Gypsy heritage is something I don't embrace—or didn't. Morgan until a few minutes ago was unaware."

Brock laughed. "You been outed brother. Secrets in a marriage are never a good thing."

"And just how would the family playboy know about that?" his brother shot back testily.

"Boys, boys…" Morgan held up her hand. "Not that I think I have a say in this discussion. But you're going to hear my thoughts anyway. I fell in love and married the man, not some heritage. But now that it's been revealed, I find it's quite intriguing. Since the family castle is in Ireland, it's safe to assume you are of Irish descent rather than the Romani?"

"Aye, you'd be correct," Shamus said in an exaggerated brogue.

Amused, Brock watched both Pepper and Gwen give Morgan a double thumbs up. He coughed to cover a snicker. Scutter men are attracted to strong women. By the same token, his sisters had married confident men, so this acknowledgment of magic heritage should be nothing more than an interesting tidbit.

However, the consequences of the children inheriting magical talent could be challenging. *Yes indeed.* He pondered the possibility of marriage and children with Gwen. Their children would definitely be strongly predisposed to inherit magic ability from both sides. A prospect that scared him…just a little…Okay honestly— it scared him a lot. Hell, he was just getting up the nerve to consider…settling down.

The door banged shut and he jerked to attention. Glancing around the smug expressions on the women's faces and his brother's absence spoke volumes. His dad remained in the chair at the head of the table, fingers tented looking thoughtful. *What did I miss?*

His mother got up from the table and began clearing the dishes. Molly and Riva got to their feet and went out to check on the boys while Gwen and Pepper assisted with clean up.

Staring directly at him, his dad nodded toward the door. "Jeremiah needed some air. You might want to join him."

Brock shoved up from the table and glanced at Lathen who was shifting uncomfortably in his seat. "Join me?"

"You bet." His friend jumped up from the table so quickly, his chair nearly toppled over before he caught it.

Walking out the door, Brock hissed. "What'd I miss?"

Lathen grinned. "Your brother called your family magic bullshit and stormed out. It was quite a scene. Were you off in la-la land?" His friend cocked his head and searched Brock's face. "He was so loud that the kids outside heard him." Lathen snorted and shook his head. "I love family disagreements especially when it's not my family."

He huffed out a breath. "I thought Mom and Dad were going to handle this." He glanced backward toward the cabin before continuing on down the path toward his brother who was grumbling and pacing up and down the path to the boathouse.

"Hey bro, what's the problem?"

"You're in on this aren't you?" his brother accused. "Even my own wife…"

Hands raised in a surrender gesture, Brock slowly reached out and grasped his brother's shoulder.

"Whoa… hang on there a second. There's no conspiracy here. Only truth—you don't want to hear."

Jeremiah shot a scathing glance toward Lathen. "You believe all this shit?"

Lathen shrugged. "Depends on what you're referring to. My wife who is a powerful witch. Myself a card-carrying shape-shifting werewolf. Your brother who demonstrates powerful Gypsy magic or… your sisters…" Lathen hesitated as the color drained out of Jeremiah's face once again. "Need I go on?"

"Bro, I think you need a stiff drink. Come on, walk down to the boathouse with us."

"There's no liquor there." His brother stiffened but turned and quick-stepped down the path. "Not even a place…"

"There will be by the time we arrive." He chuckled when his brother stopped dead in his tracks, then whirled to face him opening and closing his mouth like a codfish. No sound coming out.

Catching up with his brother, he clapped him on the back, propelling him forward along the path. They rounded the curve where the trail opened up to the wide expanse of beach and there displayed in front of the boathouse was a picnic table, wine chilling in an ice bucket, stronger adult beverages lined on the table next to a colorful bin full of ice cubes and an ice chest of bottled beer and other drinks.

His brother stood, eyes wide, Jeremiah's gaze darting from the table to the beach house and back to Brock and Lathen.

"What'd I tell you?" He meandered over to the table, grabbed a couple of bottles of beer and handed one to Lathen and offered another type to Jeremiah.

Taking the offered bottle of specialty beer, his brother turned it around in his hand peering at the label, before he popped open the lid and took a swig. "My favorite. How'd you know? Where'd you get it here?"

"Gypsy Magic. The cabin or land, I'm not quite sure how it works, knows what you need and poof." He made an explosion sign with his hand. "It's available." Brock took another swig of his beer pointing to the spread. "Can you imagine arriving here with Gwen, entering the cabin and having a full course meal on the table with no one around and well aware no one else had a key?"

The sound of footsteps, pounding of dog paws, and women's cheerful voices were the only sounds for a couple of beats as Jeremiah apparently processed the information.

"Don't overthink it, bro. Your logical mind will blow a gasket." He chortled. "It is what it is. Perhaps the magic skipped you as Mom and Dad thought it skipped me, but…I guess it takes a different form in each individual. Ever known the outcome of a case before it happened? Ever taken a loser case, only to discover a way to win?"

"It's called being a good lawyer." His brother narrowed his eyes at him.

He shrugged one shoulder. "Maybe… but from what I hear, your ability to win difficult if not impossible cases defies the odds. Believe it or not, a sobering thought is your kids may inherit the magic." He tipped the bottle of beer toward his brother. "Then what?" Gwen crept up behind him and slung an arm over his shoulder breathing a kiss at the base of his neck, nibbling her way to his jawline.

"Get a room." Lathen laughed.

"Got one." He shot back turning toward the splashing sound. Misfit was giving the gulls at water's edge a run for their money. He leaned over and whispered to Gwen. "Your dog is going to be a muddy salt-water mess."

Gwen frowned glancing at Misfit frolicking in the ocean waves. "Pepper can clean her up with a wave of her hand," she said softly.

"Need more persuasion?" Pepper bounced down the path toward them, disappeared then reappeared behind Jeremiah and tapped him on the shoulder while tossing a ball of orange snapping energy up over the doubting brother then catching it with the other hand and extinguishing it. "Witchfire. It's one of my talents."

Morgan wrapped an arm around his waist. "Good thing you married a free spirit." She kissed him lightly on the lips.

Jeremiah returned the kiss then whispered, "With a will of iron."

Throwing her head back, Morgan roared with laughter. Her long blonde hair blowing in the breeze. "Being quite the stick in the mud, aren't you? Gotta go with the flow." She picked up the bottle of wine and four glasses appeared just as the cork popped. Eyes wide, she poured the wine into the glasses and returned the bottle to the ice. Each of the women took a glass. "I wonder who gets the fourth?" The words left her mouth as Shamus sauntered along the path.

"Thought I'd better make sure Jer hadn't had a heart attack or stroked out with you guys handling his enlightenment." His father chuckled. "Kate is watching the boys, Lance is keeping an eye on Corbin and

Candy. Any questions for me?" Shamus paused for a moment. "Hand me one of those beers." Before Jeremiah could grab a bottle of beer, it launched out of the cooler, flew across the air dripping ice and water into his Dad's hand. "Now that's what I call service." Shamus shook the ice off his hand, took a swig, and grinned eying his eldest son.

By the end of the evening, Jeremiah claimed to be a believer though his talent seemed less than the others. The family discussed future vacations at the cabin, a trip to Owls Head lighthouse with the kids, and shivered as the autumn breeze blew in off the water bringing with it the scent of brine.

A roaring campfire, courtesy of the land, warmed the group as he and Gwen described the new house and discussed a house warming party. They left out the details of the Salem witch trials involved with the house. *A tale for another time.*

Chapter Twenty-Seven
Day-to-Day Obligations and a Surprise Lunch

A few weeks after the reunion at the cabin, Gwen's head was still spinning. Being part of a large family was daunting. Pepper then Lathen had been her only extended family. Life was changing quickly and she needed to change with it. Up before dawn, unable to sleep, she had poured herself a cup of tea and popped a breakfast strudel in the toaster. Normally she preferred a more healthy breakfast, but something was niggling at her mind and she couldn't quite put a finger on it.

Going through her calendar of day-to-day operations put her mind at ease. Nothing had been forgotten or overlooked. Trinity kept the Sanctuary running perfectly during all her time away. Maybe that was it. Switching from administration to hands-on in addition to her time off had skewed her sense of accomplishment. Until Brock, the Sanctuary had been her whole life. She flipped her long dark braid over her shoulder and tucked behind her ears the wisps of green and pink highlighted strands that were growing out.

Sitting in her little office in the cottage, she gave herself a little shake as a yellow-orange line spread along the Eastern horizon warning of the impending dawn. She leaned back in her chair, took a sip of tea, and listened to the sounds of the sanctuary waking up. *Soothing to the soul.* Cheerful voices of the staff calling

287

greetings to each other echoed through the outside common area. Paul's booming voice, louder than the rest, questioned the night staff on the overnight security. Another necessary change. She was thankful for the donations from Pepper's foundation.

Misfit curled up beside her, rolled over, let out a loud yawn and stretched on her back, then the dog looked up at her with inquiring eyes.

"Yes, we'll go out in a few minutes." She closed the calendar on the computer, pushed up from the desk as her cell phone played a lively tune about the devil in Georgia. A quick glance at the screen had her smiling. Needing some alone time, she'd spent the night at her cottage rather than with Brock at his new home. Which if she was willing to admit, may have been why she'd been unable to sleep. "Brock, how are you this morning?"

"Missing you. This house is too big, not to mention my bed without you. How about dinner and a movie at my house tonight?"

"Sure, sounds good. Are you still at home?"

"Yep. Had a late night at the clinic so slept in this morning."

"Oh…Nothing bad I hope."

"Bob's dog Willie tangled with a rattlesnake and lost. Snake got him twice. I had anti-venom but it was touch and go for a few hours. Once he stabilized, I went home and Willie spent the night under the watchful eye of our intern Terry. Bob will be back this afternoon to pick up his dog if he's well on the road to recovery."

"It's a good twenty-four to forty-eight hours for a dog to recover from a rattlesnake bite. Right?"

"Yep. The dog will rest better at home with Bob

than remaining at the clinic. If he's doing well this afternoon, and I see no reason why he wouldn't be. Terry said Willie had a good night and was eating and antsy this morning. All good signs. So what's your day shaking out like?"

"I was leaving the cottage to work with Lucky on her rehab. Then I gotta check on RoadTrip. The staff is having a hard time getting her to exercise. She draws into her shell when someone comes near and won't come out even for her favorite food, sloppy joe. Now don't start, I know it's not what she should be eating, but it got her on the road to recovery. So I figured it might coax her out of her shell… I'll insist she eat her greens this afternoon."

"Hey, I didn't say a word. But if she won't be bribed with sloppy joe, how are you going to get her to eat greens this afternoon?"

"I'll have a little discussion with her when no one is within earshot. She'll come around. The recent stormy weather has her foot aching and a bit stiff. She doesn't want to use it. Thusly she won't exercise. We'll set the heat coils on low with a timer under her enclosure. That'll help."

"I see. We could have dinner and go to your cottage for a movie if you need to stay close."

"Do I want to. Yes. But I'm learning to delegate so…nope. My staff is well-trained. They can call me if the need arises."

"Good. I want to talk about the Halloween party/house warming and run some decorating ideas past you."

Switching the phone to the other ear, she tied her shoes and walked toward the door. "Great. I love

Halloween. We'll have a wonderful time decorating it. Did you hear from your family? Are they coming? Pepper and Lathen will be here on Wednesday. Halloween is on Friday and they have to get back on Sunday. Still… so glad they can make it."

"All my family, including the munchkins, are coming. So we'll need to lock a few doors. Martha and Butch along with a few members of the Historical Society and The Witch Museum will be attending as well."

Her heartbeat ratcheted up a few notches at the thought of all his family attending. It was something she was going to have to learn to get used to. *I can do this. They all like me. What's to worry about? They won't unlike me. Right?* It'll be a full house." A soft giggle escaped her lips.

"I better get to work and see what catastrophes are headed my way today. Yesterday's chaos I blame on the full moon. Today… well, that remains to be seen. See you tonight at the house around sixish?"

"I'll be there." The call disconnected and she held the phone to her chest for a minute more. *I am a lucky woman.* "Come on Misfit, what you say we see what trouble can be stirred up today." She tugged on her coat, zipped it up, threw open the door, and bounded outside. Feeling energized by the crisp autumn air, she giggled at Misfit as the dog raced in circles, bouncing on her hind legs and barking while Gwen sprinted to Lucky's aviary.

The owl turned her head and blinked bright yellow eyes at her hooting as she yanked open the door. Lucky may have been less than impressed with her antic's but after she slipped on the gauntlets and raised an arm, the owl shakily flew a couple of circles around her before landing with precision on the outstretched arm.

"Good girl." Stroking the good wing gently, she offered a meat treat from a leather pouch tied on her belt loop. "Happy to see your wing is gaining strength." Forty-five minutes later the short flights were much less shaky. She ended the session using targeting and treats for wing stretches before Lucky flew off to a higher perch indicating training was finished. Laughing she conceded PT was at an end. "Okay, we'll quit for today…but tomorrow longer flights."

Trinity bustled into the aviary. "Checks need to be signed. There are a few invoices I need you to review. I think the seed vendor is trying to pad his bill."

"Lead the way." She followed her assistant to the office and looked over the invoices, corrected them and signed checks. "I'm going to work with RoadTrip, then return to the cottage, get cleaned up, and surprise Brock with lunch. If you need me, call me."

Trinity met her gaze. "Sure boss. Have a good time. I've got this."

"I know you do or I wouldn't leave." She smiled. "I appreciate everything you do." With a wave, she sauntered off to the reptile habitat.

Once inside, she flipped the switch to turn on the heat coils below RoadTrip's enclosure, opened a supply cupboard, took out a heating pad, and plugged it in setting the temperature control to low. "Okay monster, come on over and we need to talk." Opening the gate, she rattled the turtle's food bowl. Nothing. The dish was crusted with last night's dinner. RT hadn't eaten much. She took the bowl over to the sink washed it out with warm soapy water. Then she took two cubes of sloppy joe out of the freezer and warmed the food in the microwave. The ding of the oven brought the rustle of a creature plodding through the habitat's terrain and made her smile. *Works every time. Well for me anyway.* RT appeared from behind the vegetation around the pond, craned her neck to see what was going on, and ambled over to the gate still favoring her hind leg.

RoadTrip let out a gravelly hiss when she picked the turtle up and sat down with the creature in her lap on the heating pad. "Now I know you've been deliberately being difficult with the staff. That's going to stop right now. Understood?"

The turtle pulled herself into her shell with another displeased hiss.

"Pout if you want, but if you are going to be able to keep up with the other turtles, you've got to use that leg or you are going to lose what mobility you have."

RoadTrip eased her hind legs out resting them on the heating pad.

"See now doesn't that feel good?" She lightly stroked the injured leg, noting the muscle tone was getting better before TR yanked it back inside her shell.

The door *squeaked* open. Charlotte one of the veterinary student interns assigned to RT strode in. "Did I hear you talking to someone?"

She startled and turned toward Charlotte. "Just convincing RT here to cooperate with her physical therapy."

Standing hands on hips, the vet intern narrowed her eyes as if not quite sure if her boss was joking or not. "Good luck with that. She's quite stubborn, especially when the weather is bad. Good news, the eye is completely healed and infection free."

"Great. As far as physical therapy, it will help if you warm her up a bit with the heating pad before trying to get her to move around." She eased RT back into her enclosure along with the warm food. "Be a good girl."

RoadTrip took two large bites of the food, turned her head and bobbed at Gwen. Sure enough, the eye had healed well.

Charlotte's eyes widened. "Did that turtle just nod at you? Almost like it understood what you said."

"Stranger things have happened." Shrugging, she laughed off the reference as she winked at RT. A contented sound hummed in the turtle's mind. "I've got to get going, I have a lunch appointment. I think you'll find RT more cooperative now that she's warmed up. Try the target stick and get her to move around from station to station. Reward her with a few fresh sprouts at each area." After one last glance at RT, she walked out the door and whistled for Misfit.

The dog appeared around the corner of the building and trotted beside her to the SUV, then jumped inside.

After picking up lunch, she pulled into the clinic's parking lot, happy to discover only a few vehicles in the lot. "You stay." She directed the dog and cracked the back windows. "Don't want to disrupt any sick or injured animals." Closing the vehicle door behind her, she entered the clinic and dropped off a salad at the receptionist's empty desk. After waving at Bob who was sitting in the reception area, she proceeded down the hall. "Hey anyone home?" she called before pushing through the hallway door to the examining rooms.

"In here." Brock's deep voice boomed.

She followed the sound and found him reviewing a chart at his desk. "Delta stood next to him with several sheets of paper in her hands "That should be enough instructions for Bob. I explained everything to him already, so Willie is ready to go home."

"I'll take care of it." Delta waved at Gwen then quickly strode out of the office.

Brock eased up from the desk and walked over to her. "To what do I owe this visit?"

"I finished up with Lucky and RT and decided you were hungry." She smiled seductively and held out the bags of food.

"What's in those bags isn't exactly what I'm hungry for." Wrapping his arms around her waist, he pulled her to him nibbling along her jawline, across her cheek and kissing the corner of her lips.

"I'm afraid it will have to do unless you plan on taking me right here on your desk." She snickered sliding her hand over the polished desktop.

He glanced at the desk and back to her. "Not a bad idea. The door has a lock."

"And you have patients." She slipped her arms around his neck and feathered her fingers in the baby-soft hair at the back of his neck slithering against him reveling in his reaction to her.

"Talk about mixed messages." He lifted her up on the desk, slid a hand under her shirt to caress her breast, then moved between her legs. "I've missed you," he murmured against her lips.

Footsteps echoed in the distance coming closer.

"Deja Vu." She giggled, wiggling off the desk and straightened her clothes. Recalling their first interlude at the clinic also interrupted. She'd been relieved at the time—this time—not so much.

He glanced at the unlocked door. "Damnit." Moving away from the desk, he brushed his lips over hers and strode toward the entrance.

A soft knock sounded on the door. "You guys decent?" Delta's voice held a note of amusement.

The handle moved slowly at first, then Brock yanked the door open. "Of course we're decent. This is a place of business."

"Just checking." The receptionist smirked. "Your next patient moved to next week, so you have plenty of time for lunch." Turning on her heel, she closed the door with a chuckle.

"You didn't fool her one bit." She grinned while taking the food out of the bag and setting it on the desk. Turning her head, she found him standing close behind her.

"It smells wonderful." He reached around her, picked up a burger and took a bite.

She leaned against him before reaching for the chocolate malt and handing it to him.

He took a draw on the straw. With a raised eyebrow, he said, "You know what I like. Didn't realize how hungry I am." Taking another large bite, he wrapped his other arm around her.

"This is awkward. Let me go, so I can eat too." She giggled, twisting out of his hold, and kissing his cheek. "We have all evening."

Hands raised in a gesture of surrender, a hamburger still in one, he snickered. "Can't have you starving to death on my watch."

She shot him a withering glance. "Right, now, Misfit is waiting in the SUV. If it's all right with you, we're going to go directly to the house from here and figure out the decorations." When she unwrapped her burger, she frowned wrinkling up her nose. "I said no onions or pickles." Carefully, she picked off the offending veggies, tossed them in the bag, and took a bite. "Mmmm, this is good." Sticking a long spoon in the chocolate shake she slipped a taste in her mouth. "I love handmade shakes." Then she spooned up another bite.

"Great lunch. Thanks." He popped a couple of fries in his mouth.

"Of course." After lunch, she gathered up the trash and stuffed it in the bag. Making sure to wrap up a piece of her burger she saved for Misfit in a napkin, she kissed Brock. "See ya soon."

"Sounds good. I'll be right behind you. Only one more patient today and it is only for vaccines."

As her shoes squeaked on the shiny tile floor of the waiting area, she waved to Delta sitting at her desk enjoying the salad.

The receptionist held up an index finger, finished chewing, and grinned. "How'd you know I like extra croutons in my salad, no onion, and extra shredded carrots? Thank you by the way."

She shrugged. "I pay attention. You're very much welcome." Stepping on the mat at the automatic door it whooshed open. She glanced across the parking lot and noticed part of the passenger side window in her SUV fogged up. A black nose was pressed against the window with big brown eyes glittering with excitement and a happy expression on her face while her tail appeared to wiggle her body all over.

It was a far cry from the scared, untrusting dog

she'd rescued months back. Fobbing open the door, she scratched the dog's ears, gave her a hug, then banished her to the back seat and fastened her safety harness.

Chapter Twenty-Eight
Preparing for a Magical Housewarming—
Ultimately They Had No Idea

On the day of the house warming Halloween party, the sun rose in an almost cloudless cerulean blue sky. After checking her phone, Gwen slipped silently out of his bed, padded over to the window, and opened it just a crack. The sun was warm, but the breeze carried a heavy scent of brine and a fall chill. She shivered and closed the window scurrying back to the warm bed.

"Good morning beautiful. Need a little fresh air?" He grinned and held the covers up for her to climb back under.

"It looks a lot warmer than it is." She slid in beside him, snuggling up to his body.

"Always does." With a sliver of sunshine warming the bed, he slipped one arm around her then reached with the other hand for his phone on the nightstand and checked the screen. "No missed calls. No messages. Great start to the day." He left the phone on the nightstand and rolled over to envelop her in his arms and nuzzling her neck.

She brushed her lips over his. "Morning handsome." Though she whispered the words, her voice brought the sound of paws on the hardwood floor and a wet black nose at her side of the bed snuffling. Laughing, she kissed him again. "Guess someone wants out."

"We gotta get up anyway. Big day ahead." He reluctantly released her then stretched his arms above his head. On a yawn, he said, "The wooden fence around the back yard isn't dog-proof yet. It's on my to-do-list."

"Okay. I'll put her leash on." Pausing, she tapped a finger to her chin, her forehead creased. "There's a pile of leftover lumber in the garage. Might make a temporary fix. Not sure Misfit will appreciate all the costumed people in the house this evening." She shimmied into her jeans, and pulled an orange and white sweater over her head then she tugged on socks and shoes.

"Good point. I'll join you and Misfit in the yard. Together we can check the fence and the lumber in the garage." He swung his feet to the floor and walked to the closet, pulled out worn jeans and an orange plaid flannel shirt.

She glanced in the mirror as she ran a brush through her hair. "Aren't we dressed festively today?"

"Of course. We're all about the Halloween season. Right?"

Giving him a thumbs up, she opened the bedroom door and sniffed at the welcoming aroma of coffee wafting in the room. Misfit thundered out into the hall and down the stairs. "Pepper or Lathen must be up and put the coffee on. Or do you have a timed coffee maker?"

He stilled for a minute. Lathen and Pepper had arrived last night. Yet, no sounds came from the downstairs kitchen. *Strange.* "Nope, been meaning to get one, but…like the fence, it's on the to-do-list."

At the bottom of the stairs, the dog whined then barked before racing to the back door.

Gwen sprinted down the stairs through the kitchen to the back door. "I'm hurrying girl."

Socks and boots on, he followed Gwen down the steps but paused in the kitchen. The coffee maker sputtered the last of the coffee into the glass pot. He blinked and glanced around. No sign of anyone in the room.

She clipped the long leash on Misfit's harness, then opened the door. The dog dashed out into the yard and did her business. "Guess you did have to go."

The seven-foot-tall wooden fence surrounded the back yard standing guard against intruders unless they could crawl through spaces provided by several missing boards. He stood on the wraparound porch watching Gwen throw a ball for Misfit. The dog bringing it back for her to throw again and again.

On the third throw, Misfit caught the ball on the first bounce and trotted up the steps where he stood and dropped the ball at his feet, turned and bolted into the yard. "Looks like she's made herself at home." He picked up the ball and tossed it within the perimeter the dog could reach on her leash. "I'm going to check on the lumber, then we'll get a bite to eat and patch up the fence."

"We'll be right in after a couple more tosses so Misfit can burn off some of the energy she has this morning." The dog barked happily and picked up the ball this time racing around the yard as far as the leash would allow.

Inside the garage, he poked around and found several fence pickets leaning against the far wall. "Well isn't this handy?" Searching the workbench, he found a pair of leather gloves tucked inside a yellow five-gallon bucket next to a plastic box of long screws. The gloves fit perfectly. A claw-head hammer hung on the pegboard above the workbench along with a multitude of other tools he didn't remember being there earlier.

After glancing at his watch, he took the hammer off the wall along with a flat tip screwdriver, a tape measure, and put them in the bucket. He took an armload of pickets, grabbed the bucket, and strode out the door to the back yard. "Look what I found. Only take a few minutes to screw these boards in place then Misfit can stay out here while we fix breakfast."

"Sounds like a plan." She rushed over to him, took the bucket and peered inside. "These screws are the same ones Lathen used to put up the outside aviary for Kaylee in Lobster Cove."

"Did I hear my name called?" Lathen stood on the porch holding the screen door open for Pepper.

"Look what Brock found in the garage." Gwen held out the yellow bucket rattling the tools inside and pointed to the fence pickets Brock held.

"Wow." He peered into the bucket. "I've got a drill with a screw head in the SUV that will make short work of this project."

"Maybe we should eat before the food gets cold." Pepper suggested looking longingly back inside the kitchen.

Puzzled, he glanced at Gwen, then switched to Pepper and Lathen. "Did you cook breakfast?" *No that wasn't possible, we've only been out here a few minutes.*

"Nope. Thought you did. There's scrambled eggs

in a skillet on the stove, bacon on a platter on the table, and a pot of freshly brewed coffee. I was looking for mugs when I heard my name." Lathen's stomach growled loud enough for everyone to hear.

"Well by all means, we should eat." He scrubbed his hand over his face. *Deja Vu from the cabin. Does magic work anywhere there is a portal of some kind—like this house? The family cabin?* "Huh?"

"You say something?" Lathen turned to him.

"Yeah…No… If we didn't fix breakfast, and you two didn't. Who did?" he blurted out.

Pepper and Lathen chortled, with Pepper finding her voice first, "Appears your Gypsy magic strikes again."

"I don't care who fixed breakfast. I'm famished. The fence can wait." Gwen tugged on Misfit's leash and hurried toward the house.

"Yeah, Brock and I can get the fence repaired in a few minutes. I'll get my tools out of the SUV after breakfast." Lathen waited until everyone passed through the kitchen door then closed it behind him.

Just as Pepper had said, a steaming breakfast was on the stove and table. The couples filled their plates and sat down. Misfit did a couple of circles on her plush purple rug in the corner and flopped down, head on her front paws, and eyes drooping. The ball rolled slowly over beside her.

"What will your family think about your house?" Pepper scooped up a fork of scrambled eggs lightly covered with cheese and slipped it in her mouth. "Mmm, delicious."

Taking a swig of coffee from his mug, he looked thoughtful. "They'll like it. Dad will be intrigued by the architecture. Mom will love the kitchen and the magic elements as well as my sisters. Jeremiah—who knows. I'm not sure he's on board with the magic. It may be hidden too deep in him to be discovered."

"Awww we'll have another run at him tonight after all your guests leave." Pepper held her solemn expression only a few seconds before her contagious laugh filled the house.

Having been indoctrinated into magic by Pepper, he had no doubt Jeremiah would be a convert by the end of the night.

Gwen took another bite of toast. "Hey, pass the strawberry preserves. Quit hogging it all to yourself." She teased him.

He grinned and handed her the jar. "You owe me." Waggling his eyebrows, he whispered in her ear, "I'll collect tonight."

Heat rose in her cheeks. He loved it when she blushed. So rarely did he catch her off guard and cause the reaction.

Gwen busied herself spreading the delicious fruit concoction over the partial slice of toast and took another bite.

Lathen covered a chuckle with a cough. Pepper shook her head. "For goodness sakes girl, you've got to practice a poker face. Your thoughts and emotions are written all over your face." Pepper shook her finger at him. "You're bad."

A mischievous twinkle appeared in Gwen's eyes. "Oh, I believe that statement to be incorrect." Other than the twinkle, her face was void from all expression until she burst out laughing.

"Now exactly what would we be talking about?"

Pepper asked primly.

"Depends." Gwen batted her eyes at him. "You don't get the playboy reputation without the prowess to back it up. If you know what I mean." She winked at him then grinned at Pepper.

It was his turn for heat to rush to his face. "Believe we need a change of subject. How do you like the Halloween decorations? Gwen and Misfit did most of them while I was at the clinic."

"Love the blue light spider in the large window above the door. I don't think the dragon staircase is thrilled with the orange and purple sequined witch's hat you put on its head. But the spider webs woven between the balusters set a great spooky tone."

"I like the black casket in the family room in front of the fireplace. You going to prop it open and put Dracula inside?" Lathen's lips twitched.

"Nope, it holds the ice chests full of soft drinks, water, and beer, but now that you mention it, we could stick a Dracula between the coolers." He raised an eyebrow.

"Hey, not a bad idea. Where could we get a Dracula this close to Halloween?" Gwen turned to stare at the casket. "We've carved all the pumpkins, only need to set them on either side of the path leading to the house. A couple would look great on the fireplace mantel. Don't you think?"

"Yes, one at each end. Where are they?"

"In the garage. We can set them up while the guys fix the fence." Gwen winked at him.

"Slave driver." He took the last gulp of coffee and pushed up from the table. "Come on Lathen, breakfast is over." He slung an arm around her shoulder and kissed her lingering for several beats.

"Okay, guys get a room. Oh, wait a minute. You have several right up there." He rolled his eyes heavenward and laughed. "I crack me up."

The others groaned.

"But you're the only one," Gwen shot back. "Hey Brock what time is your family coming? Shouldn't they be here by now?"

"Dad said early afternoon. So by the time we finish the fence they should arrive." Taking a jacket from the closet, he shrugged into it and motioned Lathen toward the door. "Ready?"

"As I'll ever be." Lathen brushed his lips over Pepper's and caressed her cheek. "Be back soon." The door banged shut behind them.

****

Pepper sidled over to Gwen and jerked her chin toward the painting hanging on the wall. "Do you think Beth or her family will make an appearance tonight?"

"Doubt it. We've not seen nor heard from them since we were able to release them." She chewed on her bottom lip. "What worries me is who may be able to cross the veil between the living and dead tonight. Apparently, this house has quite a history."

"I hadn't considered that." Pepper frowned. "Any spirit could try... but the magic wielders at the party far outweigh any unsuspecting spirit. We'll need to stay aware."

"Yeah, might want to alert the others—including Martha and her friend Butch. I don't think the house would allow maleficent spirits access. Unless..."

"Your right. Better get the pumpkins set out. Hey, Pepper would you mind lighting them and using a bit of

305

magic to keep them lit outside?"

"Of course. Don't want to be outdone by the weather gods." Pepper snickered. "Although it's forecast to be clear and cold tonight."

As she glanced out the front window, a feeling of foreboding washed over her as storm clouds boiled up on the horizon. She shrugged it off. Sudden storms were not unusual this time of year. *Hope it doesn't snow.* Misfit gave no sign of restlessness as she had previously before storms. *The excitement of the evening is affecting my abilities.*

The sound of a vehicle engine brought her attention back to the window. An unfamiliar large white van coasted to a stop in front of the house. Kate and Shamus exited the van first, followed by Riva and her family, and Molly and hers. Behind the van, Dylan's SUV slowed to a stop. Before Dylan and Lance released their small children, Molly's three boys and Riva's two raced pass the van and up the path toward the house. For a split second, she had the urge to lock the front door and run to get Brock from the back yard.

As if Pepper knew what she was thinking, her friend winked and strolled toward the door. "You got this girlfriend."

With a thought, she made sure the rooms the boys shouldn't have access to were locked. A calm settled inside her and she eagerly tugged open the door greeting Brock's family. "Welcome everyone. Come on in. Let me take your jackets. Did you have any trouble finding the house?" As the words poured from her lips, the boys tossed their coats at her and rushed through the house.

"Not at all," Shamus said.

"Boys!" Molly's husband Talbert bellowed. "Stop where you are or spend the rest of the day in the van." The three boys leading the pack screeched to a halt causing the two younger boys to smack into them. "That's better. Pick up your coats and hand them to Gwen. Then come over here and stand with us. You know better than to behave like this."

"Yes, sir." Molly's three boys echoed sheepishly returning to their parents.

Way ahead of Talbert, Riva caught up with her two boys, grabbed them by the shoulders and yanked them into place beside her and Caleb. "Sorry about that. Long car ride equals pent up energy."

She pointed toward the back door. "Oh, I understand. The guys are in the backyard dog proofing the wooden fence. You can let the boys out there to get the wiggles out."

"Thank you. I'll take them out. Don't think Brock will want to supervise and work on the fence." Talbert motioned for the boys to follow him.

"You could get roped into helping on the fence," she warned with a giggle.

"We'll see," Molly's husband called over his shoulder on his way out the door.

"Suit yourself." She surveyed the rest of the family. "Is Jeremiah not coming?"

Kate rolled her eyes and glanced at her husband. "Last minute law firm business. He and Morgan will be along later."

Lathen and Brock came trudging in the house. "Took longer than we thought. The boards at the far end of the yard were rotted. One bounce from Misfit and they would have splintered into pieces. So we checked all the wood. Good news, there were enough pickets in the garage to fill all the holes and the fence is solid now."

"We put large barrel locks on the inside of the gates, to prevent them from being accidentally left open."

He held up two sets of keys. "I've the keys on my key ring and will leave a set in the key box in the laundry room."

"Good idea." Gwen glanced at the back door. "Where's Talbert and the boys?"

"Out in the back yard playing catch with an old ball they found. Wish I had the energy those boys have." Brock hugged his dad, mother, and sisters. Shook hands with Caleb and Lance. "Glad you made it. Gwen, did you give them the tour?"

"Only the downstairs, I was headed upstairs when you came in." He glanced at the clock on the wall. "How about we finish the tour of the second floor after we shower and get cleaned up for the party?" He brushed the dirt from his jeans and took screws out of his shirt pocket. "Noticed snacks and drinks are set up in the kitchen, courtesy of the house." He winked at his mother who was still carrying a wrapped package.

Kate handed the box to him. "A family crest. We brought one over from Ireland for each of you kids. Thought it would be a great housewarming gift." His mother raised her eyebrow. "Appears your house has magic of its own. Still, it'll ward away evil spirits." She smiled knowingly. "Now you kids go get cleaned up. We'll hold down the fort until you get back."

"Thanks. We'll hang the crest above the fireplace for all to see." Then he waggled his eyebrows at Gwen.

She giggled. "Lead the way."

"We're going to take this opportunity to do the same." Lathen and Pepper climbed the stairs behind them.

Chapter Twenty-Nine
A Halloween Party With a Dash of Magic and Surprises

Lighted pumpkins lined the path to the house. The fence fixed, Misfit was allowed out in the back yard as the guests began arriving. With Gwen at his side, Brock stood at the front door to greet Butch and Martha as the first guests to arrive dressed as a witch and blacksmith. Several members of the Witch's Museum and The Historical Committee followed shortly after.

Friends and staff from his clinic and the Salem Sanctuary dropped by in costumes ranging from vampires to characters from popular movies with a few witches and ghosts thrown in. Finally, Jeremiah and Morgan made an appearance dressed like a pirate captain and fairy from a famous childhood tale. His parents came dressed in original colorful Gypsy costumes as did his sisters.

A multi-course buffet lined one wall of the dining room, finger foods and snacks lined another, and yet another table held spiced cider, hot chocolate, and coffee or tea along with plates, mugs, and silverware. Carved jack-o-lanterns glowed from each end of the fireplace mantel as the fire burned merrily in the hearth. The large rectangular oak dining table was covered by a crocheted black table cloth with shiny silver threads running through it.

Silver candelabras placed at each end and the middle of the table held burning black flame candles. An eerie sight if he did say so himself. He and Gwen gave tours of the house, then circulated most the night chatting with family and guests, discussing the history and craftsmanship of the house. Dressed as normal humans, Talbert, Caleb, and Lance took turns supervising the children in a room set up for them with a big-screen television, video games, snacks and soda.

His nieces and nephews would have to be scraped off the ceiling with all the sugar they were consuming. Just then a thought occurred to him, his family was spending the night, so it would be his ceiling they'd be scraped off of. *Oh well having my family under one roof, my roof, was worth it and a long time coming.*

Gwen touched his shoulder as they passed through the kitchen checking on the food and supplies. "I've checked on Misfit twice, she seems to be enjoying the peace and quiet outside on the porch, but it's dark now, so I'm going to bring her inside. Think she'll be all right upstairs in our room—alone?"

"Sure." He grabbed a package of dog snacks off the counter by the door. "Rewards to help her through the crowd on the way upstairs."

Handing her a jacket, he shrugged into his and accompanied her outside. "Need a little fresh air myself." Reminiscent of a Halloween picture, the full yellow moon hung in a dark sky sprinkled with twinkling stars. Chuckling, he half expected the silhouette of a witch riding a broom to appear crossing the celestial body. *Pepper would not appreciate that image*. Wrapping his arms around Gwen's waist, he pulled her against him nibbling at her neck, trailing kisses across her cheek until his lips reached her full warm lips and murmured, "Beautiful night."

She cocked her head and stared quizzically up at him. "What has you so amused?" Not waiting for an answer, she wrapped her arms around his neck and shivered. "Don't you feel that? Something feels…for lack of a better word…wrong." Misfit blinked sleepily at them from the corner of the porch under the swing.

"I don't. But…"

"Come on girl, time to go inside." Gwen shook the bag of treats.

The dog stretched and yawned getting slowly to her feet then came to attention nose in the air sniffing. Suddenly the fur on the back of Misfit stood straight up, she took an aggressive stance, and a low snarl rose from the pup's throat.

"What is it, girl?" He scanned the back yard, seeing nothing, he released Gwen, took a few steps backward and reached inside the door and turned on the floodlights. Again he scanned the backyard. Nothing. Holding the door open as Gwen clipped on the leash and tugged Misfit inside. "She's feeding off your unsettled feelings."

"It's more than that, I can feel it."

He glanced at his watch. *Eleven thirty. A half-hour before midnight and Halloween would be over.* Someone clapped him on the shoulder and he whirled around, fist clenched, and arm drawn back.

"Whoa, there Brock." His friend Butch grinned. "A little jumpy on this Halloween night?"

"No, no not at all." He lied. "Just deep in thought."

Members of the Historical Society and The Witch's Museum gathered around the front door. He hurried over. "Ready to leave so soon?"

"Yes, we've had a wonderful time, but it's late…"A member of The Witch's Museum said on a yawn.

"Past our bedtime" Another person added jokingly. "Great house you have here."

"Thank you and thanks for coming." He escorted his guests to their cars while Gwen took a defiant Misfit upstairs to their room. A thin cloud floated across the full moon in the star-strewn night sky. A twinge of anxiety niggled at his gut as he breathed in the crisp autumn air. *Maybe Gwen's right.* He hurried inside. The door slammed behind him and locked.

Gwen raced down the stairs.

His gaze was drawn to the wall where the painting hung. Earlier in the evening, he'd noticed that no one was in the painting…now the chairs contained members of Beth's family and she stood next to the fireplace inside the painting. *Didn't they all cross over? Could spirits come back after crossing over? Shit! Gwen was right, something is brewing.*

Pepper and Lathen stood grim-faced next to Gwen. His mother and father crossed the room to join the little group. Butch helped Martha on with her coat then paused as the back door slammed and locked. The shutters banged against the house. Butch reached for the door handle, an eyebrow raised as the deadbolt slid into place.

"Son, I think your house is trying to tell you something." His mother peered at the stairway where Dylan, Riva, and Molly stood.

Jeremiah and Morgan stepped out from behind the staircase. "What's going on?" Jeremiah wanted to know, wrapping a protective arm around Morgan pulling her close. "It feels like all the air is being sucked out of this room." His brother's face turned ashen white as Beth's ghostly form took shape in the center of the room.

Brock moved to the little group gathered and glanced at the grandfather clock standing in the hallway. *Fifteen minutes until midnight. The witching hour on All Hallows Eve.* A nervous chuckle rose up in his throat. *How cliche. His brother would be a believer after this night.*

He cleared his throat and wrapped an arm around Gwen's waist. "Can we help you, Beth?" Misfit's howling could be heard clearly from the upstairs bedroom.

"No, but I hope we can help you." Beth glanced back at the painting and sadly shook her head. "The ghost of Judge John Hathorne stands outside ready to curse or worse all those involved in sullying his reputation. The house stands between all of you...protecting—" The ghost's hand and arm made a sweeping motion toward their group, "— against his magic ability."

A soft almost hysterical giggle burst from Gwen. "Doesn't he know that by his actions this night, he has not only outed himself but proved the rumors and article are true?"

"I don't believe he's considered that point." Beth's ghostly grim face twitched into a half-smile. "He's bent on revenge, but apparently had trouble passing through the veil this evening." She pointed to the clock and then laid a finger on her lips.

Seven minutes until midnight. Brock opened his

mouth to speak, but Pepper beat him to it.

"Isn't there some way to banish him forever while he walks among the mortals? I don't have my spell book with me. Guess I should travel with it after all the recent experiences with you gypsies." A slight giggle slipped out between her lips.

The somber tone in the room eased for a minute. "I mean, in your painting don't you…"

"You're on the right path. That's why I'm here." Beth smiled wide. "You can't battle him outside this house. But with the protections afforded us inside the abode, with our combined magic and grandmother's grimoire we would be able to do exactly as you suggest. Do we have your full support?"

"Of course." The group chorused with the exception of Jeremiah, still shell shocked leaning against the wall. But Morgan was all in pumping her fist in the air.

Lance stuck his head out of the upstairs room. "Need us to help?"

"No," Dylan called up to him. "Protect the children. We got this."

"Good enough." Lance slammed the door shut.

A trail of mist floated out of the picture, around the room, and settled beside Beth taking the shape of an older woman holding a thick book spread open. "Granddaughter. Are we ready then? We've located the…um…." The elderly ghost switched her gaze from the pages of the book to outside the window. "…proper page." Then the ghost jerked her chin toward the painting where previously all the Colson family had been but now they gathered in the center of the room inside the painting.

"Let's do it." Gwen shared a glance at the clock with him. "Only—"

Beth again put her finger to her ghostly lips and shook her head.

The elderly ghost began to read from the book.

"We are witches, this is our creed. We will help where there is need. Days of old, wrongs to right. Let the truth be known this night. Forever banish from all realms Judge John Hathorne's spirit and soul are bound. So mote it be."

The book closed with a loud clap, tendrils of red and black mist floated from the book, over the room and right through the windowpane. Jeremiah rushed to the window, touching the glass with his fingers. The rest of the group followed in time to see the tendrils expand and circle a ghostly shape in top hat and suit, the ground beneath its feet glowed as if molten lava bubbled up from the earth's core. With a snap, the tendrils and their prisoner sank into the ground leaving no trace except a stench of sulfur seeping into the old house.

The elderly ghost slumped against the wall that held the picture and turned into a white mist returning to the painting.

The door locks clicked, the shutters banged open and the full moon shone brightly in a cloudless star-strewn sky.

"Anyone care to take a peek outside?" Brock asked cautiously reaching for the door handle.

Beth's ghostly hand rested on his. "Give it a minute." She bent over and picked up a poppet that lay singed on the floor. It crumpled in her hand and turned to ash. She gently blew the ashes into the fireplace. "It is done. We will take our leave but our gratitude will be forever yours." The ghost faded away.

All eyes looked to the painting but no one was there. Heads turned to the hallway as the old grandfather clock began chiming the hour of midnight.

At the clock's final stroke of twelve, he squeezed Gwen tight against him. "Well? Halloween is over. Any premonitions or feelings of doom now?"

She smiled relaxing against him. "Not a one."

"It's quite a house you have here." Jeremiah clapped his brother on the back. "I'd like to say you crafted all this for my benefit, but I know better. You all have made a believer out of me." He wrapped an arm around a grinning Morgan. "The next family reunion should be at the castle in Ireland. Who's with me?"

Aye's sounded from each family member.

"I for one am wiped. If you'd direct us to our bedroom, we'll retire for the night." Jeremiah glanced at their bags lined against the wall.

"As you know the bedrooms are all upstairs. Pick one. I'm afraid the boys will have to share the biggest bedroom. Unless you want them to share your bedroom." He glanced at his sisters.

"No. The men can take turns sleeping in the boys' room." Molly smiled sweetly at her husband Talbert. "Leaving them unsupervised is not an option."

"Since sleeping arrangements are all set, Gwen and I are going to step outside for a little fresh air and let Misfit out. We don't do puddles in this house."

As if on cue, a plaintive howl rose from upstairs. "I'm so glad we didn't leave her outside." Gwen sighed and sprinted upstairs to release the pup. Moments later

Misfit came thundering down the stairs, through the house, and whined at the back door.

He turned on the outside floodlights, cracked the door, and stepped outside to make sure the yard was safe. Opening the door wider, he released the dog. Gwen joined him on the porch, bundled up in her parka then settled into the swing.

Walking across the porch, he fingered the small square box in his jacket pocket. *Now or never.* A warm feeling of contentment swirled through him as he sucked in a deep breath and knelt down on one knee in front of her. "Gwen the last few months has been a whirlwind of challenges, excitement, and pure fun. I've never been happier."

Gwen's eyes were the size of saucers her lips formed an "O" as he spoke never taking her gaze off his face. "Happiest day of my life...so far," she managed to squeak out.

"I want to spend the rest of my life with you. If you'll have me." He offered the small purple velvet box to her and flipped the lid open. A marquise diamond ring sparkled in the moonlight.

"Are you asking me to marry you?" she whispered as if the sound would break the spell the full moon and stars had woven around them.

"You bet I am." His warm breath formed a white cloud between them in the frosty air.

Nodding, she pulled her hands out of her parka pockets, he slipped the ring on her finger, and she wrapped her arms around his neck. "Of course, I'll marry you." On tiptoe, she closed her eyes and brushed her lips over his. "You know fate set us up."

"I don't know about that, but there's no doubt we

belong together and in this house." His lips pressed against hers, then gently covered hers deepening the kiss.

Suddenly the dog barked in surprise as the door flew open. His entire family plus Pepper and Lathen stood in the doorframe clapping.

"We knew you were up to something." His father exclaimed pointing to the finger on Gwen's left hand.

"She said yes." His mother smiled clapping her hands together like a child at Christmas. "It's been decades since the family castle in Ireland was the location for a good old fashion Irish wedding."

He leaned his forehead down on hers. "The joys of a large family."

"You are so lucky," Gwen whispered.

"Remember they're your family now too." He retorted. "Mom, give us a chance to breathe before you go planning the wedding. Gwen may not want to be married in Ireland. Her whole world is here."

Pepper shoved her way through the crowd and hugged Gwen then Brock. "What a wonderful beginning to the holiday season."

A word about the author...

Tena Stetler is a best-selling author of paranormal romance. She has an over-active imagination, which led to writing her first vampire romance as a tween, to the chagrin of her mother and delight of her friends. After many years as a paralegal, then an IT manager, she decided to live out her dream of pursuing a publishing career.

With the Rocky Mountains outside her window, she sits at her computer surrounded by a wide array of witches, shapeshifters, demons, faeries, and gryphons, with a Navy SEAL or two mixed in telling their tales. Her books tell stories of magical kick-ass women and mystical alpha males who dare to love them. Travel, adventure, and a bit of mystery flourish in her books along with a few companion animals to round out the tales.

Colorado is home; shared with her husband of many moons, a brilliant Chow Chow, a spoiled parrot, and a forty-five-year-old box turtle. When she's not writing, her time is spent kayaking, camping, hiking, biking, or just relaxing in the great Colorado outdoors. During the winter you can find her curled up in front of a crackling fire with a good book, a mug of hot chocolate, and a big bowl of popcorn.

http://www.tenastetler.com